MW01420282

Angelica Syndrome
The Last Seed

David Campo

PublishAmerica
Baltimore

First printing

Photograph of city used on the cover was taken by Miranda Prather.

Softcover 9781462632350
PUBLISHED BY PUBLISHAMERICA, LLLP
www.publishamerica.com
Baltimore

Printed in the United States of America

To Heather
Any thing is Possible

Dedication:

I dedicate this book to my family. They have always been there for me. Especially to my late grandfather who has recently passed at the tender age of 97. The things he must have seen, from horse and carriage to cars, planes, and a man on the moon.

(CHAPTER ONE)

May 10th 1959, that is when it all started. It was not a significant day for any reason, other than it was the day that Benjamin Stone was brought into this world. Though this day meant little to anyone except his parents, it would someday become a day that the human race as a whole would never forget.

Benjamin Stone was the second of three children. His mother was a home maker and his father was a carpenter. His family lived a middle life existence, not poor, not by any means wealthy. The Stone family was an average family, an everyday nothing special, nothing unusual family. At least that was until at a very early age Benjamin exhibited signs of being different, of being very unusual.

At the age of two years, Benjamin was able to read. And by read it is not meant that he was able to identify a word here and there, but that he was able to read at the same level as his eight year old sister Rebecca whom was in third grade. One day his sister, while doing her homework, noticed that her brother appeared to be reading. She thought it was cute. That is until she realized that young Benjamin was *actually* reading. She ran to her mother to let her know that Benjamin could read. For the next hour Benjamin, his sister, and his mother sat at the kitchen table while young Benjamin entertained them by reading everything they handed him. When his father came home the process continued. Nobody could believe what they were seeing, but they were in fact seeing it.

Benjamin's father began to ask him to spell some words. To his surprise young Benjamin did. Each word became progressively harder and yet each time young Benjamin got the spelling correct. This went on for over an hour, until finally his father had to use a work dictionary to check the spelling. Each time the results were the same, the spelling was correct.

Over the next few weeks both of Benjamin's parents had him read and write for them. They also started testing him at math. To their astonishment, but not to their disbelief, young Benjamin was also able to do some math. The problem Benjamin's parents had found themselves faced with was what to do with him. A problem that any parent would have if faced with a child prodigy.

As previously stated the Stone family was an ordinary family, with ordinary problems, and limited resources. Not only did they not know what to with him, they could not afford to do anything even if they knew what to do. And so life went on for the Stone family.

Benjamin's parents had another child, a boy they named Nathanial. By now Benjamin was five years old. His mother and father both had been working with him trying to challenge him, but that was becoming ever so difficult.

(CHAPTER TWO)

Finally, the time had come to send young Benjamin to school. He was going to be attending first grade. On the morning of his first day, young Benjamin stood in line along with all the rest of the first graders. He had in his hand a lunch box and a bag full of school supplies. The bell rang and the children were led into the school in an orderly fashion. Benjamin was assigned to his first grade home room teacher. Her name was Mrs. Tate.

Mrs. Tate started by taking role. Once she was satisfied that all her students were present she started the day by trying to find out how much they knew about reading, writing, and mathematics. She had no reason to believe that they would know anymore than any other class she had taught, but never the less it was a standard procedure that she would follow.

While writing on the chalk board, quizzing her students at random, Mrs. Tate asked the question, "Does anyone think they can solve the math problems I have written here on the chalk board?"

Young Benjamin was about to explode from his seat. He could solve those math problems! Benjamin's hand flew up. His mind was racing pick me, pick me. Very slowly, Mrs. Tate turned to Benjamin and said, "If you think you can solve my math problems come up to the chalk board and solve them." Mrs. Tate was surprised that someone volunteered. In all her years teaching, not one student had *ever* volunteered on the first day of first grade.

Benjamin approached the chalk board completely confident he could answer the questions. He reached for a piece of chalk and began to solve Mrs. Tate's math problems. He solved them with ease. Mrs. Tate looked at him with her head slightly cocked and said, "Would you like to try solving some problems that are harder?" Benjamin responded by saying, "Yes please." Mrs. Tate erased the chalk board. This time the math problems would be on a third grade level. Once again, Benjamin solved all of Mrs. Tate's problems. Not only were they all correct, he asked if he could please do some more. Benjamin was having fun. At this point Mrs. Tate wanted to give him some problems that she was certain he would be unable to solve. This time Mrs. Tate put junior high school math problems on the chalk board. She knew with full certainty that Benjamin would be unable to solve the problems. Young Benjamin smiled back, "Yes Ma'am" to her complete astonishment he solved the problems. This process continued until Mrs. Tate had reached the limits of *her* mathematical skills. Benjamin solved every problem asked of him. He was having fun.

Mrs. Tate asked Benjamin to return to his seat. For the remainder of that day, Mrs. Tate wondered what to do with a student of Benjamin's caliber.

At the end of the day Mrs. Tate spoke to the principal, Mr. Kants, about what she had witnessed in her classroom. After a long drawn out conversation the principal wanted to see for himself. The next morning, Mrs. Tate brought Benjamin to the principal's office where Benjamin repeated for the principal what he had done just the day before. The principal was almost speechless. He was in a state of disbelief. When he finally was able collect his thoughts, he told Mrs. Tate to go back to class and to take Benjamin with her. From this point on Mr. Kants would do everything in his power to see to it that any child of this nature was properly educated.

Mr. Kants had Benjamin's parents come to school where they could discuss Benjamin's needs. Needs that could not be tended to by a normal school environment. Mr. Kants, with the permission of Benjamin's parents, started contacting educational facilities from around the country. Mr. Kants desperately needed someone to fund *and* educate Benjamin in a manner fitting his intellect.

Several prestigious schools stepped forward, all sending their representatives to test Benjamin. After testing him, they *all* wanted to fund his education. To have a child prodigy in one's educational institution speaks well of the institution. It was Harvard University in the end, that won the privilege of educating young Benjamin. Harvard was chosen for several reasons. First being that during the time Benjamin was being tested; his mother felt that the Harvard representative connected with Benjamin, her husband, and herself more than the other school representatives had. Another reason was that Harvard University offered to pay for the family to move to Boston, to give Benjamin's father a job in the their maintenance department, as well as educating Benjamin as long as Benjamin and his parents wanted him at Harvard University.

It was the fall of 1965, Benjamin, his mother; his father, sister, and little brother were in the family car headed for Boston. Benjamin could not have been more excited he was going to Harvard University. He just knew he was going to have fun. After two days on the road, the Stone family reached Boston. By now they all were road weary. Benjamin's parents just wanted to settle down into their new home.

The Stone family was met upon their arrival in Boston, by a Harvard representative, the same one they had meet at

Benjamin's testing. He took the Stone family to their new home that was provided for them by the University.

The house was a two story brick home with four bedrooms and two bathrooms. Benjamin's mother could not have been more pleased. She was in her new home, which was conveniently located on the University grounds. Her son was going to receive the education he could only have at a facility of this type, and her husband had a new job. The family was in good shape. Now for her son Benjamin, his education was about to start. She hoped that the pressure would not be too much for young Benjamin.

The Stone family was allowed to settle down for a few days before Benjamin began his education, and before his father began his new job. The last thing the University wanted to do would be to put too much pressure on the family.

It was time; almost a week had passed since the Stone family had arrived in Boston. Benjamin's father was told to report to the maintenance department to receive his assignment and begin his new job.

When it came to Benjamin, the school told his parents he would be provided a permanent escort. This would be someone who picked him up in the morning and got him through the day, taking him from place to place, and seeing that he was safely taken home. Benjamin's mother especially liked the idea that her son would be cared for. This took quite a bit of pressure off her knowing her son would be safe.

On that fateful morning, day one of his education, young Benjamin could hardly sit still. He kept asking his mother, "Is she here yet? Is she here yet?" Finally, from the window that Benjamin had been standing in front of, he saw her coming up the walk. "Mother, *she's here, she's here*!" Benjamin was like a kid in a candy store. His mother told him to be patient and wait for her to knock on the door. As Benjamin stood at the door with his hand on the door knob, the next minute seemed to take forever. Finally, there was a knock at the door. Benjamin immediately opened it and there before him stood his personnel escort. She introduced herself as Mrs. Janice Whitmore. She was a twenty six year old, graduate of Harvard University with a PHD in child psychology. Her job was not only to escort Benjamin to and from school, but was also to see to it that Benjamin was at no time being pushed too hard or pressured too much. Though she was hired by the University, if at any time she felt it necessary, she could remove Benjamin from any situation they were not comfortable with.

It was time to go. Benjamin's mother gave him a hug and a kiss. She told him to be a good boy and to do what was asked of him. Mrs. Whitmore took Benjamin by the hand leading the way. They walked to the administrative building which would be their first stop.

Upon arriving at the administrative building they were met by the Dean of Students. This would be the first time that Mr. Pearl had met Benjamin Stone. Mrs. Whitmore and Benjamin approached Dean Pearl. Benjamin extended his hand, "Hello, my name is Benjamin Stone, I am very pleased to meet you and I would also like to thank you for allowing me to attend your University". The Dean shook Benjamin's hand, thanking *him* for the privilege to be able to take part in educating him. All the while, Dean Pearl was taken aback by the adult like manner in which Benjamin had presented himself.

Dean Pearl asked Benjamin if he was ready for his journey to begin. Benjamin responded "yes sir!" Dean Pearl extended his hand and in response Benjamin took his hand and he was then led into a large room with a very large table. The room was full of people, lots of people. Benjamin and Mrs. Whitmore were seated, and Dean Pearl took his place at the head of the table. Benjamin glanced around the room. Every seat at the table was taken. Those who weren't seated stood off to the side observing.

The Dean started to introduce Benjamin to the faculty. One by one he worked his way around the room introducing him to all the heads of the various departments. Benjamin smiled and graciously said, "I am very pleased to meet you," all the while under the watchful eye of Mrs. Whitmore.

After all introductions had been made, Dean Pearl told Benjamin that the main reason and *focus* of the meeting today was to try to evaluate him. He stated that this would allow them to be able to better format an educational schedule best suited for a student of his needs. The initial goal was to get Benjamin through grades one to twelve before completely saturating him with college courses.

It was then that Dean Pearl turned to his right, looked at one of the gentlemen seated at the table, and nodded. The man began to speak. He introduced himself as Professor Bret Hollinger. He stated that he was the head of the mathematics department. Professor Hollinger asked Benjamin if he had heard of him. Benjamin responded by saying, "No I have not, but I am sure that you are very good at your job." The entire room, though only momentarily, erupted in laughter. "Well thank you for that compliment Benjamin. If it would be ok with you, I would like to see for myself what skill levels you posses in mathematics." Benjamin smiled and responded by saying, "Ok."

Professor Hollinger asked Benjamin to join him at the chalk board. Benjamin approached the chalk board with the stature and grace of a person much older in years than himself. Professor Hollinger started by having Benjamin solve some elementary math problems, which Benjamin accomplished quite easily. From there they moved on to basic algebra. Professor Hollinger placed a few problems on the board. Once again Benjamin completed these problems in short order. Professor Hollinger was impressed and now he was going to try Benjamin's hand at advanced algebra. Professor Hollinger felt that if Benjamin could answer these questions correctly that he did indeed have a mathematical child prodigy on his hands. After having placed the problems on the chalk board Professor Hollinger looked at Benjamin and asked, "Do you think you can solve these problems Benjamin?" Benjamin looked at Professor Hollinger, smiled and then approached the chalk board. Benjamin quickly completed the first two questions, and then it seemed to Professor Hollinger as well as the rest of the faculty in the room that Benjamin was stuck on the third question. Mrs. Whitmore was prepared to remove Benjamin from this awkward situation. Mrs. Whitmore waited for a signal that the two of them had already agreed on. Benjamin was to scratch his nose and at the same time make eye contact with Mrs. Whitmore. No signal came. Instead Benjamin looked at Professor Hollinger with somewhat of a puzzled look and then he stated "The third question has no correct answer because of the way it has been written. There is no way a proper answer can be given."

Professor Hollinger's face lit up. He became very excited. "*That is right Benjamin*" exclaimed Professor Hollinger! "There is no correct answer, I was trying to trick you" he said. Benjamin smiled. Professor Hollinger wanted to continue with even more advanced questions, but Mrs.

Whitmore felt that Benjamin had done enough mathematics for now.

With the permission of Mrs. Whitmore, Professor Hollinger did have a question that he wanted to ask Benjamin. What Professor Hollinger wanted to know was, exactly how, Benjamin had learned algebra. Benjamin told Professor Hollinger that his mother had bought a book on advanced algebra at a yard sale for twenty five cents. She thought her son might enjoy looking through the book. "How old were you when your mother gave you the algebra book?" Professor Hollinger asked. "I was five years old," replied Benjamin. Professor Hollinger smiled, and then returned to his seat all the while mumbling to himself "Simply amazing, simply amazing."

Dean Pearl took control of the meeting once again and asked Benjamin if he needed a break or if he was prepared to continue. Benjamin said he was fine and that he didn't need a break yet because he had gone to the bathroom before he had left the house. Everyone in the room smiled. As intelligent as Benjamin was, he by all accounts was still a six year old boy whom did not yet posses the higher social skills of an adult.

Dean Pearl then introduced Benjamin to the head of the English department. Once the introduction was made. Professor Diana Coller asked Benjamin to read for her. They started at the first grade level and then quickly worked their way up. Professor Coller increased the reading level until she felt that Benjamin had reached the limits of skill level. Professor Coller then had Benjamin move onto spelling. Again, she let Benjamin continue until she felt had reached the limits of his skill level.

This process continued from professor to professor, all the while under the watchful eye Mrs. Whitmore. The entire testing process lasted for three hours. At the end of those three hours, it was determined by the staff that Benjamin had a twelve grade equivalent at math, a seventh grade equivalent in reading, a fourth grade equivalent at spelling, a fourth grade equivalent in his writing, and had little to no skill level at geography, social science, history, or biology. It was believed that the reason for a lack of skill level in these areas was simply due to a lack of exposure.

At the end of the meeting, Dean Pearl, as well as the faculty had the information they needed to properly format an educational program best suited for Benjamin's needs. The current goal was to get Benjamin through grades one to twelve in compliance with current state laws before moving on to his college education.

Benjamin and Mrs. Whitmore would spend the rest of the day exploring the University. To Benjamin the University seemed endless. Benjamin especially liked the cafeteria. He had never seen so much food. Benjamin also liked the fact that everywhere he and Mrs. Whitmore went, people would stop then just to meet him. It seemed that he was a bit of a celebrity on campus. Word of him coming to Harvard had preceded him.

After having spent several hours walking about the campus, Mrs. Whitmore took Benjamin home to his mother. That evening Benjamin told his family about the day he had spent at the University. Benjamin told them everyone he met treated him like a celebrity.

Benjamin's father also told of his day at work. How everyone he met asked him about his son. They all had so many questions, "Was your son always this way," "Where do you think he gets his intelligence," and Benjamin's fathers favorite question was "What is it like to know that your son that is six years old and is already smarter than you?" It was then that Benjamin's mother reached over to put her hand on her husband's hand, as if to let him know that everything would be ok. One can only imagine the feelings a parent would experience having such a child. As far as Benjamin's father was concerned, he was willing to endure the feelings of inferiority if it meant that his son would receive the education that only a University such as Harvard could provide.

The next morning Benjamin was up and ready well before he needed to be. Finally he spotted Mrs. Whitmore coming up the walk. Benjamin shouted to his mother, "*Here she comes! I have to go!*" Benjamin's mother reminded him that he needed to show more self control, as well as patience.

Benjamin apologized to his mother and stood patiently by the door waiting for the knock that seemed to take *forever*. When Mrs. Whitmore came to the door, she asked Benjamin if he was ready to go to school. Benjamin replied, "You bet I am." Mrs. Whitmore smiled and they were on their way. From this point on, his day would be filled with an aggressive schedule of learning, challenging him *every* moment.

From time to time Mrs. Whitmore would step in to demand a break for Benjamin if she felt that he was being pressured too much, or if she felt that Benjamin just needed time to play, to wonder around the campus, or just time to be a *normal* child; or at least as normal as a "prodigy" child could be. To Benjamin the entire campus was a playground. Benjamin was allowed to go anywhere he wanted and do almost anything he wanted to do. It seemed for the most part, no one minded he was there. There was one occasion during summer break when Benjamin and his sister Rebecca decided to play hop scotch on the sidewalk leading to Dean Pearl's administrative office. Dean Pearl did not find that very amusing considering it took several attempts to remove the chalk leading up the walkway to his office. Finally it had to wear off on its own. After the Dean contacted Benjamin's mother, Benjamin apologized and promised *not to do that again, ever*.

(CHAPTER THREE)

As time went on, Benjamin's education would progressing rapidly he was well over half way completed with the curriculum he needed to achieve his twelfth grade education, and he was *only* eight year old.

It was during this time that Benjamin was introduced to the game of chess by his mathematics teacher, Professor Bret Hollinger. It was felt by Professor Hollinger that by learning the game of chess, Benjamin would learn how to solve higher mathematical problems with constantly changing variables. As Professor Hollinger had explained to Benjamin, the game of chess was nothing more than a complex math problem from beginning to end.

Benjamin took to the game of chess as a fish took to water. He quickly learned the game. With each session Benjamin became more proficient. After a few months of playing the game of chess, Professor Hollinger asked Benjamin if he would like to play against some of the student members of the Harvard Chess Club, which Professor Hollinger was in charge of. "Of course", Benjamin agreed. After all he was more than up to the task and was excited with the prospect of playing some of the older students. Professor Hollinger made the arrangements for Benjamin to have a chess match with one of the students on the chess club. All the while he would be under the watchful eye of Mrs. Whitmore.

Benjamin, Professor Hollinger, and Mrs. Whitmore, as well as the chess club in its entirety, were gathered in Professor Hollinger's class room. Professor Hollinger wanted to challenge Benjamin as much as possible. He felt in order to do this it would be best to have Benjamin play the reigning champion, Adam Caldwell.

Adam Caldwell was a child prodigy in his own right. He was only eighteen years old and already had completed his Masters Degree in Physics and was currently working on his Doctorate.

Benjamin was seated at a table where a chess board was already set up. Across the table sat Adam. Benjamin spoke first. "Hi, my name is Benjamin Stone. Professor Hollinger said it was ok with you for us to play a game of chess together." Adam sat motionless for a moment, looking at Benjamin in a very curious manner. Here sat before him an eight year old boy, whom Professor Hollinger felt was worthy enough to challenge *him* to a game of chess. Adam Caldwell was the reigning Chess champion not only at Harvard, but he was also the current National Chess Champion.

To Adam this entire event seemed beneath him, or at the very least bizarre. Finally Adam spoke, "Yes, I agreed to play a game of chess with you. Are you ready?" Benjamin responded, "Yes, I am ready."

The game began. Adam moved first and then Benjamin. As it would continue on, it became apparent to Adam that Benjamin was going to give him a chess game he had not expected. This child, this small boy of only eight years old, was staying with Adam move after move. At one point Adam thought he might even lose, but the end results would leave Adam's ego intact *Benjamin lost* the match.

Adam started to get up from the table, when Benjamin asked him, "Would you like to try your luck *one more time*?" On some level, this infuriated Adam! How dare this child speak to him as though he might have won the chess match only thru some sort of luck! On the other hand, he himself knew that at one point he *had* almost lost the match. Before Adam could respond Professor Hollinger spoke

"Adam, I would appreciate it if you would let Benjamin have a rematch. I believe he has shown all of us that he is worthy." All Adam could do in order to save his dignity would be to allow the rematch. "Of course Professor Hollinger, we can play all day if Benjamin would like or until everyone's curiosity is satisfied". Professor Hollinger looked at Adam with a look of disapproval. Adam knew that his comment was unwarranted. "Continue playing" said Professor Hollinger. The second game was closer than the first game, but once again Adam managed to win. Benjamin and Adam continued to play, and game four was to be the end for Adam. He had *finally* lost. It had taken four games for Benjamin to figure out his opponent.

Benjamin had just beaten the national chess champion, this was *huge*. Everyone was clapping and telling Benjamin what a great job he had done! That is everyone *except* for Adam who was visibly upset. Adam stood up and asked everyone to calm down and that it was *he* who now wanted a rematch. It was then that Mrs. Whitmore stepped in and said that Benjamin had enough chess for one day, and that he would be able to continue at a later time, but not today. As a child psychologist Mrs. Whitmore felt it would be best if Benjamin stopped playing at this point, especially after his win. This would be a huge boost to his self esteem. As for Adam Caldwell's self esteem, he was older, more mature and would have to deal with his feelings of inferiority on his own for the time being. All Benjamin knew was that he had fun playing chess with Adam, even though he had lost three games, he did win one. Everyone in the room seemed to be so excited by his one win. Benjamin did not give much thought to it. Benjamin did ask Professor Hollinger if he could join the chess club. Professor Hollinger told Benjamin that since he was not at Harvard University in the capacity of a college student (at least for now) he needed to get through his high school curriculum first. Then once he was enrolled in college, *if and only if* it did not interfere with his other studies, he would be allowed to join the chess club. This pleased Benjamin a great deal, and from this time forward he was on a mission to finish his high school curriculum, get into college, and join the chess club where he could spend time with his new friend, Adam Caldwell.

Professor Hollinger had a long talk with Adam. He explained that he understood how Adam must have felt to have been beaten at a game of chess by an eight year old child. Professor Hollinger went on to tell Adam that though he had lost a chess match, he did only lose one out of four matches and that he needed to keep in mind that Benjamin was not your average eight year old child. As a matter of fact, he was not your average anything! You must understand Adam, people like yourself, me, and *especially* Benjamin, were in a minority.

Adam your IQ has been rated somewhere around one hundred and ninety putting you in the top one percent of the human population. As far as Benjamin is concerned, we regularly test his IQ. Each time the test is given his score goes up. We estimate, and I hesitate to use that word, but our best educated guess is that his IQ, as of right now, is probably somewhere around two hundred and thirty. You and I are by all accounts geniuses. He is rated a super genius. So Adam, what I am asking of you, *not* demanding, is to see if you can help me with Benjamin's development. There are very few people who can understand this kind of genius, but you are one of them. I would like you to be friends with Benjamin, become a mentor to him, to help him grow. It is up to you Adam. I would just ask that you give some thought to what I have asked of you. Adam processed the information provided to him by Professor Hollinger. He paused for a moment, then spoke, "Professor Hollinger everything you have said about Benjamin is true, as well as everything you have said about the way I felt having been beaten by an eight year old child. I suppose that I have let my emotions get the best of me. The only thing I can say in my defense is that when I came to Harvard University I was fourteen years old and had quickly become accustom to being the center of attention around here. But as usual Professor Hollinger you have once again become the voice of reason, and I admit you are right. Therefore, I will do what you have asked of me. I will try to be friends with Benjamin. I will try to be a mentor to him, and who knows, if I keep an open mind, I will more than likely learn something from him."

As Professor Hollinger had hoped, Benjamin and Adam became friends. Adam would set time aside from his schedule twice a week, a few hours each time. They would spend this time playing chess or just talking. Benjamin had asked Adam what degree he was pursuing in college. Adam told him that he was pursuing a degree in Practical Physics. Benjamin then asked Adam if he could borrow some books on the subject so that they would be able to have more detailed conversations. Adam reached into his back pack and handed Benjamin a book titled Practical Physics. Benjamin thanked Adam for the book and promised he would read it so that next week they could have a better conversation. It was then that Mrs. Whitmore interrupted the conversation to tell Benjamin that they must go; otherwise they would be late for his biology class.

As promised by Benjamin the next time the two of them met, Benjamin had read the entire book. Not only did he read the book, *but he understood it!* Adam knew then that Professor Hollinger was right, that Adam was standing in the presence of a "Super Genius". As far as Adam was concerned, the icing on the cake was the fact that Benjamin did not care to learn about physics, he just wanted to be able to carry on a conversation with his new friend. As mentioned before, Benjamin was on a mission to join the chess club and the only way to do that was to graduate twelfth grade and officially become a college student. Two years have passed and Benjamin is now ten years old. He has just finished the curriculum needed to graduate high school.

He was now ready for college but most importantly he was ready for the chess club. Benjamin's friend Adam Caldwell has also finished his schooling. He has acquired his Doctorate Degree in Physics and at twenty years of age, through Harvard University, he has landed a job at NASA. Adam Caldwell is officially the youngest physicist in the world, as well as the youngest physicist to have ever worked for NASA. Benjamin was just as happy for his friend Adam, as he was sad to see him go. Adam felt likewise but it was his turn to make his mark in life. Adam did make Benjamin promise him that he would not pursue a career as a Physicist. They both had a good laugh with that comment. Benjamin was now *officially* a college student. As for Benjamin, the first order of business was to join the chess club; the second order of business would be to complete his prerequisite courses, then to pursue a Doctorate Degree in Mathematics.

As the youngest member of the chess club, Benjamin would have to prove himself by playing all of the other members, which he did in short order. Benjamin not only played all the other members, Benjamin proved that he was a *superior* player. By midterm he had become the captain of the chess club at Harvard University. The chess club was playing in tournaments against other universities from around the Eastern Seaboard. The top chess clubs would play each other for a regional championship. Then the regional champions would play each other for a national title. With Benjamin onboard, Harvard University would go on to compete in the National Championship his freshmen year, but in the world of chess this was not enough. Each competing club was then to put up their top champion to play through the process of elimination amongst *all the top club champions*. They would play each other until only one was left. The one left standing would be the national champion, a title that would be held for the entire year.

Well, as you have probably already guessed, Benjamin *was* going to be that champion. The Harvard chess club was not surprised, because they already knew of Benjamin and his ability at chess. It was the rest of the world that was taken aback by this child prodigy. He was in every major news paper in the country. The world had "officially" been introduced to Benjamin Stone. The question weighing in on every one's mind is would Benjamin fare as well when he played on the international chess level. Those competing would play for the title of World Champion Chess Player. Before Benjamin left for Sweden, Dean Pearl came to see Benjamin and his parents. Dean Pearl wanted to let Benjamin and his parents know how pleased the university was with how Benjamin had been representing himself, the chess club, *and* the university. Dean Pearl went on tell Benjamin and his parents, that because of how pleased the university was that they would like to send Benjamin's parents, his brother, and his sister, the entire family, to Sweden for a family vacation as well as to support Benjamin in his bid to obtain the World Chess Champion title. Benjamin's parents accepted the university's offer. They were all so excited, and *so* proud of Benjamin. Before Benjamin knew it he was in Sweden.

Benjamin's family was very excited to be in Sweden. They had never taken a family vacation before. They did not know where to start or where to go. The university had made arrangements for the family to stay at a very nice hotel. The family would be accompanied by Professor Hollinger. He was, after all, the head of the Harvard chess club. The first two days in Sweden were to be spent just unwinding and taking in some of the local sites. The third day was business for Benjamin, no more playing. It was time, time to see if Benjamin was as good as Professor Hollinger believed he was.

The international chess tournament would be a process of elimination. Benjamin would play his first game against a young woman from England named Carrie Thorton. She was the current chess champion in the United Kingdom. They were seated at a table, the chess board was ready, and the mood in the room was very serious. It wasn't just Benjamin being seated to play his chess match but rather numerous games being played at one time. Just as the officials were preparing to start the tournament, Benjamin blurted out "Hi, my name is Benjamin, have you been here before?" The officials gave Benjamin a stern look, as well as Professor Hollinger. The young lady, Carrie Thorton, from the United Kingdom smiled and politely told Benjamin that she had been here before and there is no talking during the tournament. Benjamin was somewhat embarrassed by the whole event and apologized to the officials.

It was now time to play and play Benjamin did. He easily won the first chess match as well as the other three matches he played that day. Benjamin it seemed by the end of the day, if he had not already been a celebrity, he now most certainly was. The competition continued for three more days, each day ending the same for Benjamin. He would win every chess match that he played. Not only was he winning, he was destroying the competition. On day five, Benjamin was positioned to play the current champion, his friend Adam Caldwell. This was causing Benjamin a great deal of stress. He did not want to take from his friend what he had worked so hard for. The night before the final chess match, the match that would determine who would be the champion for the next year. Benjamin insisted that he be allowed to speak to his friend Adam. Professor Hollinger told Benjamin that he felt it would be inappropriate for Benjamin to have a meeting with the current champion the night before the championship match. Even though Benjamin understood, no matter how many times Professor Hollinger explained to Benjamin the implications' of such a meeting, Benjamin *insisted* on seeing Adam. Benjamin went as far as to tell Professor Hollinger that if he did not talk to Adam before the chess match, that there would be no chess match. Finally, under pressure from Benjamin and with great reluctance, Professor Hollinger took Benjamin to see Adam. When Benjamin and Professor Hollinger arrived at Adam's room, he too was surprised to see the both of them standing at his door. Adam felt the same as Professor Hollinger, a meeting between the current champion and the challenger the night before the chess match, could be interrupted in an unfavorable light. Never the less, Adam invited the both of them into his room. Benjamin asked Adam if he could speak to him in private. Adam asked Professor Hollinger if he minded stepping onto the balcony for a few minutes. He turned Benjamin and said, "Alright Benjamin now that Professor Hollinger is out of the way, what is so important that you had to see me tonight?"

"Adam I hope you are not mad at me", Benjamin asked. Adam told Benjamin that he was not mad, but that he really shouldn't be here. He told him to leave and that the two of them could talk tomorrow after the chess match! Adam, "I have to talk to you", Benjamin insisted." What is so important that it can't wait Benjamin?" " You don't understand Adam, I do not want to play you tomorrow and I do not want to take your title." "Benjamin; that is what this is all about? First of all, keep in mind I only have the title because *I* took it from someone else. Secondly, do not be so sure that you are going to win; after all I have beaten you before. Remember?" "Adam I *let* you win. You have *never* beaten me. What you and Professor Hollinger don't know is that I let people win sometimes so that they will play me. I like playing the game of chess, but I know that *no one* can beat me. So I lose on purpose sometimes so people will still play with me. I don't get to play with kids other than my brother or sister and the game of chess gives me the opportunity to play with other people and everyone seems to make such a big deal out of me winning the way I do. To be honest with you,sometimes I wish I wasn't as smart as I am, but I am and I can't turn it off no matter how much I wish I could. If I play you tomorrow and I lose there will be a lot of people disappointed in me. If I play you tomorrow and win, which I could if I wanted to, then I will feel bad, because you are my friend and you have worked very hard to be the World Champion Chess player that you are. As for me, I don't have to work hard at it. All I do is play for fun.

"Now Benjamin, that was a mouthful and I know chess comes easily to you. Though I would like to have thought that the few times I had beaten you. I had done so by my own skill and not by you letting me win, but I am not surprised you have done that. Benjamin I can tell you that I also have wished from time to time that I was not as smart as I am. It can be a curse at times, but like you said, I am smart and I can't change that. As far as the championship game tomorrow, as my friend, if indeed you are my friend, I expect you to give me one hundred percent, because if you don't and you were to let me win, the victory would be hollow. It would mean nothing to me. Now as your friend and I am indeed your friend, I will guarantee you that I am going to give you one hundred percent. I will try with every bit of skill I have to beat you! I want you to promise me two things here tonight. The first is that you will indeed give one hundred percent when we play for the championship. The second is that you never give less than one hundred percent no matter who you think you may or may not be offending. *You must always be true to yourself Benjamin.* So the question is, Benjamin, not only can you promise me you will do these things, will you do those things?" Benjamin looked at his friend Adam, he smiled and then nodded indicating that he could and would do what Adam had asked of him. It was then that Adam signaled for Professor Hollinger to come back inside. Professor Hollinger asked Benjamin are you ok, are you satisfied? Benjamin smiled and said that he was fine then asked, Professor Hollinger to take him back to his room. Again, Benjamin smiled and laughed as he left the room.

The next day there was a mood of excitement in the convention center, were the event was being held. When Benjamin walked into the room escorted by Professor Hollinger, his mother, father and siblings, all eyes were on him. Benjamin walked directly to the table were the chess match was to be played. His friend Adam Caldwell had already seated himself. Benjamin took his seat and after a few minutes the officials started the match. This would also be the first year that the World Chess Championship was to be televised. No doubt because of the fact that a twelve year old child prodigy by the name of Benjamin Stone, had taken the world of chess by storm. It was also no surprise to anyone when Benjamin *won* the chess match, defeating his friend and current champion. Benjamin was to be crowned the new World Champion Chess Player of 1971 and the first person to congratulate Benjamin was his friend Adam Caldwell.

Everyone was eager to meet Benjamin, to talk to him, to be seen with him, just to have their picture taken with him. Benjamin was indeed without dispute a true celebrity.

When Benjamin arrived back home it was not different, the attention continued. Benjamin did several interviews that were set by the university, all the while under the watchful eye of Mrs. Whitmore.

It didn't take long for those in the advertising community to begin contacting Benjamin's parents to see if it would be possible to have Benjamin endorse their products. Benjamin parents decided to leave that decision to Benjamin. It would be entirely up to him whether or not he wanted to endorse a particular product. Benjamin decided that if it was a product that *he* liked, a product that *he* used, that it would be okay to tell people they should try it. In the end, Benjamin would only end up endorsing a few products. He would do an ad for Cheerio's (his favorite cereal). The cereal company had Benjamin's face plastered on millions of boxes of Cheerios. Benjamin also decided he would like to endorse Pepsi Cola. This was after all his favorite soft drink, even though his mother would only let him have one maybe two Pepsi's a week. Another company Benjamin did an endorsement for was a tennis shoe company called Kid Flyers. They so happened to be the brand of shoes that he wore. (Benjamin thought they would make him run faster and jump higher.) If Benjamin or his parents wanted they could endorse everything that was offered to them making a great deal of money, but this was not the case. Benjamin only endorsed the three products he liked. The money he made from the endorsement was a *substantial* amount. Benjamin's parents were putting all the money in an account for Benjamin to use when he became older. They told him they would turn all the money over to him, but for now Benjamin was not allowed to spend *any* of it.

Benjamin was aggressively working on his degree in mathematics. Yet all the while, he was continuing to play chess, not to mention defending his multiple titles.

When Benjamin was thirteen years old, he asked Mrs. Whitmore if she could arrange a meeting for him with the Dean of Students, Mr. Pearl. On the day of the meeting, upon entering Mr. Pearl's office, Benjamin asked Mr. Pearl if he was okay with Mrs. Whitmore attending our meeting. Mr. Pearl was more than happy to accommodate Benjamin's request. Now Benjamin asked Mr. Pearl, What exactly is the purpose of you needing to have a meeting? "Benjamin took a deep breath, he looked at Mrs. Whitmore then back to Mr. Pearl, "The reason I have asked for a meeting is to discuss the possibility of not having Mrs. Whitmore escort me throughout the day." Benjamin turned to Mrs. Whitmore to tell her that it was definitely not something she had or had not done. That is was all about him and how he felt. Benjamin proceeded to tell both Mrs. Whitmore and Mr. Pearl that he was at the age where he wanted to become more independent that having Mrs. Whitmore as a escort made him feel childish. Before Mr. Pearl could respond, Mrs. Whitmore told Benjamin that she had been anticipating this for some time. That she was surprised Benjamin had taken as long as he had. Benjamin told Mrs. Whitmore that he had wanted to say something for almost a year, but he was afraid that it would hurt her feelings. Mrs. Whitmore told Benjamin that not only did it not hurt her feelings, but quite the contrary, she was proud of him. "The fact that you want to be on your own, shows growth on your part, Benjamin."

By the end of the meeting, Mr. Pearl agreed that Benjamin was of the age were he should be allowed to attend school unescorted and completely responsible for himself.

As time went on, Benjamin continued his pursuit of a PhD in Mathematics. Benjamin also continued to defend his chess title. By now Benjamin, at just fifteen years old, had set himself on a pace to secure a PhD in mathematics by the end of the school year, just days after his sixteenth birthday.

Prior to the end of the school year, Benjamin would be challenged by no other than MIT, another prestige school of higher learning. It seems that some students at MIT had programmed a computer to play chess. They claimed that no one could beat their computer at a game of chess, not even the great child prodigy of Harvard University Benjamin Stone. It seems that the gauntlet has been thrown down. Benjamin readily accepted the challenge.

The students at MIT, working hand and hand with Dean Pearl, they made arrangements to have the chess game televised. This was not just *any* chess game; it was going to be a televised match between Harvard and MIT. It was a match that would be seen by millions of people worldwide. In reality it would be MIT and Harvard that were to be matched against each other. Each one of schools would be putting up their own. Benjamin would be representing Harvard, and a computer was going to be representing MIT. There was a lot of buzz in the academic community as to whether or not a person could beat a computer. It seemed that people were firmly split down the middle on their choice of who the champion would be. The match was going to be held at MIT; after all it would be easier to have Benjamin go to MIT than to have the computer brought to Harvard.

On the day of the match, while Benjamin was being interviewed by one of the commentators, he was asked if he believed he would be able to beat the computer. Benjamin stood before the commentator pausing for just a brief moment before answering the question asked of him. (To many his reply bordered on arrogance, but then again as a child prodigy perhaps he had earned the right to be arrogant.) “No” replied Benjamin, “I do not believe I am able to beat a computer, but then I am not playing against a computer. I am playing against a computer program, a program written by a person or persons. The program is only as good as the people who wrote it and I do not believe that the collective knowledge of the MIT students at the game of chess is adequate to beat me. Chess is a game that I have mastered above all others.”

After answering the question, Benjamin turned and walked away. The commentator stood silent for a moment before composing himself; after all he was caught off guard with the comment he was just given.

The match would begin with a coin toss to see who would make the first move. Benjamin won the coin toss; he would make the first move. Every time Benjamin made a move, the MIT students would type it into the computer to make it aware of the move. Then the computer would process the information, thus coming up with a counter move. The first game ended in a draw. The MIT students, as well as Benjamin, would both claim victory since neither one had been beaten. Both parties decided to continue playing until one or the other has lost.

The next two games ended as the first, in a draw. It seemed to everyone that the computer would be unable to beat Benjamin, as well as Benjamin unable to beat the computer. That is to everyone *except* Benjamin. Benjamin had been doing something that the computer was unable to do. He had been studying the computers moves, studying the computers programming flaws. The computer's programming would only allow the computer to make a move based on probable outcome *not* on experience. This was the program's Achilles Heel.

The fourth game had begun with the computer making the first move, a move that was a predictable one. The next move was Benjamin's. It was a move the computer would deem mathematically impossible, unable to think beyond its programming, the computer would make a move based on probable outcome. Six moves later Benjamin had finally beat the computer.

There was an *explosion* of excitement throughout the room, at least for the people whom were there to support Benjamin. The MIT students were huddled around their computer wondering what had gone wrong. Professor Hollinger was beside himself, he seemed to be doing some sort of strange victory dance. The dance seemed to Benjamin to be reminiscence to that of early man dancing around a tribal fire which was lighting up the evening sky.

After a few minutes, the room slowly began to settle down. The MIT students approached Benjamin to congratulate him on his victory. Benjamin gracefully accepted the congratulations that the MIT students had bestowed upon him.

Throughout all the excitement surrounding Benjamin and his victory, he himself stayed composed, showing little to no emotions. He was not feeling the urge to celebrate with a victory dance as Professor Hollinger had done.

Dean Pearl approached Benjamin telling him he needed to do yet another interview. Benjamin was then led over to where the commentators table was located and sat to the right of the commentator. The MIT team leader would be seated to the left of the commentator.

The interview began by congratulating Benjamin. Then the commentator quickly turned to the MIT team leader asking what had gone wrong? The MIT team leader commented that Benjamin has simply beaten the computer, but he also went on to say that he was confident that with some modifications to the program he believes the program could beat Benjamin. That is if Benjamin were up to a rematch. The commentator turned to Benjamin asking a series of questions all at once without giving Benjamin an opportunity to respond to the questions one at a time. "Well Benjamin it seems that MIT wants a rematch. Are you willing to try your luck at a rematch? Or do you feel that you have nothing to gain, after all as of today you are the undisputed world champion chess player. Perhaps you are not willing to risk that with a rematch, or are you? Well Benjamin what is your response to all of this?"

Benjamin who was always a well mannered and mild tempered individual took exception with the tone and the manner of questioning by the commentator. After all, to suggest that Benjamin was the "undisputed" World Champion Chess player was a complete discount to the fact that he *already* held that title. Benjamin began by telling the commentator that he found his method of questioning to be rude, insulting, without substance, and lacking intelligent thought. "As to how I feel about winning here today? Well, according to you, it was just *today* that I was declared the "undisputed World Champion Chess Player." Since it is obvious you are incapable of *proper* research, I would like to inform you that prior to today I was already the undisputed World Chess Player. A title I have held since the age of twelve. As to whether or not I am willing to risk my title or try my luck at a rematch, there is no risk on my part because as I stated in my previous interview "*I cannot be beaten.*" As far as "lucky", luck has nothing to do with it. Now I hope I have answered all the questions you have asked of me. Furthermore there will be no rematch. I would like to take the opportunity to make an announcement. As of today, I will no longer play the game of chess competitively. I do herby relinquish all chess titles that I hold." Benjamin went on to say that he felt that he has taken the game of chess as far as he could. That to continue playing held no interest to him, nor did he feel that it would be fair for him to continue playing and holding on to titles that so many people working so hard to achieve sought to have.

The second interview ended much like the first. When Benjamin was finished he stood up walked away with no further comment. As he walked past Dean Pearl and Professor Hollinger they looked completely stunned by what they had just witnessed. Professor Hollinger said nothing. Dean Pearl on the other hand put his hand on Benjamin's shoulder as he walked by, asking "Benjamin what have you done?" Benjamin committed, "I have done what I feel needed to be done with my best interest in mind." Benjamin walked up to his mother and father, whom were always supportive of whatever decision Benjamin made concerning him, and asked if they could go home. Not pressing Benjamin as to why his mother simply said, "Of course Benjamin, let's go home."

(CHAPTER FOUR)

In the days that followed, the faculty at Harvard University treated Benjamin somewhat awkwardly since Benjamin refused to offer an explanation as to exactly why he had walked away from the game of chess or at least an explanation that the faculty could live with. Dean Pearl and the rest of the faculty felt it was best not to press Benjamin any further at this time, giving him some time to rethink his decision may allow for him to change it.

It was around this time that Benjamin's mother told him that his younger brother Nathanial had been diagnosed with Leukemia. Benjamin found this to be very troublesome. Even though Benjamin and Nathanial were not very close, and they shared no common interest, Nathanial was still after all Benjamin's younger brother.

Benjamin pressed forward working on his thesis to complete his PhD in Mathematics. Benjamin thesis would be ground breaking. Benjamin turned his thesis into Professor Hollinger. It was titled: The mathematical probability of natural occurring worm holes, as well a potential for manmade recreation of same.

Professor Hollinger looked at Benjamin's title and then at Benjamin asking, "Is this what, I think it is?" Yes," replied Benjamin. "Do you feel that you have actually solved this problem Benjamin? Mathematicians, as well as Physicists, have been doing theoretical work in this field for decades. Benjamin you need to keep in mind in order to get your PhD that your thesis cannot be a theoretical problem it has to be a solvable problem." Benjamin told Professor Hollinger that he was aware of that and that his thesis would outline the problem, as well as gives a concrete solution. Benjamin told Professor Hollinger that if he had any problems understanding the thesis all he needed to do is contact Benjamin who would supply him with clarification. Professor Hollinger knew it would take quite some time to dissect Benjamin thesis; as well as some help from the physics department.

Shortly after Benjamin sixteenth birthday, Benjamin was told by Professor Hollinger that not only would he be receiving his PhD in Mathematics, but that he would also be having his thesis published for the scientific community to review. Scientist worldwide will argue for years to come about Benjamin's thesis. Some will claim Benjamin to be decades ahead of the rest of the world. Others would claim his thesis to be erroneous and unproven.

Benjamin was preparing to sign up for more classes. He now wanted to pursue a degree in Cellular and Molecular Biology with a minor in Chemistry. When Dean Pearl told him that the members of the Board of Trustees from Harvard University have requested that Benjamin appear before them, he asked Dean Pearl if he knew what it was about. Dean Pearl told Benjamin that though he was not sure, he believed it was about Benjamin having relinquishing his chess titles. Benjamin asked Professor Hollinger if he would care to attend the meeting with him. Professor Hollinger agreed he would be there for Benjamin.

The day of the meeting was upon them, Benjamin, accompanied by Dean Pearl and Professor Hollinger, entered the Board room. The chairman of the board Mr. Montgomery introduced himself then asked everybody to be seated. "Benjamin the purpose of the meeting today is to determine whether or not Harvard University should continue to fund your education, especially in light of your decision to relinquish your chess titles. Now Benjamin, perhaps you can shed some light on why you have chosen to relinquish your titles and why you feel that Harvard should continue to fund your education. Before you answer any of these questions Benjamin, I need you to keep in mind that your decision to relinquish your titles did not set well with the Board of Trustees."

"To us Harvard is a business and that is how we must view it. Your decision has cost us money in the form of endowments provided to us by people of wealth and influence, whom happen to be fans of the game of chess. Now that you have all the information you need please enlighten us Benjamin."

Benjamin started by telling the Board of Trustees that he apologized for any inconvenience or undue stress that he may have caused anyone. At this point he went on to tell Mr. Montgomery that he preferred to be addressed as Doctor Benjamin Stone or at the very least Doctor Stone, after all he had earned that right. Mr. Montgomery looked at Benjamin curiously then apologized for not giving proper credit where credit was due. Please continue Doctor Stone, replied Mr. Montgomery.

"I truly mean no disrespect, but I do not know how else to explain myself. For me to continue playing chess would be the equivalent of having you enter into a shoe tying contest with a group of three year old children then run around declaring yourself to be the world champion shoe tier." What an accomplishment. How good you must be, knowing that you, a full grown man had beaten a group of three year old children at a shoe tying contest. Ridiculous is it not? Well that is how I feel when competing in chess. Mr. Montgomery replies that he did not realize that competing in chess had become such an arduous task. But to Benjamin that is exactly what it had become.

Benjamin was not sure if his explanation would suffice or not, but it was the best he could give. Mr. Montgomery moved on asking no more questions about chess. Instead he asked Benjamin what he planned to do next. Benjamin told Mr. Montgomery and the Board of Trustees that he was interested in pursuing a degree in Cellular and Molecular Biology with a Minor in Chemistry.

"What do you plan to do with such a degree Doctor Stone" asked Mr. Montgomery. "As you may or may not know, my brother Nathanial was recently diagnosed with Leukemia. I truly believe that all the ailments that plague the human race are curable. I would like to apply my intellect to helping the human race. I may or may not be able to save my brother Nathanial. The truth be known with the time restraints at hand it is not likely, but perhaps I can save the next Nathanial from a disease that I know in my heart and mind *can and must be cured*."

"Mr. Montgomery you mentioned at the beginning of the meeting that the Board of Trustees may choose to stop funding my education, that you see Harvard as a business. If that is true, then from a business point of view you may wish to continue funding my education, thus ensuring that you share in my accolades. If you do not continue my funding, it will sadden me to leave Harvard, but I will explore my options and continue to further my education elsewhere. At this time I feel that it will no longer serve either one of us to continue this meeting. You will either decide in my favor or not. Thank you for your time." Benjamin stood up and walked out of the room, with Dean Pearl and the professor just a few steps behind.

Professor Hollinger was trying to get Benjamin to stop. Yelling down the corridor to him, "Benjamin; Benjamin would you please stop for a moment!" At that moment

Benjamin stopped, just standing there in the middle of the corridor. "Benjamin you *must* get out of the habit of walking away from interviews and meetings just because you are finished. You have to stop and think that just maybe the other party has not finished. Do you understand that Benjamin?" "What I understand," replied Benjamin, is that when there is not more pertinent information to exchange I am through with the interview.

Profession Hollinger told Benjamin that he may very well be the smartest person on the planet, but you have a lot to learn about social graces. "With your permission I would like to go back into the board room and talk to the members on your behalf." Benjamin replied, "If it pleases you to go back into the room then by all means go back into the board room, but if not to that would by equally fine as well. Now, please excuse me, I would like to return to the library, there are several textbooks I wish to review. "Dean Pearl took a deep breath and then told Benjamin, "By all means, Doctor Stone I would not want to keep you from your research." With that Dean Pearl went back into the board room. When Dean Pearl re—entered the room it suddenly became silent. Mr. Montgomery looked at Dean Pearl and asked if maybe he could explain to the board exactly what is going on with Benjamin. "I am sorry it seems that I once again stand corrected, what I meant to say is Doctor Stone." Though by now Mr. Montgomery's look was one of agitation, his voice seemed to show signs of aggravation.

Dean Pearl was in full damage control mode, "Mr. Montgomery as well as members of the Board I apologize for Doctor Stone. What you witnessed today were the oddities and the quirks of a genius. There is no doubt that Doctor Stone comes off as a *very arrogant* individual, though he does not do it intentionally. For Doctor Stone the line between arrogant and confidence is blurred to the point that one is not distinguishable from the other. I cannot defend the fact that Doctor Stone, posses little to no social skills, but what I can defend is the fact that Doctor Stones is a genius. The thesis that Doctor Stone prepared in order to receive his PhD in Mathematics is nothing less than monumental. Physicists from around the world have been trying to solve this theory for decades. My office has been flooded by people who want access to Doctor Stone. *Everyone from NASA to every prestige's think tank in the world!* Yet Doctor Stone so matter of factually turns down all opportunities to be interviewed or to give a lecture on his thesis about worm holes. Doctor Stone walked out of this meeting, for the same reason he refuses to grant interviews, or give lectures. The reason being that once Doctor Stone has determined that *he* is finished with a particular subject and has gotten out of it all the pertinent information he needs he is simply done and he moves on. This is the way Doctor Stone's mind works. I ask you not to understand this, but I would ask that you accept this. Not I, not any member of this Board, not you Mr. Montgomery, and perhaps not a single person on this planet, can truly understand the inner workings of Doctor Stone's mind. In this respect Doctor Stone *does* truly walk alone. I would ask you Mr. Montgomery as well as your fellow board members to consider the continuation of Doctor Stone's education. Keep in mind that with the intellect that Doctor Stone posses, only good can come from a mind such as his. I truly believe this. I also truly believe that Harvard University would like to share in Doctor Stone's future accomplishments." "Mr. Pearl, I believe that I speak for the entire board when I say that you have stated a strong case for Doctor Stone's continued education here at Harvard. The Board will notify your office of our decision in due time. Now, if you would excuse us so that we may discuss our findings."

With that Dean Pearl excused himself from the board room. For the next few days while waiting to hear from the Board, Dean Pearl would ask his secretary three or four times daily if she had heard from the board. As for Benjamin he was where he seemed to always be, the library. Benjamin spent so much time in the library the head librarian had assigned Benjamin to a table of his own. This way Benjamin could come and go as he pleased leaving his numerous textbooks spread out in a manner that only made sense to Benjamin. After the better part of a week had past, Dean Pearl was finally notified as to the Board of Trustees decision. The Board of Trustees decision would be in Benjamin's favor, a decision that both relieved and pleased Dean Pearl. He asked his secretary to locate Doctor Stone. She informed Dean Pearl that he was at the library and that she had sent word that he was requesting to see him. A short while later Doctor Stone sent word back that he was in the middle of something and at this time would be unable to comply. Dean Pearl stood up abruptly, telling his secretary that if Doctor Stone would not come to him, then he would go to Doctor Stone! Upon entering the library he saw Benjamin at once. There he was at his table where he could always be found. Doctor Stone could you please stop reading for just a moment, after all it is I who came to you. Finally after another moment or two Benjamin looked up, "Yes Dean Pearl how can I help you?" "Well Doctor Stone I thought you might like to know that the Board of Trustees has decided to continue funding your education." Benjamin looked up and asked him to thank the board for him, and he appreciated the fact that the Dean took the time to personally deliver the message. Then in a manner that only Benjamin could get away with, he simply turned his head down and once again began reading his text. Dean Pearl stood there shaking his head saying out loud to himself, "Only you Benjamin, Only you."

(CHAPTER FIVE)

By the fall of 1975 Benjamin had become more and more consumed with his studies. For the most part he was not required to attend class along with the other students. He was allowed to study independently, apart from the rest of the student body.

Benjamin spent his time between the laboratory conducting experiments and the library. It was not uncommon for Benjamin to spend five or six hours a day in the library seven days a week, *even* on holidays.

Benjamin's mother was concerned that he was spending too much time with his studies, he had no social life. His own mother would readily admit that even she did not understand the inner workings of a genius such as Benjamin. Never the less, she wished that her son would not push himself so hard. She also knew that forcing Benjamin to slow down would be a futile effort. If he were not at the library or the laboratory then he would only be in his room reading.

Benjamin's mother was very happy when Adam Caldwell called their house wanting to speak to Benjamin. Unfortunately, she had to tell Adam that he was not home. Instead he was at his usual place in the library on a Sunday afternoon. It was then that Benjamin's mother hatched the plan to have Adam come for a visit. Adam agreed. Benjamin's mother hoped that a visit from Adam would distract Benjamin from his studies, even if only for short period.

With a plan in place, Benjamin's mother made him promise that he would be home on time for dinner at six o'clock Friday night. He asked her, "Why, what is so important about dinner this Friday, compared to any other Friday or even any other night?" Benjamin's mother knew that Benjamin was looking for a rational, *logical* answer to her request. Instead, he received something he rarely experienced, "Because I said so Benjamin, that's why," his mother replied. "I know that is not what you want to hear, but I am not going to explain myself to you, not this time. All you need to know is that I'm your mother and I have asked you to do something that is important to me and as my son that should be enough." Benjamin did not know exactly how to respond. It was almost unheard of his mother to be so demanding. The only thing Benjamin could say was that he promised that he would be home at six o'clock on Friday night, "Whether or not I understood your motives is not important. You are my mother and I will do as you ask."

As promised at six o'clock in Friday night Benjamin walked into the house. To his astonishment he saw Adam Caldwell standing in the living room talking to his father. Before Benjamin could speak Adam said, "Hello Doctor Stone." This made Benjamin smile and prompted him to return the pleasantry by saying, "hello Doctor Caldwell." They both smiled at each other, but before the conversation could go any further, Benjamin's mother interrupted by saying "This is the reason that I insisted you to come home on time tonight. I have invited Adam to dinner. I thought you could use a break from your studies, aren't you surprised?" Benjamin was surprised; he had not seen his friend Adam nor spoken to him in quite some time. The four of them stood in the living room for a few minutes engaging in some light conversation. Benjamin's mother then exited the room leaving the three men alone to carry on. After fifteen or so minutes, she came back to let them know that dinner was ready.

Everybody was gathered at the table, the mood was light, the conversation was good, and mother's cooking was excellent as always. Towards the end of dinner, Benjamin and Adam began to engage in a conversation about Benjamin's thesis on worm holes. At that point Benjamin's mother stopped the two of them by telling them both that at some point she had no doubt that the subject matter would end up involving something that only the two of them could possibly understand, and that should be a conversation they have alone after dinner. Benjamin's father commented that no matter how old or how smart a person becomes it is hard to argue with mom. They all just smiled at each other and his comment.

After dinner Benjamin and Adam returned to the study. Benjamin asked Adam, "Maybe now you can tell me what really brings you here tonight." Adam told him about a phone call some weeks earlier, and how his mother had invited him to come to dinner. Adam told Benjamin that his mother had become concerned that he was too consumed with his studies. Benjamin asked Adam if there was more to the visit that he not telling him. Adam confided in Benjamin that he was also there on behalf of NASA they had been pressuring him to contact Benjamin since he refused any and all attempts to be interviewed by NASA, about his thesis on worm holes.

Adam went on to ask why he refused to be interviewed by anyone about his thesis. He then told Benjamin that he had a two part question for him. "First, why would you refuse to be interviewed or give a lecture on your thesis and second, if I ask you to let me interview you am I putting our friendship in jeopardy?" Benjamin commented to Adam, "Those are two very good questions. One easily answered the other one not so easily. As far as your first question goes I find it to be a very daunting task to have to explain myself to people who are unable to understand the information I have provided for them. In my mind, if someone is unable to comprehend what I have given them, then perhaps they are not ready to receive the information in question. I mean no disrespect to you Adam, nor do I mean to be so seemingly arrogant. It is just that at times I feel like I am trying to explain quantum physics to a group of grade school students, who are by no means able to understand what I am telling them. The way I see it, science will someday catch up to me, and someday the scientific community will come to understand what I have given them. Adam, I want you to know that there is *nothing* you could ask of me that would compromise our friendship, for you may be the *only* friend I have."

"Having said that, as a favor to you on behalf of NASA I will explain to you whatever you do not understand about my thesis on worm holes." Adam was grateful that Benjamin was not offended by his request. Adam told Benjamin that he had gone through Benjamin's thesis *countless times*, and he did understand eighty percent of what he read; however, it was the twenty percent of the thesis he could not understand that troubled him. Adam told Benjamin that neither he *nor* his colleges at NASA could get past that twenty percent. Benjamin just smiled, telling Adam they would start at the beginning and that is just what they did.

At one o'clock in the morning Benjamin's mother came into the study telling the both of them that they had solved enough problems for one evening. Now as far as Benjamin and Adam were concerned, neither one of them wanted to stop, but at Benjamin's mother insistence they put the notepads and pencils to rest for the evening. The next morning after breakfast Benjamin and Adam picked up right where they had left off. Their marathon of the higher probability of mathematics continued all day and into the evening. Once again Benjamin's mother stopped them when she felt they had been at it long enough. Sunday morning was no different. After breakfast Benjamin and Adam went at it again. Benjamin's mother must have realized that having Adam over had not stopped Benjamin or even slowed him down. At best, it redirected his focus onto something else for a short period.

On Sunday afternoon Adam finally had what he wanted and what NASA *needed*. It suddenly all became clear to him, why he had not seen it. Adam was very grateful to Benjamin. Adam asked Benjamin if he could call on him for any future clarification he might need. Of course Benjamin had no problem with that.

Benjamin's mother was preparing dinner when Adam came down from upstairs with luggage in hand. "Adam will you be staying for dinner?" asked Benjamin's mother. "No ma'am", replied Adam. "I need to get back to NASA. Besides with the information Doctor Stone has given me my colleges at NASA will be eager to receive the news." Benjamin smiled and said "goodbye Doctor Caldwell. I consider this to have been a relaxing, pleasant, and productive visit on both our parts." Adam replied, "I could have not stated it any better myself Doctor Stone", and with that he left.

For Benjamin Monday, as most days, meant back to the laboratory, and back to the library. The next few years, went by with little to no change in Benjamin's life or daily routine. Then one day while in the library, his sister came into see him. This may not seem strange on the surface, except Benjamin's sister had *never* come to see him at the library before. Now Benjamin was not a person who lost focus easily nor was he a person who generally noticed what was going on around him. However, when he heard his sister's voice he knew something was wrong. "Rebecca", replied Benjamin, "What is wrong? Why are you here?" "Mother sent me to get you, it's Nathanial." With that, Benjamin dropped the book he had been reading and took off running towards home. Benjamin ran into the house, hollering "mother, mother where are you!" It was then that Benjamin's father appeared in the entry way to the kitchen. Before his father spoke Benjamin knew, he just knew.

Nathanial would be laid to rest four days later. Benjamin's mother would never be the same. She changed. It seemed that in part she had died along with Benjamin's brother Nathanial. As far as Benjamin, he blamed himself in part for his brother's death. If only he had more time, if only he could have somehow found a cure, or even away to delay the disease, but he did not and he would have to live with this whether or not his guilt was real or imagined.

Benjamin would now spend all of his time in the laboratory, evenings, weekends, and holidays. It mattered not, the days blurred into weeks, the weeks to months, and the months became years.

(CHAPTER SIX)

It is May 1979, and Benjamin had just celebrated his twentieth birthday. It somehow seemed fitting that just days after Benjamin's twentieth birthday, he had completed and turned in his thesis. His thesis was being reviewed by the Biology staff. The only problem is that his thesis was more advanced than the Biology staff reviewing it. Yes, once again it seemed that Benjamin had delivered a thesis so advanced, so ground breaking, so absolutely mind boggling that even his most hardened critics' had to come to terms with the fact that Doctor Benjamin Stone, at the age of twenty, a two time PHD recipient, was a person to be reendowed within the Scientific community. Benjamin's thesis was titled "The Genome of the Varies Human Breeds and Sub—breeds". The title alone cause confusion and as usual Benjamin's work would require a great deal of explanation. After repetitive insistence by Harvard's Board of Directors, Benjamin finally agreed to give a lecture on his latest thesis.

The lecture would be held at Harvard University. On the day of the lecture, just twenty minutes before it was to begin, there was no sign of Benjamin. Dean Pearl was in a panic and he asked if someone could please find Doctor Stone. Benjamin's sister, Rebecca was standing near Dean Pearl and overheard his request. Rebecca quickly volunteers and in just a moment she was off and running. Rebecca knew where to find Benjamin. You could always find Benjamin was in the laboratory. When Rebecca arrived at the laboratory there was Benjamin just as she thought he would be. With a great deal of excitement Rebecca hollered, "Benjamin you are going to be late for your lecture". Benjamin response was his typical just one minute; I am in the middle of something. “No Benjamin”, Rebecca responded your lecture is supposed to start in less than ten minutes. As if a light bulb had just been turned on in Benjamin’s head, his eyes opened wide, he responded “Oh no, I forgot”. With that the both of them were off and running. When they arrived at the back stage of the auditorium Benjamin had less than two minutes to prepare for the lecture. A lecture he was to give to a diverse group of the most brilliant scientific minds in the world. Benjamin stood before Dean Pearl and Mr. Montgomery of the Board of Directors looking un—kept, un—groomed, and ill prepared.

“*My god* Doctor Stone, just look at you” barked Mr. Montgomery. “You look as if though you slept in these clothes, your hair is a mess, and where are your notes?” Now it was Benjamin turn to bark back. “Mr. Montgomery,” He replied, “The first thing you need to remember is that it was *your* idea for me to give this lecture and the only reason you want this is so *you* can get some free public relations out of my work. As to my appearance I am not here to give a lecture on fashion. I am here to give a lecture on the human genome. Now if you will excuse me I have less than one minute to prepare myself.” Benjamin walked up to an undergrad student and asked to borrow his lab coat, which he then put it on. Benjamin then turned walking toward the stage as he approached the curtain. He could hear Dean Pearl introducing him, ladies and gentlemen it is my pleasure to introduce Doctor Benjamin Stone whom is here today to enlighten us on his thesis “The Genome of the Varies Human Breeds, and Sub—breeds.” Ladies and Gentlemen I give you Doctor Benjamin Stone.

Benjamin walked across the stage to the podium and thanked Dean Pearl for the introduction. Benjamin then went on to thank the audience for taking time out of their busy schedules to attend the lecture. Benjamin started by telling everyone in the audience that he would prefer an open question and answer session over that of a traditional lecture format. Everyone in the audience knows who I am, so when you are called on please introduce yourself as well as letting me know what field you are currently working in. It will make it helpful to me if I knew what your area of expertise is, so that I might be able to tailor my answers to best meet your individual needs. Everyone in the audience has had ample time to review my thesis. There will be no surprises here today, only clarification on the material as needed. Now, let us begin.

The first person Benjamin called on introduced himself as Doctor Burstein. He said he was currently working on a genome project of his own. He asked, "Doctor Stone, in your thesis you claim that there are only four breeds of humans, three of which are sub—breeds to the original breed. Is that correct?" "Yes, that is correct," replied Benjamin, "and what would be our question." "My question is more one of a personal nature. As a Jewish male, you give no assigned breed to the Jewish community." "Doctor Burstein what you have done is make a common mistake and that is to confuse ethnology with breed. To answer your question the Jewish community has been assigned to a breed, the Arabic's. Now what everybody must remember is this is pure science and emotion needs to be removed. No matter what the past, present, or even the future relationship between the Arabic community and the Jewish community may be the Jewish people and the Arabic people are one and the same, under the skin that is. I hope that helps to answer your question." "Yes it does Doctor Stone. Whether or not I agree with is another question." Benjamin seemed completely indifferent to what Doctor Burstein had said, and he quickly moved on.

Benjamin scanned the room for the next person to call on. He spotted a young lady who caught his eye; not just because of her physical beauty, but because amongst the others in the audience she also stood out for her youth. Benjamin pointed, to the women in the fourth row towards the end, “What is your name and your question?” “My name is Doctor Angelica Web. I am currently working in the field of research and development in the pharmaceutical industry.” My question is, “do you see the possibility of drug’s being developed, and tailored to specific breeds of humans?”

“Yes I do, for example the Negroid breed suffers from Sickle Cell Anemia, and Hypertension to a larger degree than others. Once the trigger in their genome is found, I believe that specific drugs can be tailored to relieve this breed of ailments. I hope that answers your question. Yes Doctor Stone, thank you, No Doctor Web it is I who thank you for your well stated, and obviously well thought out question.

Benjamin felt some sense of embarrassment for having openly flirted with a member of the audience, prompting him to *quickly* move on. You sir, what is your question?

“My name is Doctor Anickey and my field is Cellular Biology. What I would like to know is if you could start at the beginning, and explain how you determined that there is only one true breed, along with what you call the three sub—breeds.

Doctor Anickey I would be glad to explain the “original breed”, not the *true breed* as you have called it, but the original breed, as well as the three subsequent sub—breeds. To start off, the oldest breed is the Negroid breed, making it the original breed. Mankind branched out moving around the planet. Because of the environment he inhabited, and over a period of tens of thousands of years, branches of the original breed began to distinguish themselves, thus the three sub—breeds come in. The first sub—breed is the Asian breed. This breed will account for the Eskimos, the American Indians, the Hispanic people of South America, all of the Island inhabitants, Polynesians, etc…, and of course the Asian people. The second sub—breed would be the Arabic breed. This would cover the people of India, the Jewish people, the Italians, the Greeks, the Egyptians, and all the other Arabic people. The third and last would be the Caucasian breed, this breed as with the Negroid breed, are easily identified. Does this help to clear things up for you, Doctor Anickey?" "Yes Doctor Stone it does. Your answer had been very helpful."

Benjamin picked another person to ask a question. This time it was to be an older woman who was trying very hard to be noticed, with both her arms raised waving about. "Yes," "You, the women in the front. It is obvious that you badly want to ask a question," commented Benjamin. "Yes, Doctor Stone I do want to ask you a question. My name is Doctor Sylvia Lance. My current field is that of Theology. Doctor Stone you have commented that it took tens of thousands of years for what you call the three sub—breeds to make their presence known." "That would be correct," responded Benjamin. "As a theologian, hearing you make comments of that nature tells me that you have totally discounted the events of the human experience as laid out before us in the Bible. Your comments, in my mind, go even further. They give no credit to God, no credit to a higher being, no credit to the world God has created for us. It seems to me that you have chosen to instead credit our very existence to random chance or dumb blind luck. Is that right Doctor Stone?" "Doctor Lance, I am here today to discuss scientific fact and scientific fact is the *only* thing I will discuss. You obviously have an agenda. You seem to be here today to press your point. Fortunately, today is set up for me to press *my* point."

"You sir, I saw your hand up earlier, what was your question?" The gentlemen asked his question and Benjamin answered. The event went on like this for nearly two hours. Finally Benjamin told the audience that the lecture was concluded and that for anyone who cared to attend there would be appetizers and cocktails at Roosevelt Hall for the next few hours at which time he would be circulating throughout the crowd for some one on one conversation.

Benjamin then left the stage by the same manner he had entered it. When he went backstage he was greeted by Mr. Montgomery, and Dean Pearl. They both seemed pleased by the way the lecture had gone with the exception of the religious questioning that had been aimed at getting Benjamin to comment to his belief in the existence of God. It was felt that Benjamin handled the questioning very well.

Benjamin reluctantly attended the meet and greet session that the university had put together for him. Benjamin worked the crowd wanting nothing more than to get out of there and get back to his laboratory. He saw an opportunity to leave and leave he did. Benjamin exited Roosevelt Hall through a stairway at the back of the hall. In Benjamin's mind the day's events could be put behind him and he could now make more productive use of his time. It was then Benjamin heard the voice of a woman, "Doctor Stone, Doctor Stone," Benjamin kept going at first then once again he heard her voice. "Doctor Stone please wait". Benjamin began to slow down not because he wanted to be asked any more questions, but because the women's voice calling him was soft and inviting. His curiosity was getting the best of him. Finally, Benjamin stopped and waited for the women who had been chasing after him. When Benjamin caught sight of her, it turned out to be the young lady in the audience that he had clumsily been flirting with. “Doctor Stone, could you give me a moment of your time”. Benjamin stood saying nothing. It seems that for the first time in Benjamin life he had been smitten. “Doctor Stone did you hear me?” Suddenly Benjamin came back from where ever the sight and sound of this young lady had sent him. “Yes, I heard you, but before you ask anything of me. I would like to introduce myself to you”. I already know who you are, you are Doctor Benjamin Stone. “No I am not, not here not now I am simply Benjamin, and if memory serves me right you are Angelica.” That is correct Benjamin, my name is Angelica. Benjamin had little to no experience with women. He for the most part found them to be emotional and lacking in logic, but for reasons he could not rationalize he found himself to be unable to focus, unable to clear his thoughts. “Benjamin, can I have a moment of your time? There are a few more questions I would like to ask you.” Benjamin responded by telling Angelica that if she would join him for dinner, he would answer her questions. Well I suppose that would be ok. Where would you like to go Benjamin? You leave that to me, I am going to take you to my favorite place in this area to get a good hardy meal. Angelica just smiled and told Benjamin to lead the way. The two of them walked for twenty minutes, talking. Benjamin had taken Angelica to Barney’s Burger Barn.

They went inside and seated themselves. Angelica looked at Benjamin and commented, “So this is your favorite place to have a meal?”

Benjamin replied, “It is close to campus, the owner is friendly and I am comfortable coming here. Not to mention the burgers are great!” Just then the owner walked up to their table. “I have not seen you in months, Benjamin. If it were not for you having food delivered, I would never hear from you.” Benjamin just smiled and said, “I just don’t seem to have much spare time.” “Well Benjamin I see that you have made time tonight, and judging from your company I can see why.” I am sorry Barney this Doctor Angelica Web. She is an associate of mine.

“Of course Benjamin, an associate, and what a delightful associate she is.” “Hello Angelica, my name is Barney. Any associate of Benjamin is a friend of mine. Now, what can I get for the two of you?” Angelica replied first, “Benjamin this is your favorite place to eat. So why don’t you order for the two of us.” “Barney we will have the Big Barney burger, an order of fries, and chocolate malts for each of us.” “Benjamin as always you have made an excellent choice. Now while the meal is being prepared the two of you need to get back to “associating” with each other.”

While waiting for their meal Angelica continued to ask Benjamin questions. Do you really feel that there is no difference between ethnic groups such as Jewish people compared to the people of Iraq or Saudi Arabia? Of course there are differences, but they are very subtle. Think of it this way, dogs have many breeds, but all dogs are members of the canine family. A German Sheppard, whether it is black, white, brown, or brown and black it is still a German Sheppard. The differences are more a matter of characteristics, subtle differences that make one German Sheppard different from another, but in the end they are still German Sheppard’s. Benjamin, the explanation you just gave me was so simple, but yet so elegant, and yes it did help. The conversation continued over their Big Barney Burger, fries, and chocolate malts. The conversation went from light to serious, back and forth. Then Angelica brought up the religious assault that Benjamin had endured while at the Podium. Benjamin told Angelica that people are too quick to discount science. It is easier to just say "God did it" instead of looking for an explanation or a reason. I seek knowledge and in the quest for knowledge I question all. If I want to know why people have different skin colors, I can look in the Bible and find a story of how God did it and why, but if I seek a science based answer, it would have to do with environment and evolution. As a scientist I know that if I put a group of black people in Iceland, with a large enough breeding base, isolated from all other people, this group of black people in a period of thirty five to forty thousand years would turn white. I also know that if I isolated a group of white people in Africa under the same circumstances that in a period of thirty five to forty thousand years they would become black. This is not blasphemy, nor is it racial. It is simply a matter of fact, a matter of science. At the moment Benjamin suddenly realized that he may have offended Angelica after all he didn't know what her religious views were. Angelica, if I offended you with my commits it was not my intention. No Benjamin you haven't offended me, I share your views when it comes to science and religion. Benjamin felt as if though a large weight had just been lifted off his chest, now he could breathe again. The two of them continued uninterrupted, until Barney told them that he was closing. Neither Benjamin nor Angelica noticed, but they had been at Barney's Burger Barn for *five hours*!

Benjamin told Angelica that he was within walking distance of his home, but wondered where she was staying, and how she would get there. Angelica told Benjamin that she was staying at the Ramada Inn, and that she would call for a taxi to take her back. Benjamin asked Angelica if it would be ok for him to ride along with her just to see that she made it back safely. Angelica smiled in a very approving manner, telling Benjamin that she would appreciate that. When the taxi arrived at the Ramada Inn, Benjamin walked Angelica to the front door they exchanged pleasantries, and then as Benjamin was walking away Angelica asked Benjamin if he cared to join her in her room to continue their conversation, she was not ready for the evening to end. Without hesitation Benjamin agreed and the two of them went to her room. They stayed up all night talking, and *only* talking.

When the sun came up Angelica told Benjamin that she had an early flight back to New York, and that she needed to get ready. Benjamin told Angelica that he had never had a night filled with such stimulating conversation. Then for the first time in Benjamin's life, he asked a woman for her phone number. A few minutes later Benjamin was on his way with her phone number in hand. For the next few days, weeks, all Benjamin could think about was Angelica. Benjamin was spending so much time thinking about Angelica that his work was starting to suffer and he knew it. For the first time in Benjamin's life his mind was clouded, he was unable to focus. This disturbed Benjamin; this caused him great stress, which led to confusion. Benjamin determined after a great deal of thought that the only thing to do, the only he could do to once again compose himself was to throw Angelica's number away, and get back to work, and that is exactly what Benjamin did.

The weeks continued to pass in a seemingly uneventful manner, Benjamin as always could be found in the laboratory. It was now October 1979, during this time Benjamin was under even more increasing pressure by Dean Pearl, whom was bringing word down from the Board of Directors telling Benjamin that he had to give the university a format as to the direction his research was headed. Benjamin resisted as always. All Benjamin wanted was to be left alone to do as he pleased. In Benjamin's mind his research could change direction at any time, depending on what he discovered. Benjamin finally explained to Dean Pearl what direction his research would hopefully take him. Dean Pearl would go back and forth between Mr. Montgomery, the Board of Directors, and Benjamin. After several weeks of trying to get some sort of coherent information out of Benjamin, as to the direction he was headed and trying to satisfy Mr. Montgomery along with the Board of Directors, a meeting was set. The meeting would be between Benjamin, the Board of Directors, and the Center for Disease Control, which was an agency for the United States Government. The CDC as a matter of practice would fund research at varies universities, giving grant money with no strings attached, other than wanting to know what type of research the money would go to. Dean Pearl would also be attending the meeting.

The stage was set; Benjamin entered the room accompanied by Dean Pearl. At the table before Benjamin sat the Board of Directors in its entirety headed by Mr. Montgomery. Also, at the table was a gentleman who represented the Center for Disease Control. Once Benjamin and Dean Pearl had seated themselves the introductions began. The meeting would be headed by Mr. Montgomery. He began by introducing Benjamin to Doctor John Welch who was there to represent the Center for Disease Control. Doctor Stone, I appreciated the introduction by Mr. Montgomery, but you need no introduction as your reputation precedes you. I am here today to determine whether or not the Center for Disease Control will give grant money to Harvard University to fund your research. I have been briefed as to the research you plan to undertake. If what I have been told is true, what you are attempting would be *monumental*. The implications of such research if proven to be true would be one of the greatest discoveries ever made by mankind. Now, I need you to explain to me in a very thorough and precise manner what your research is, where you think it may led you, and what benefits it will have for mankind as well as for the taxpayers of the Unites States. Benjamin knew that the only thing between him, and an endless flow of grant money, would be convincing Doctor Welch that his research was worth the investment. "Doctor Welch, I appreciate you having taken time to be here with us today. I would also like to add that your reputation also precedes you. Your work at the Center for Disease Control is well known. You have asked me for a thorough and precise explanation as to my research, in addition to exactly what benefits there would be to mankind, and the taxpayers of the United States. What I am attempting to solve is a problem that mankind has sought an answer to throughout recorded history. That would be the quest to find the fountain of youth. Doctor Welch I plan to find the mechanism in the human body that causes aging. Once I find this mechanism, I plan to find a way to alter the aging process. The aging process is the key to everything. If that process can be slowed down, then a person who has a catastrophic illness, someone who has been given only a few years to live, well then this person's life could be extended, three, maybe four times, what they would have previously had. This would give the scientific community more time to find a cure to the various ailments that plague mankind. Beyond that, my personal long term vision for mankind whether people are willing to accept it or not is that in the distant future mankind be able to outlive his body.

I am willing admit that this seems more science fiction than science fact, but keep in mind that very few people if given the choice would be willing to die. If there were an alternative, even if that alterative was to be an android body, people would chose life over death. Now, as I have stated, that is my long term prediction for mankind. As for now Doctor Welch the cure for aging is where my research is headed. Doctor Stone what you have laid out before me is exactly what I expected from you, nothing less. I do believe that someday you will cure the aging process. There is no reason for me to believe that your vision of the future is incorrect, my scientific side tells me that you could possibly be correct. However, my humanistic side hopes you are wrong because this is not a world I would care to live in. Doctor Stone I do hereby officially concede that the grant money needed for Harvard University to fund your research will be forthcoming. I also wish you the best of luck in your research. There is no doubt that your research, no matter where it takes you, will provide mankind with a wealth of knowledge and a far greater understanding of how the human body works. I would like nothing more than to stay for awhile to get to know you better, unfortunately my schedule doesn't allow for that.

After Doctor Welch had left the room, everyone was congratulating Benjamin for having acquired the grant money needed to fund his research. After a few moments things settled down and Mr. Montgomery declared the meeting to have been a victory for Benjamin as well as Harvard University. Mr. Montgomery declared the meeting to be over and that in a few weeks the university would present Benjamin with some budget numbers. Mr. Montgomery may have declared the meeting over but there were a few demands that Benjamin wanted everyone in the room to be aware of. Demands he was *sure* that Mr. Montgomery and the Board of Directors would not like. As Mr. Montgomery began to stand up, Benjamin spoke, "Mr. Montgomery there are some things we have not covered." Mr. Montgomery sat back down and he looked at Benjamin in an inquisitive manner. What is it that you do not feel we have covered here today Doctor Stone? "The first thing is that I need it to be understood that I have *complete and total control* over my research. There will be *no* interruption from *any* outside source *including* the Board of Directors from Harvard University. *No one* will tell me how to conduct my research or how to run my laboratory! I will be given the equipment I need, when I need it. I will be free to hire whatever staff I need without the pre—approval of the university." You could see by the look on Mr. Montgomery's face that he was very agitated. "Are you done Doctor Stone," "No Mr. Montgomery I am not? In addition to having total control over my research I want a written contract to be drawn up between myself and Harvard University stating that I would receive a thirty percent share of any proceeds made from my research." "Now are you done Doctor Stone?" "Yes, now I am done."

"To address your first demand, you will be given free reign when it comes to your research. As far as not needing pre—approval Doctor Stone you will have to stay within the budget the university gives you. Are we in agreement on your first demand, Doctor Stone?"

"Mr. Montgomery as long as I am free to run my research uninterrupted by outside sources, and all you require from me is that I stay within the budget given to me, then yes we are in agreement."

"Alright Doctor Stone then on the first demand we are in agreement. Now to move on to your second, and may I add unheard of demand, that you share in monetary gains for research you are being paid to do by Harvard University. No matter what the source of the research funding is, no one has ever shared in monetary proceeds for research they are being paid to do nor will Harvard University open Pandora's Box and begin such a practice. You will also receive all credit for your work, but you will not be given a percentage of any proceeds this is *not negotiable*!"

"Mr. Montgomery I feel that it is important you know I have been contacted by numerous people from around the world, some of which represent large pharmaceutical companies. Please keep in mind that if Harvard University is unwilling to compromise and allow me the right to share in the monetary gains derived from *my* research; research that with no doubt *will* generate billions of dollars, I will go elsewhere if both my demands are not completely satisfied. It will pain me to do so, because I have a great deal of respect for the university, for all they have done for me. Make no mistakes about it Mr. Montgomery I will go elsewhere."

"Benjamin I believe I speak for the entire Board when I say that it pains me to hear you speak this way. Harvard University had invested a great deal of money and time in your education. Not to mention the fact that we have given your family a place to live and we have given your father a job. Have you considered your family and have your decision to leave Harvard may impact them?"

"Yes Mr. Montgomery I have, and no matter what my decision my family will be taken care of."

"Doctor Stone, once again I believe I speak for the entire board. It is my sad duty and with my deepest regards, to tell you then you have thirty days to change your mind. In the mean time your father may keep his job, your family will be allowed to stay in the house the university has provided; but you Doctor Stone, during this period, will *not* be granted access to Harvard University. Facilities, your laboratory, the library, etc… I remind you Doctor Stone *again*, you have thirty days to change your mind not a day more! In the event you decide to stay we can put this behind us. In the event you decide to leave, your father's job will be terminated and your family will be asked to give up the house we have provided. Doctor Stone I now consider this meeting to be over. We will be expecting to hear from you."

With that Benjamin stood up thanked everyone for their time, excused himself, and left the room. Dean Pearl followed Benjamin out of the board room. Dean Pearl expressed to Benjamin how the meeting had gone from an absolute high point, to an *absolute low point*. In addition, he along with all of Harvard University hoped that Benjamin would change his mind and stay at the university. Benjamin had been given an ultimatum; this was an ultimatum that he could not give into. Benjamin went home and when he walked into the house, his mother wanted to know to what she owed the honor of Benjamin being home so early. Benjamin told her that he was going to his room and when father gets home let him know and he would explain everything then. I just don't want to explain what is going on more than once. Benjamin is everything ok? Everything will be fine, let me know when father gets home.

When Benjamin's father came home, his mother called for him. Benjamin came down stairs, he took his parents into the dining room; and once they were all seated, he explained how the events of the day had unfolded. When Benjamin had finished, his father spoke first telling him that he would support any decision that he made and don't worry about his job, I can always find work, and your mother and I will be just fine. Benjamin's mother likewise supported Benjamin in his decision.

From this point on; thru the next few weeks Benjamin was contacting everyone, who had contacted him. There were numerous job offers, all of which were willing to pay more than Harvard was willing to offer. After weighing his options Benjamin had settled on an offer given to him by Aspen Pharmaceutical Company. Benjamin was offered a job at their main research facility. Aspen Pharmaceuticals main research facility was located in South Carolina in a midsized town called Leesburg. They offered Benjamin a ridicules salary *and* thirty percent of any profits from his research. In addition they agreed to give Benjamin a state of the art research laboratory with any equipment he felt that he might need. They agreed to give him an *unlimited* budget for research with no interference from them as long as Benjamin agreed to quarterly briefings to let everyone know about any advancement in his research. Benjamin was in complete agreement with everything that Aspen Pharmaceutical had proposed.

It would take a great deal of convincing to get Benjamin's father to agree to move to Leesburg, South Carolina. It would take even more convincing to get Benjamin's father to retire. Benjamin's father was fifty—two years old; he had always been there for Benjamin even though he quite often did not understand what Benjamin was doing. Money was not a problem. The salary that Aspen Pharmaceutical was paying Benjamin alone would be *more than enough* to support his parents and his sister. His father invested a large portion of Benjamin's money in an up and coming new company, Wal—Mart. Benjamin's father had been buying Wal—Mart stock for Benjamin for a number of years and the already large amount of money Benjamin had was now doubled many times

(CHAPTER SEVEN)

It was early December 1979, when Benjamin and his family arrived in Leesburg, South Carolina. While in Leesburg negotiating his contract with Aspen Pharmaceutical, Benjamin bought a large two story Victorian house, complete with large white pillars in the front. When they pulled up to the house, Benjamin's mother was almost speechless. She had never seen a house this beautiful, at least not in person. They were greeted by the real estate agent who Benjamin had bought the house from. The agent gave Benjamin and his family a tour of the property.

The house itself was breathtaking, Benjamin's mother loved it! Benjamin's father liked the house, but seemed more impressed by the one hundred and forty—six acres of land it sat on, complete with an old style two story oak barn. After the family saw as much as they could soak up in a single day, with a nod from Benjamin, the real estate agent presented Benjamin's parents with the deed to the house and property. Benjamin's mother almost fainted and she began to cry. Benjamin's father looked at him, putting his hand on Benjamin's shoulder saying nothing just patting his shoulder. Benjamin's father then turned and walked away. He was headed for the barn. Benjamin' father was a proud man, a man of little education, a man who had earned his living from the sweat of his brow. Benjamin knew that his father could not express himself the way he would like to, but that would be okay because knew how his father felt, even if he could not express it.

Benjamin took the next few days off to get settled in, to get familiar with the area. When Benjamin reported for work, his research laboratory was almost ready. There were just a few more pieces of equipment left to install. Benjamin would spend the next week organizing his new work place. It also seemed that where ever Benjamin went in Leesburg, people already know him. Leesburg after all was not a very large community and Aspen Pharmaceutical was the largest employer in the county.

Once the laboratory was complete and ready for business Benjamin was in need of a staff. Benjamin was asked by Aspen Pharmaceutical to try to fill any positions needed from Aspen's current employees' base if possible. Keeping this in mind Benjamin conducted interviews for weeks; Aspen did indeed have a large base of qualified people to choose from. Benjamin had filled all the positions he needed with the exception of one. Benjamin needed a head lab chemist; this was probably the most important job next to Benjamin himself.

Benjamin interviewed half a dozen candidates, none to his liking. Just when Benjamin was about to give up he was approached by one of the administrators at Aspen Pharmaceutical. Benjamin was told of a young chemist who in her own right, was doing great things in the research and development field. Benjamin said that it would be fine, he would be glad to interview her. Benjamin was then told the young ladies name was *Doctor Angelica Webb*. Benjamin sat motionless, his jaw gaped opened, and he was truly stunned by what he had just heard. The administrator noticed that Benjamin seemed to suddenly be acting strangely. He had become unresponsive, "Doctor Stone did you hear me?" Benjamin looked up at the administrator, then back down to the top of the desk that he was currently occupying. Once again the administrator asked, "Doctor Stone did you hear me?" Finally, Benjamin responded, "yes I heard you." The administrator commented, "If you wish I can schedule the interview for you." "That will be fine, have Doctor Angelica

Webb here in my office tomorrow morning at ten o'clock. That is unless you feel the time frame will not work for Doctor Webb, Doctor Stone." I am sure that ten o'clock will be just fine. If not I will let you know, the administrator then excused herself, leaving Benjamin alone. Benjamin was still seated at his desk. To any outsider who may have passed by at that exact moment, it could have appeared to them that Benjamin was frozen and taking on more of the characteristic of a statue, then a human being. At one point Benjamin considered having the interview canceled. Benjamin reconsidered that notion knowing that it would not be fair to Doctor Webb, or fair to his research to discount her as a potential candidate. This was going to be tough for Benjamin, after all Angelica made him feel something that no women had ever made him feel before.

Benjamin left the laboratory early that day; he seemed to have lost the ability to properly focus. Both his mother and father were surprised to see him home at such an early hour. Benjamin asked his mother if she could make sure that he had a nice shirt and good pair of slacks ready for him to wear for the next day. Benjamin's mother informed him that if he would look thru his clothes and stop wearing the same two or three outfits he would discover that his closet had several pair of slacks as well as nice shirts ready to wear. Benjamin just looked at his mother and smiled. Benjamin is there any particular reason you are home early or any particular reason you need to look you best tomorrow? Benjamin told his mother that until his laboratory was completed, and until his staff was in place there was not much to be done. The reason I wanted to know about the slacks and shirt is because I have to start dressing a little nicer. At least that is what Aspen Pharmaceutical had requested. Well Benjamin thank god for Aspen Pharmaceuticals. I have been trying to get you to pay a little more attention to your appearance for as long as I can remember. Once again Benjamin just smiled at his mother and walked away.

For Benjamin getting a good night sleep would be impossible. Benjamin woke up at twelve o'clock, one—thirty, four—fifteen, and finally again at five—thirty. Benjamin took a long shower, shaved then spent the next hour trying to decide which way to comb his hair, and finally getting dressed. Benjamin went down stairs to find his mother already up and in the kitchen making coffee. Benjamin if you were not my son I am not sure I would recognize you; you should always dress like that. Benjamin just smiled and asked, "Do you like it? Do you think I look ok, How about my hair, is it ok?" Benjamin Stone you have never asked me what I thought about the way you look in your life. If I did not know better I would have to say there is a young lady out there somewhere causing you to act this way. Mother, I told you, I need to start dressing in more of a professional manner, that's all! Benjamin's mother smiled and laughed at him telling him that she was just teasing.

Benjamin left for work that morning over an hour early. When he arrived at his office he found a package on his desk. The package contained the file that Aspen Pharmaceuticals had put together for Benjamin to review on Doctor Webb. She was a graduate of Yale University and had a Ph. D in Chemistry. (Doctor Webb had completed her Ph. D by the age of twenty three.) Upon graduating from Yale University Doctor Webb was recruited by Aspen Pharmaceutical to work in the research and development field for Aspen Pharmaceuticals.

Benjamin was constantly looking at his watch. As the time grew near Benjamin became more and more anxious. He wondered if Doctor Webb would be mad at him, he wondered if she even cared one way or another that he never called, he wondered if his hair looked alright, or if maybe he should have worn a different shirt. Then, at ten o'clock sharp Doctor Angelica Webb entered Benjamin's office.

Benjamin immediately stood to greet Doctor Webb, almost tripping over himself. "Hello Doctor Webb, it is nice to see you again. I understand you are interested in taking a position of head chemist in my lab."

"It is nice to see you again as well. You are correct; I am interested in the position of head chemist."

"Well, I have briefly read your file, and it seems to me that you are *more* than qualified for the position. However there are a few things I did not see in your file."

"Anything that you cannot find in the file you may feel free to ask."

"Where you were born?"

"I was born in a small town in upstate New York."

"Where did you go to high school, what are your likes, and dislikes? Tell me a little something about yourself."

"Doctor Stone exactly what is it that you are looking for?"

"Doctor Webb, before I give my blessing for you to work in this laboratory I want to know more about *you* than what your degree is."

"Alright Doctor Stone, it is just that I am not sure what you want me to tell you."

"For instance are you involved with anybody?"

"Doctor Stone!" I am sorry, but your line of questioning seems to me to be inappropriate. You have no reason to know if I am involved in a relationship."

"Doctor Webb though you may find my line of questioning to be inappropriate I can assure you I mean no offense, and I hope none was taken. I want to know about your personal life, your romantic involvement with others for one reason, and one reason only. If you are to work in this laboratory you will be expected to work long hours, evenings, and maybe from time to time weekends. In my mind if you are romantically involved then you are going to want more time off work than this position will allow. If that is the case then you would not be a good candidate for the position of head chemist."

"Doctor Stone I apologize, you are right. I did not consider your explanation of the questioning, please forgive me. The answer to your question is no, I am not currently seeing anyone. Nor have I in quite some time. My work keeps me busy and relationships require a great deal of time, something I seem to be in short supply of."

"Doctor Webb after having gone over your file, along with the recommendations you have received from Aspen Pharmaceuticals, and having interviewed you, I do believe that you would make an *excellent* choice for the position. If you would like, the position is yours most definitely."

"I would love nothing more than the opportunity to work with you."

Benjamin stood up walked over to the door in his office that led to the laboratory. He looked at Doctor Webb who was still seated, and asked her if she cared to see her office. Of course she replied. She then got up and followed

Benjamin into the laboratory. Benjamin took Doctor Webb to the other end of the lab, where he showed her the office and her laboratory. "I would like you to begin immediately."

"That sounds fine Doctor Stone. I will need a few days to tie up some loose ends before I begin. I am looking forward to being part of your team. Take as many days as you need Doctor Webb because once you start there will not be much time off. I am somewhat a workaholic and I expect the same from the people around me."

"Of course, I understand. I am prepared to do what it takes to be part of your team."

Aspen Pharmaceuticals decided to have a function celebrating Benjamin going to work for them; as well they wanted to show recognition to the project that Benjamin was preparing to undertake. All the important people from Aspen Pharmaceuticals were there, plus the who's who in the community. The local media was present. Benjamin made sure to invite his family. The function was held at the newly fitted laboratory that was provided for Benjamin. At the beginning of the ceremony Benjamin was asked to give a speech. Public speaking was not on the top of the list of things Benjamin cared to do; but as an employee of Aspen Pharmaceuticals, it was expected of him. In normal Benjamin fashion no speech was prepared nor rehearsed.

He started by saying, "I would like to thank everyone for being here tonight. I would especially like to thank Aspen Pharmaceuticals for having given me the opportunity to work for them, and for funding my research. I truly believe that the research we are preparing to pursue will provide nothing less than unprecedented medical advancement for mankind. I would also like to thank the team of professional and highly dedicated people I will be working with even though they truly do not realize just how much of a task master I am. In the end when we have accomplished what we set out to do the long nights at work, the days on end without time for yourself, will be but that of a distant memory. Once again, I would like to thank everyone for being here. Please enjoy the food, drinks, and feel free to mingle."

After the speech Benjamin's mother told him that she thought he did a very nice job, but before they could talk any further Doctor Webb approached them. "Hello Doctor Stone, I would like to congratulate you on your speech. I was quite eloquent." Benjamin responded by saying that I am glad to hear that, because *I do not* like public speaking. She of course told him what a great job he did, and the two of them stood there talking to each other to the point they had stopped noticing the people around them.

Then suddenly, they were interrupted by the sound of someone clearly their throat. It was only then that Benjamin realized the sound was coming from his mother. Benjamin quickly responded by telling his mother that he was sorry and introducing her to Doctor Angelica Webb, "Doctor Webb this is my mother Christine Stone. I would introduce you to my father except I see he is busy at the buffet and I am not sure where my sister is."

"Benjamin did not tell me that he had such a lovely lady working for him."

"Mother", barked Benjamin; but before he could any further he was interrupted by Aspen Pharmaceutical's CEO. It seemed that he wanted to introduce Benjamin to some of the more influential people who were in attendance. As he was walking away he looked at his mother and told her to be nice. Which really meant please do not embarrass me.

"So Doctor Webb have you known my son for very long?"

"Mrs. Stone, please call me Angelica."

"Only if you call me Christine, I insist".

"I first meet Doctor Stone earlier last year when I attended a lecture he was giving at Harvard."

"I see; now could you do me one more favor? When we are talking about my son could we refer to him as Benjamin?"

"I am sorry! It's that I am just used to calling him Doctor Stone, you have to forgive me."

"So you meet my son last year?"

"Yes, as I said I meet him during a lecture at Harvard. When I heard Doctor Stone, I am sorry I mean Benjamin, was going to work for Aspen Pharmaceuticals, and the nature of his research I *immediately* knew that I wanted to be part of the team he would assemble. Benjamin granted me an interview, and I was fortunate enough to have been selected for the position of head chemist."

"I see, now that is very interesting, I wish the both of you nothing but good luck. Oh, here's my husband. Doctor Webb I would like you to my husband, Robert."

"Hello, it is nice to meet you, but please call me Angelica."

"Well, Benjamin did not tell us that he had such an attractive young lady on his team."

"*Robert* don't bother Angelica, I am sure she has someone special out there already."

"It's alright, he's not bothering me, and no I do not have someone special out there. I spend too much time at work to have time for a relationship."

"I do not know of any person who spends as much time at work as my son Benjamin. If what you're telling me is you also spend that kind of time at work; then Angelica, you and Benjamin would be *perfect* for each other."

"Christine, what do you think you're doing?"

"Oh Robert; we are just two women having a conversation, isn't that right Angelica?"

"Yes, Christine that is right."

"Perhaps sometime we could have you over for dinner, if that would be ok with you."

"Thank you Christine I would like that; only one problem, getting Benjamin to agree to take time off work."

"Angelica, don't you worry about Benjamin, as his mother, I still have *some* influence."

Just then Benjamin approached from nowhere. Doctor Webb I hope my parents didn't pry too much into your personal life. "Not at all Doctor Stone, they have been just delightful."

"Doctor Webb if you don't mind there are some people I would like to introduce you to. Mother, father, I will talk to the both of you later." Benjamin's mother stood there smiling, "she has a glow about her." It was then that Benjamin's father spoke up, "what are you up to? You need to mind your own business, and leave those two alone."

“Oh Robert those two young people where meant for each other. Didn’t you see the way they keep looking at each other?”

“Our son doesn’t need a match maker.”

“*Our son* may be one of the smartest people on the planet, if not the smartest, but he knows nothing about what a woman wants. That is something he cannot learn in a text book. So Robert if it makes you feel better, all I am trying to do is give the two of them a little push in the right direction.”

“You had better be very, *very* careful.”

“Robert, I know what I am doing, after all I caught you.”

“When trying to catch a bear you need to use the right bait, and dear you where using the right bait.” Benjamin’s parent’s laughed at that comment and then shared in a small kiss. It was then that Benjamin’s father wanted to know where their daughter Rebecca was. After scanning then room, Benjamin’s mother spotted Rebecca talking to a young man. Now Benjamin’s mother could tell from the way they were standing in relationship to each other, by their body language, that they were enjoying each other’s company. Benjamin’s mother looked at Benjamin’s father and told him, “There is your daughter, and judging by the way things look, I have my work cut out for me.” Benjamin’s father just rolled his eyes, and then excused himself for a second round at the buffet. This was Benjamin’s mother’s queue to approach her daughter.

“Hello, Rebecca I have been looking for you, who is your friend?”

“Doctor Todd Cavanaro this is my mother Christine; mother this is Doctor Todd Cavanaro.” Once again the process began, the process of a slightly meddlesome well intended mother looking after her children.

In Benjamin's mother's mind the evening was a success, she saw potential for both her children. Finding someone they could share their lives with, someone they could be happy with. When the evening finally ended, everyone who had not meet Benjamin before tonight, found him to be exactly what they had been told. Everybody who met him for the first time tonight and those who already had known him were sure of one thing; Doctor Benjamin Stone would be successful at whatever he chooses to pursue.

The following day Benjamin dove into his work, and as expected he was a demanding task master. For all who were on his team, time off work and short days would be far and few between. Benjamin's mother was having very little success getting Benjamin to agree to take time away from work. She was trying to give Benjamin a push in what she considered to be the *right direction*. Now, when it came to his sister Rebecca things were moving right along. Rebecca and Doctor Todd Cavanaro were spending more and more time together. Always under the watchful eye of Benjamin's mother, the weeks went by then the months went by. All the while, Benjamin was working diligently on his project. Finally, Benjamin's mother forced him to attend a dinner she was preparing, the dinner was being held at his parents' home. The occasion; Rebecca and her boyfriend Doctor Cavanaro wanted to make an announcement. Everyone was *sure* what that announcement would be. In attendance would be Benjamin, his parents, Rebecca, her boyfriend Todd, his parents, and last but not least Angelica. Benjamin's mother was not ready to give up so easily. Benjamin himself did not know that his mother had invited Angelica.

(CHAPTER EIGHT)

Now June 1981; Benjamin had just turned twenty—two years old. In the eyes of his mother he had everything. He had money, success, and recognition, but he needed something more, he needed a woman in his life. Benjamin's mother hoped that getting Benjamin away from work and into more of a social setting that he and Angelica might have a chance. She would use this dinner as a method of at least *trying* to achieve her goal.

The dinner was set for six o'clock. Benjamin's mother asked Angelica if she could be there around five o'clock, to give her hand if needed. Now, Benjamin's mother knew that she needed no help; she just wanted Angelica to come early so they could talk, and to possibly spend some time with Benjamin outside of the office.

The house was somewhat chaotic in the hours before the dinner; Rebecca wanted everything to be perfect. Rebecca had Benjamin and her father rearranging furniture, bring extra chairs up from the basement. Although this was a special dinner to Rebecca, it was work to Benjamin and his father. At five o'clock sharp the door bell rang, Benjamin hollered, "I'll get it". To his surprise when he answered the door it was Angelica. "Doctor Webb I didn't know you were coming". We are not at work today Benjamin, you can call me Angelica. Well Angelica, can I help you with what looks like my favorite double crust apple pie. (That would be the dessert Benjamin's mother told Angelica to bring.) She *obviously* knows her son's favorite pie, and hoped this would spark some interest by Benjamin. "No thank you," Angelica replied, "I can handle it, just point me in the right direction." Benjamin led Angelica to the kitchen were his mother was busy with last minute preparations.

"Hello, Angelica I'm glad to see you could make it."

"Thank you Christine, I would not have missed it for anything." Benjamin then chimed in, "Mother I was caught off guard by Angelica being here today, you did not tell me she was invited. Not that I mind, because I don't. Quite the opposite it is a pleasant surprise."

"Well Benjamin, Angelica and I have become friends; and it seems her boss rarely gives her time off work. So I do not get to see, or talk to her very often. I thought today would be on opportunity for use to catch up. Now Benjamin you need to get of my kitchen and go see if your sister needs you for anything."

He left the room, but only to come back from time to time, always making some lame excuse to be there. Every time he would come and go Benjamin's mother and Angelica would just look at each other and smile. After one such event Benjamin's mother turned to Angelica, and asked her point blank, "are you interested in my son?" All Angelica could say was *"Christine!"* Christine told her she didn't have to answer the question and that she already knew the answer. She also told her that if she wanted a little advice when it came to her son, perhaps she could help.

Angelica replied, "I'm listening"

"Well, to begin with Benjamin is not exactly a social butterfly. A life of constant education and the pursuit of knowledge has left his social skills somewhat undeveloped. If you are interested in Benjamin, like I know you are, you may have to be one to take control of things. Benjamin likes you, I already know this. A mother can *always* tell, but as I said you may have to nudge him in the right direction."

"I understand, I think I can handle that."

"Ok dear, the ball is firmly in your court. Now it sounds like the rest of the guest are arriving. If you don't mind you can help me finish setting the table."

Once everyone was there and all of the introductions had been made, Todd asked Benjamin's father if he could have a word with him in private. They went into the den were they could have some privacy. Once in the den, Todd was noticeably nervous. Benjamin's father told him, "I believe I already know what you want, so feel free to ask." With all the courage any young man who is in this position could muster up Todd told Benjamin's father that with his permission he would like to ask for his daughters hand in marriage. Now, that wasn't so difficult was it?

"No sir."

"Of course you can have my daughters hand in marriage, welcome to the family! However, there in one thing you need to know. Rebecca is my baby girl and if you *ever* lay your hands on her for *any* reason they will never find your body! Now let's go share the news with the rest of the family." Todd was completely taken back by what Rebecca's father had just said to him, however he knew that he was just a father showing love for his daughter.

As they exited the den the entire group stood before them waiting; especially Rebecca. Todd had orchestrated the dinner party with the help of Benjamin's mother. Even though he would never say for sure what the purpose of the two families getting together was, everyone had a pretty good idea. Todd saw no one else in the room except Rebecca. Though he was aware of their presence Todd paid no attention to them. He walked straight to where Rebecca was standing, and took her hand. Everyone was on the edge of their seats waiting for Todd to speak. Benjamin's mother as well as Todd's mother had already begun to cry, and Rebecca was trembling. Finally, as if a lifetime had already passed, Todd spoke. "Rebecca I take your hand in mine, after asking your father's permission and having had it granted to me." Then dropping to one knee he looked up to her and said "I love you with all my heart, will you marry me." *"Yes"* Rebecca exclaimed in a voice that could heard by neighbors! Todd put a ring on Rebecca's finger that was appropriately large enough to make Rebecca the envy of all who knew her. Benjamin turned to his right to see Angelica wiping tears from her eyes. Benjamin then quickly turned away before Angelica knew he had noticed. Benjamin took part in congratulating Todd and Rebecca along with everyone else. After enough congratulations' had been bestowed upon Todd and Rebecca, everyone went into the dining room for dinner. Benjamin's mother made sure to seat Angelica next to Benjamin.

The evening went well by all accounts, Benjamin and Angelica seemed to spend more time noticing each other, more so than the other people at the dinner party. By evenings end it was determined that Rebecca and Todd would marry before the next spring.

The night grew long, and it was time for Angelica to leave. Benjamin's mother thanked Angelica for coming, and for her help. Benjamin escorted Angelica to her car, all the while under the watchful eye of his mother, whom was peeking through the drapes. Benjamin's father was trying to get Benjamin's mother to stop spying on their son but this would prove to be difficult on the part of Benjamin's father." Benjamin and Angelica stood at her car door for several minutes exchanging pleasantries. He let Angelica know that he appreciated her coming to dinner and he enjoyed the time he had spent with her that evening. Benjamin took

Angelica's hand, and once again thanked her for everything. He was completely prepared to end the evening on a hand shake, however this in Angelica's mind would not do not by any stretch of the imagination. Angelica decided to take the advice of Christine and take charge of the situation, to push Benjamin in the right direction. As Benjamin was preparing to break away from the hand shake, Angelica pulled him in close, giving him a full blown kiss on the mouth. Benjamin did not resist the initial move by Angelica to bring him in close, nor did he hesitate to respond to the kiss by kissing her back. When they pulled apart, and before Benjamin could speak Angelica told him she would see him tomorrow, jumped into her car driving away. Benjamin stood slightly motionless, watching Angelica drive away. Even when Angelica had driven out of sight, Benjamin was still standing in the same place where Angelica left him. In the same place they had shared their first kiss.

After Benjamin regained his senses, he headed back towards the house, wearing a grin from ear to ear. Finally, at the last moment Benjamin's mother abandoned her lookout point at the window. The rest of the evening would be spent by Benjamin's parents talking about all the events that had transpired concerning both of their children. Benjamin fell asleep that evening remembering the kiss he had shared with Angelica. Angelica on the other hand, fell asleep that evening not remembering the kiss they had shared, but hearing wedding bells. No matter how distant the sound of those bells might be for now, Angelica could clearly hear them ringing as she slipped away for a pleasant night's sleep.

From this point on Benjamin and Angelica would either be working together or spending whatever precious little time they had away from work with each other. There may have been one aspect of their relationship Angelica wished might change, but in her heart knew would not. It was the part of their relationship that while at work Benjamin treated Angelica in a cold and calculating manner always the task master, always the perfectionist. Benjamin was the type of person who absolutely was able to separate his professional feelings, from his personal feelings for Angelica.

Benjamin and his team continued working on the research that Benjamin had determined to undertake. Weeks went by with no noticeable progress for Benjamin and his team. Before anyone knew it, and quicker than expected, it was Spring.

Just as planned Rebecca and Todd were going to be married, the date was set. Their wedding would be June 2, 1982. Benjamin would turn twenty—three a month earlier.

It was decided the wedding would be held at Benjamin's parent's home. Large tents had been erected and Benjamin's father personally built a large gazebo where the ceremony would be held. Todd had asked Benjamin to be his best man and Rebecca had asked Angelica to be her maid of honor. There would be more than four hundred people in attendance on their big day. Todd had invited a large number of people from Aspen Pharmaceuticals, numerous family members from around the country, as well as the friends they had made since moving to Leesburg, South Carolina.

The wedding went off as planned, the ceremony was flawless. Of course; Benjamin's mother, Todd's mother, along with some of the other guests in attendance were having a tearful moment as expected. At one point Benjamin even saw his father brushing away the tears, but being the type of man he was, he was able to contain himself.

The wedding was followed by a celebration for the couple. A good time was being had by all. Benjamin was seated next to his sweetheart Angelica. There was not a person in the crowd who could say these two were not a couple. After the majority of the guests were done eating, it was time for Benjamin's speech. He was normally not fond of public speaking, but on this occasion Benjamin would be speaking from his heart. "Excuse me I would like to have everyone's attention please. Today is a day of celebration for both the Stone and Cavanaro families as well as those guests who have helped to make this a truly special occasion. My sister Rebecca has always been there for me and I hope today is the beginning of a wonderful life for both Rebecca and Todd. I would like everyone to raise their glass, and join me in toasting Mr. and Mrs. Todd Cavanaro."

After Benjamin's speech, his mother could be found talking to some of the other women about Benjamin and Angelica. They were wondering when they would tie the knot. After the festivities had ended, Todd and Rebecca took off for their honeymoon, two weeks in France. It was someplace Rebecca always wanted to go.

As for Benjamin, he dove head first into his research. Benjamin was more fixated on work than he had been in a long time. As time passed Benjamin's habit of staying at the laboratory for long periods at a time was causing concern for everyone. Benjamin would sleep on the couch in his office, a few hours here a few hours there, and working in—between. Angelica was concerned, and she had just cause on one occasion. Benjamin stayed at the laboratory, not going home once for three days. Angelica knew that Benjamin was on the road to self destruction if he was allowed to continue on the way he had been. Behind Benjamin's back Angelica went to Aspen Pharmaceuticals to make them aware of exactly what was going on. Angelica knows the only way to get Benjamin out of the laboratory was to *force* him out. Just as Angelica had hoped, Aspen Pharmaceuticals stepped in and Benjamin was forced to no longer spend more than ten hours a day in the lab for no more than six days a week. This also extended to the team of people who worked with Benjamin. To make sure the new policy was adhered to, a security guard would come to the laboratory every evening, making sure all personal were gone at the appropriated time. This *infuriated* Benjamin! Did Aspen Pharmaceuticals want something positive to come out of his research or not?

Luckily for Angelica, Benjamin was never aware of the fact that *she* was the one who went over his head. For Angelica she felt she risked it all; her job on Benjamin's team, perhaps even her relationship with Benjamin; but in order to save Benjamin, she was willing to hurt him. Whether Benjamin knows it or not it was for his own good. Even though Benjamin was upset, after a few weeks he quickly settled into his new routine. Angelica commented to Benjamin that his mood seemed to be better and even Benjamin could not argue with that. It was like Angelica told Benjamin there is always a plus side, we get to spend a little time with each other away from work.

The months past with very little progress, then finally in August 1984, Benjamin and his team had inadvertently stumbled on a discovery. They had come up with a topical cream that if applied daily would completely relieve the systems related to Psoriasis. As if this were not enough for Aspen Pharmaceuticals who knew the financial rewards for this discovery were going to be significant; however, after further research it was discovered that if the cream was applied twice a day, it would also remove wrinkles by eighty percent in just a few months. Now this was cause for celebration for Benjamin, his team and Aspen Pharmaceuticals.

The discovery would make Benjamin more money than he could spend in a life time. The news of the pending topical cream for psoriasis and wrinkles drove the price of Aspen Pharmaceuticals stock up *twenty—three percent* in just one day.

In the months to follow the stock would double. Aspen Pharmaceuticals named the topical cream Stones' Psoriasis and Wrinkle cream. This *should* have been an honor to Benjamin, but he considered if to be more of an insult than an honor. If things were not bad enough in Benjamin's mind one of the major newspapers reporting the discovery printed across the front page, "Doctor Wrinkle along with Aspen Pharmaceuticals gives relief to Psoriasis suffers, and to all who suffer from unwanted wrinkles." "Doctor Wrinkle," this made Benjamin furious! The last thing he wanted to be known as was the Doctor who cured wrinkles. Aspen Pharmaceuticals saw it as a major financial success, knowing that the wrinkle cream would out sell any other product they produced. After all, nobody wants is wrinkles.

Angelica finally calmed Benjamin down after a few days. She explained to him that his research into the human genome and trying to break the human body down to a sub atomic level in order to find out exactly what caused aging and how to slow it down, would inadvertently produce unintended discoveries. She also let Benjamin know that his research had given relief to millions of people worldwide who suffered from Psoriasis, people who would forever be grateful for what he had done. Angelica wanted Benjamin to know that as she grew older she would most certainly appreciate "Doctor Wrinkle", and his topical cream. Finally, after a few days Benjamin calmed down even though every time he heard the phrase "Doctor Wrinkle" the hair on the back of his neck would stand up.

Benjamin continued his research in the subsequent months with little success. This gave Aspen Pharmaceuticals little to no concern because of the massive profits they were making due to his discovery. They would continue to pour as much money into Benjamin's research as he needed in the hope that Benjamin and his team would inadvertently stumble upon something else while on their quest for their true research to alter aging.

Benjamin had decided he wanted to do something for his family. It had become a custom for Benjamin, Angelica, Rebecca, her husband Todd, and Benjamin's parents to have Sunday dinner together every week. So on one such occasion Benjamin announced that he would like to send the entire family on a vacation; that is everyone *except* for himself and Angelica. They had too much work going to get away for any long period of time. Benjamin told the four of them to get together and decide where they would like to go and not to give the cost any consideration. He also insisted that where ever they go, they fly first class and stay only at the nicest hotels. The four of them planned their trip for several weeks before finally settling on what they wanted. At their normal Sunday dinner, Benjamin's mother announced that they had decided to go to Italy, Greece, France, and for their final destination they would go to Israel. Benjamin's father picked Italy, Rebecca picked Greece, Todd picked France, and Benjamin's mother picked Israel. The trip would last for six weeks, everyone seemed to be excited. It was then that Rebecca and Todd decided to let everyone know that she was pregnant. The baby would be born sometime in December. Benjamin's entire family, whom just moments before thought they were excited, had just become overly excited. The conversation went from the trip they were planning to talking of a baby shower, what sex the child would be, should Todd and Rebecca buy a largerhome to make more room or remodel the current home. It seemed that the three women in the room had taken control of the conversation. The trip had for now become a side bar; the main focus was Rebecca's pregnancy.

Things finally settled down as the weeks passed. It was now the night before the big trip, all the arrangements had been made, and everyone was packed. Benjamin told his mother make sure to send Angel and I post cards from each of your stops. Benjamin's mother gave him a very curious look. "Did you just call Angelica, Angel?"

"Yes, I did." Replied Benjamin, "it is something I have been doing in private for awhile; after all she is my Angel."

"Well Benjamin I am glad to hear that. Now when do you think you might make the big move?"

"Mother I will or will not make the big move when I am ready."

"Alright, Benjamin but I am not getting any younger, and I would like to enjoy my grandchildren." Fortunately for Benjamin, Angelica walked into the room, ending the somewhat awkward conversation he had suddenly found himself in with his mother.

Benjamin and Angelica took the four of them to the airport early the next morning, well five of them if you count Benjamin's unborn niece or nephew whichever the case might be. While unloading the luggage, Angelica commented to Rebecca, that she had luggage exactly the same. Rebecca looked at Benjamin; Benjamin looked at both Angelica and Rebecca and said, "Angel it's time for a confession, I had you spend the night so that I could get Rebecca to go to your house and pack some of your stuff for a surprise trip. I hope you're not mad."

"Benjamin what are you talking about?"

"You and I are going to visit your father. You said you have not seen him in almost two years."

"Does he know we are coming?"

"Yes, I spoke to him weeks ago, he seemed very excited." Angelica lit up with excitement. She then gave Benjamin a hug and kiss while everyone exchanged their good—byes. Benjamin made his mother once again promise to send postcards daily. She agreed.

Once Benjamin and Angelica were on the plane she wanted to know everything. "What about work, Benjamin?"

"Don't worry Angel, I know the boss. And he said we have earned a few days off."

"How did you know where to contact my father?"

"I got that information out of your personal file. Your father is on there as your emergency contact."

"Well, why a trip, why now and why to visit my father?"

"Angel you ask a lot of questions. I felt like a trip, why not now and I knew you would like to see your father. Besides I have never met him. Oh, your father said he would have someone pick us up at the airport. I feel bad I don't want him to spend his money on car service for us."

"Benjamin there is something I need to tell you. Benjamin looked somewhat puzzled, after a slight pause Angelica preceded. Benjamin it is not that I have been hiding things from you. It is just that I don't particularly care to talk about how I was raised."

"Angel I don't care where you raised, or how you were raised. I most certainly do not care if your father doesn't have a lot of money."

"Well Benjamin, I do appreciate the fact that you love me no matter what my background or my father's financial status is but the fact is my father is a wealthy man, and I do mean *wealthy*. Now before you say anything Benjamin, please let me finish. My father is the CEO of one the largest banks in the United States. I have already told you about my mother passing away when I was three years old. After that it was just my father and I. I was raised on a large estate in upstate New York. We had a housekeeper, grounds keeper, and a nanny. Her name was Margret; she was my best friend growing up. Then there was Carl, he served as my father's personal chauffeur. If my father said he was sending a car to pick us up, then it should be Carl. When I was younger, Carl took me everywhere. He was more like an uncle to me then just someone who worked for my father. Carl always called me sunshine; he said it was because my hair was so blonde when I was younger. Now Benjamin, you know everything well almost everything. I told you my father lived in New York City; well he does at least during the week. My father has an apartment that he keeps in the city that is where he stays during the week, along with Carl and a housekeeper. Not to be confused with the housekeeper that lives at the estate. I hope you're not mad at me; it is not that I didn't tell you about myself. It's just that I didn't tell you everything. I suppose that I have always been somewhat embarrassed by my father's wealth. I just don't talk about it; I don't want people to think I am bragging. Now you can speak Benjamin, and please do not be mad at me."

Benjamin sat silent for a few moments with a look of complete puzzlement on his face. Then he spoke, "Angel I suppose I can understand why you didn't tell me everything in the beginning. I told you that I would love you no matter where you were raised or no matter what your father's financial situation was and one thing is for sure; your father being very wealthy will definitely not make it any harder to love you." Angelica smiled and then gave Benjamin a big kiss. They did not speak much more about what they had just talked about, or for that matter about anything else for the rest of the flight. When they arrived at the airport, they were greeted by Angelica's fathers' chauffeur Carl, just as Angelica predicted. When Carl spotted Angelica he quickly approached her, calling out there is my "Little Miss. Sunshine". Angelica responded by giving Carl a hug and kiss to the cheek. Angelica told Carl that he looked wonderful and he hasn't changed a bit. Carl smiled, always my "Little Miss. Sunshine." They both laughed, leaving Benjamin in an awkward position, it seemed as if though he had been forgotten. Then suddenly as though it was an afterthought she said, "Benjamin I am sorry, I was caught up in the moment I didn't mean to forget you". Benjamin let Angelica know that there was no need to apologize; he knew she was just happy to see Carl, happy to be going to her childhood home for a visit. Carl this is Benjamin, Benjamin was quick to shake Carl's hand and tell him how pleased he was to meet him. Carl was slightly more reserved than Benjamin; he took Benjamin's hand, shaking it in a firm manner, holding on to Benjamin's hand as he spoke.

"Benjamin you need no introduction, little Miss has told her father all about you. Besides that you have been in the newspaper, as well as on the TV news. It seems they have come to call you Doctor Wrinkle."

"Yes, they have, and I suppose that is something I have to live with." All the while Carl was still griping Benjamin's hand in a firm manner. Benjamin there is one more thing you need to know, Little Miss means a lot to me, she is the daughter I never had. If you should ever hurt her in anyway, well let's just say the outcome would not be favorable for you. With that the hand shake ended as fast as it had started it. At that moment Carl suddenly turned into a chauffeur. Carl handed the bags to a porter who took them to the limousine. Carl walked to the door opened it for them and once inside he closed the door and the window between the driver's seat and the back of the limousine. Benjamin looked at Angelica and commented on how meeting Carl had left him somewhat bewildered. "Benjamin, Carl doesn't mean any harm; he has always been very protective of me. He has always been more like an uncle to me. He can be very professional and very serious about his job."

It was an hour and half ride to the place where Angelica grew up. All the way from the airport to her to her childhood home Angelica played tour guide. Showing Benjamin all the high points along the way, and then suddenly Angelica became very excited. There it is; that's where I grew up! "That's where you grew up commented Benjamin?" It was difficult for Benjamin to take it all in as they turned off the winding road onto the private gated road leading to the house. The word house may be an *understatement* when describing the apparent mansion that Benjamin could see off in the distant.

The private road leading to the mansion was about half a mile long; both sides of the road were lined with large oak trees, everything was landscaped and well groomed. There was a large water fountain in front of the house, which was the focal point of the circle drive in front of the mansion.

When they pulled up, they could see Angelica's father standing at the bottom of the steps waiting eagerly for the limousine to come to a stop. Just as the limousine came to a stop, and before Carl could get out and open the door, Angelica's father was at the back of the limousine opening the door himself. When Angelica exited the limousine, her father immediately gave her a hug telling her how much he had missed her and that she shouldn't wait so long between her visits. Angelica's father started leading her up the steps towards the house. Once again, Benjamin was left standing alone; seemingly forgotten about. They made it half way up the steps before Angelica turned back to look for Benjamin. As soon as she had realized what she had done, she instantly turned going back to retrieve Benjamin. Of course, Angelica was once again very apologetic. Letting Benjamin know how bad she felt for having forgotten him twice in one day, even if for only a moment. Angelica did calm Benjamin down quickly by making mention of the fact that she would make it up to him later that evening. The fact that Benjamin was a super genius did not mean that even he was impervious to the charms of a young lady.

Angelica introduced Benjamin to her father. Even though they had spoken on the phone they had never personally met each other. Benjamin this is my father, Joseph Webb, father this is Benjamin Stone. "It is a pleasure to meet you sir," commented Benjamin, Angelica's father told Benjamin that he would prefer to addressed as Joseph. Benjamin agreed, only if Angelica's father would address him as Benjamin. It seemed that both men had come to an agreement. After exchanging a few more pleasantries, the three of them went into the house. Once they were in the house Joseph asked Benjamin if Carl had read him the riot act concerning Angelica. Benjamin just smiled and responded, “Yes, I suppose you could call it that.” Well Benjamin, Carl is not just my chauffeur; he has been my friend for more than thirty years and when it comes to his “Little Miss Sunshine”, Carl is very protective. Carl looks to Angelica as the daughter he never had. So I hope he did not offend you. “No Joseph, Carl did not offend me. Just the opposite, I was glad to see that Carl thought that much of Angelica.”

“I am glad to hear that Benjamin, because Angelica thinks of a lot Carl and if I read my daughter right she also thinks a lot of *you* Benjamin. Well, enough talking for now, why don’t you join Angelica upstairs; she can show you to your room. When the two of you are all settled in, come downstairs for cocktails.”

Benjamin headed upstairs. When he came to the top of the stairs he was greeted by one of the household servants. His name was Albert. He looked at Benjamin and told him that his luggage had already been placed in his room. He told him to follow him and he would show him to his room. Benjamin followed Albert down a long corridor, at the end of that corridor Albert opened the door leading to Benjamin’s room. As Albert was walking away Benjamin asked where Angelica’s room was. Albert pointed down the corridor. Ms. Webb’s room is located at the opposite end of the corridor just as her father had requested. Benjamin just smiled as Albert walked down the corridor turning to go down the steps.

As Benjamin went into his room he could hardly believe what he saw. The room was larger than most homes people live in. When entering the room Benjamin first came into a sitting room, some thirty by thirty feet, with a twelve foot ceiling. From the sitting room Benjamin went into the bedroom. The bedroom was equally as spacious if not larger. The bed itself was no doubt the largest bed he had seen in his life. All the furnishing in the bedroom and throughout the rest of the rooms was nothing less than the best. Finally one more room to see was the bathroom. Once again Benjamin was speechless, the bath tub resembled a small Roman bath where there looked to be room for four people, *comfortably*. After Benjamin had given himself the grand tour he then decided to go to Angelica's room.

Benjamin left his room, taking the long walk to Angelica's, all the while taking note of the paintings, the furnishings, and ornate wood work in the hallway. This most definitely was *not* a house but a mansion. When Benjamin finally arrived at the other end of the corridor to Angelica's room, he felt like he had just walked a marathon. Upon arriving at Angelica's door Benjamin knocked, the patiently waited for her to answer. When Angelica came to the door she was wearing nothing but a bath towel. *Benjamin*, my father would not think it to be very appropriate of you to be at my door. "Well, are you going to let me in?" Benjamin quickly surveying the room, noting that Angelica's room was just as lavish as the room he was occupying. Benjamin took this opportunity to remind Angelica how she had ignored him on two occasions earlier that day and just as quick to remind her that she had promised to make it up to him. Angelica smiled, and then she took Benjamin by the hand leading him to the bed. As far as Benjamin was concerned Angelica had more than kept her word, and he was more that satisfied once the playfulness had ended. Angelica told Benjamin that he needed to leave her room before someone noticed that he was in there. She told him to go downstairs and make himself at home, and when she finished dressing she would join him.

Benjamin managed to slip out of Angelica's room undetected by anyone. Benjamin then did as he was told and went downstairs and made himself at home.

Benjamin was now giving himself a tour of the house, going from area to area looking things over. Benjamin had only heard of homes such as the one he was in. He had only heard of people who had such great wealth up until this point. It was then that the thought crossed Benjamin's mind, he was fast becoming a person who would no doubt acquire such wealth. Benjamin after all was already a multi—millionaire. Considering his own wealth somehow calmed Benjamin down. Knowing that he was not a poor man gave him the confidence to talk to Angelica's father Joseph without being intimidated.

Benjamin continued his self promoted tour of the house. As Benjamin was walking down a long hallway he came upon an open door. Benjamin walked into the room looking it over. It was filled with books, almost from floor to ceiling on all four walls. There was a table in the center of the room with four chairs around it. On the table there were a few books lying there open. Benjamin walked over to the table to get a better look at the books lying there. While Benjamin was looking over the books, Joseph entered the room, actually startling Benjamin.

"I am sorry Benjamin; I did not mean to startle you."

"No, Joseph I am sorry if I am someplace in your home I do not belong. But Angelica suggested that I come downstairs and make myself at home. When I came down I did not find anyone, so I was giving myself a self guided tour of your home. Then when I came upon your library the door was opened."

"Benjamin you need to stop apologizing. You are not only a guest in my home; you are my daughter's boyfriend, and as a father if I know my daughter's mind as I think I do, her feelings for you are more than that of just those of a simple boyfriend."

"Joseph I hope you are right, because there would be no better time than now to talk to the father of the woman I love. It was not until the plane ride to New York that Angelica told me what you did for a living and the manner in which she had been raised. I am not sure why Joseph but Angelica seems to be somewhat embarrassed by your wealth."

"Well Benjamin that is probably my fault, I brought her up, not to flaunt her lifestyle in the face of people who were less fortunate. Benjamin you must remember that I started with nothing. When Angelica's mother and I married, I was but only a bank clerk. Through shear will and determination I forced my way to the top but I have always tried very hard to remember where I came from. I have always tried very hard to remind Angelica where her family came from, and not to go around believing that because she comes from wealth that she is better than the people around her. So Benjamin I suppose because of that Angelica has somewhat guarded her family's wealth."

"Joseph I would like to say first of all that I admire and commend you for the way you have raised your daughter. And for the fact that even though you are surrounded by lavish wealth, you do make a conscious effort to remember where you started. Joseph now I need to ask you something, something that is very important, something that I believe is very important to the both of us."

"What would that something be Benjamin?"

"That something would be Angelica's future happiness. Joseph, the reason, I wanted to bring Angelica for a visit is to ask your permission, face to face if it would be alright with you if for me to ask for your daughter's hand in marriage?"

"Benjamin you not only have my permission you have my blessing. Now along with my blessings comes a grave responsibility. *My daughter is worth more to me that all the wealth in world!* Angelia's happiness and safety are going to be in *your* hands. Benjamin, I am not personally a violent man by nature, but as for Carl that is a different matter. I have known Carl for many, many years; he has always been a loyal friend *and* employee. Carl has no children of his own, but has always looked at Angelica as if though she were his daughter."

"Joseph, I am well aware of how Carl feels, he has made that very clear to me. I can personally assure both you and Carl that I will do all in my power to always protect Angelica as well as make her happy."

"Benjamin, have you thought about where and when you were going to ask my daughter to marry you?"

"With you permission I would like to ask her at dinner tonight."

"Benjamin if I could ask a favor of you, I would appreciate it."

"Absolutely Joseph, you may ask whatever you want of me."

"I would appreciate it if you could wait until tomorrow night. You see I have asked several close family members and friends over for a dinner celebration, many of who have not seen Angelica for quite some time. This way her family and friends could share in the celebration."

"That would be fine with me sir, it does not really matter when or where I do it, I will be just as nervous."

"Do have a ring with you?"

"Absolutely Joseph, I have come prepared."

"Well then, do you mind if I ask you to see the ring?"

"No, not at all Joseph, the only problem is I do not have the ring on me. It is upstairs in my room."

"That's fine; perhaps you could show it to me later." Just then Angelica came down the hallway calling out Benjamin's name. "What are my two favorite men doing? Talking about me perhaps?" "No Angelica," exclaimed Benjamin! Your father was telling me about the party he was having tomorrow night, in *your* honor. "Father, what is Benjamin talking about?"

"I have invited some friends and relatives over for dinner tomorrow night. After all, it has been awhile since you have come home. I hope you and Benjamin don't mind." Both Benjamin and Angelica assured Joseph that neither one of them minded.

The rest of the evening went well, they had dinner and drinks. The three of them sat up until the early morning hours talking about any number of topics. The next morning was uneventful, Benjamin and Angelica slept in, not coming down for breakfast until almost ten o'clock a.m. After breakfast they spent most of the day touring the property on a golf cart, or hanging out around the swimming pool. Angelica told Benjamin that the quests were due to start arriving at six o'clock p.m. It was now about four 'clock and Angelica felt that the two of them should start getting ready for the dinner party. Benjamin was of course ready well before Angelica.

While Angelica was making her last minute adjustments, Benjamin thought it would be a good time to find Joseph to show him the ring that he planned to present to Angelica. He once again found Joseph in the library downstairs. When Benjamin entered the room, Joseph asked him if he were holding up ok. "I will be fine, Joseph. I am just a little bit nervous. I came downstairs to find you while Angelica was getting ready. Would you like to see the ring?"

"Most defiantly Benjamin, that's if you don't mind." With that Benjamin reached into his pocket and produced a small box handing it to Joseph. Joseph took the ring box; all the while smiling, Joseph looked at Benjamin and then opened the ring box ever so carefully. Once Joseph saw the ring he looked at Benjamin with a look of complete approval. After all, there was nothing to disapprove of. The ring was magnificent in its size, luster, and beauty. Benjamin, "If you do not mind asking, exactly how many carats is the ring.

"It is an eight carat center diamond with three carats of smaller stones around it." Benjamin also told Joseph that he had hoped the ring he had chosen was not too much and that Angelica would like it, and not find it to be gaudy. Joseph told Benjamin that the ring was that of rare beauty and flawless quality. Joseph assured Benjamin that there was not a woman on the planet who would not fall in love with that ring. This made Benjamin feel better, it helped to ease his nervousness.

Joseph suggested that they go to the study, where they would be in a better position to greet Angelica when she comes down the stairs, as well as to greet the guests as they arrive.

Just as scheduled, the guests started arriving at six o'clock and by six thirty the last of the guests had arrived. There were twenty—three guests in all. As they were arriving Benjamin had never seen so many limousines. It seemed that no one drove themselves. The house itself was filled with a larger than normal staff. There were men and woman walking around serving drinks and offering hors d'oeuvres.

Benjamin was introduced to all the guests one by one, each one of them nicer than the next. That was a surprise to Benjamin; he had always had a preconceived notion about the wealthy. Benjamin thought they would be a bunch of "stuffed shirts." That notion could not have been more wrong, they were very nice, pleasant, and easy to talk to. Perhaps the super wealthy only act pompous when they are not around there own kind. At any rate Benjamin found the whole experience to be pleasant. The last person Benjamin was introduced to and the last person to arrive was Angelica's grandmother. Angelica introduced her grandmother to Benjamin as Elizabeth Webb. Benjamin very gracefully took her hand telling her that is was his pleasure to meet her. Angelica's grandmother told Benjamin not to be so nervous, that she would not bite. She also stated that she insisted he call her Elizabeth.

By now it was seven o'clock. One of the servants came into the room speaking to Joseph. Who then announced to all the guests, that dinner was ready to be served. The entire party was relocated to the dining room. Now this was unlike any dining room Benjamin had ever seen. There was a table that would seat forty people. The room was lavishly decorated with only the highest quality furnishings. The dinner was going well and after the main course, and while dessert was being served, Benjamin stood up walked around to the end of the table. As Benjamin was approaching Angelica he was very nervous. His face became flush and his hands started to sweat. Joseph noticed that everyone was involved in conversation, not noticing Benjamin, or at the very least unaware of what Benjamin was preparing to do. Joseph took this as his queue to tap his glass with his fork until everyone stopped talking. Then Joseph looked Benjamin simply saying Benjamin I believe you have everyone's attention. Angelica looked up at Benjamin. "What is going on Benjamin?" Benjamin dropped to one knee before Angelica, and began to speak. "Angel I believe I know how you feel about me, and I hope you know I feel about you. I love you more than anything or anyone I have ever known. I spend my days and nights thinking about you. Thinking about all the possible scenarios' about what might be. I can only come up with one plausible conclusion, and that is I not *only* want to spend the rest of my life with you, I *need* to spend the rest of my life with you. Would you please do me the honor of being my wife?"

"*Oh my God, Benjamin it is beautiful!*"

"Does that mean yes?"

"*Yes, Benjamin*!" Benjamin slipped the ring onto Angelica's finger. Angelica was weeping, they were tears of joy. The room *erupted in applause and cheer*. Benjamin was trying to not notice the rest of the room, trying to *only* notice his Angel.

After a bit of time had gone by and congratulations' had been extended to the two of them Joseph took Benjamin and the rest of the men back to the study to have a drink. The women were left in the dining room to admire the ring Benjamin had presented to Angelica, as well as leaving them to start planning the wedding because that is what women do.

Joseph let Benjamin know that all expenses would be covered by him and that Benjamin might as well settle into the fact that as a man, as far as your wedding, you are just along for the ride. Angelica has been planning her wedding since childhood. If you wish to survive the whole ordeal just go along for the ride. There is something else Benjamin when you are married you can either be right or you can be happy. I suggest that you be content with being happy. All of the gentlemen laughed at the comment.

The last guest left around one o'clock, after that Benjamin, Angelica, and Joseph stayed up for a few more hours talking. At one point when Angelica left the room for moment, Joseph looked at Benjamin telling him I know you are engaged to my daughter, but out of respect for me, make sure while in my house until the marriage you spend the night in your rooms, *alone*!

Benjamin readily agreed and did as Joseph had asked of him. The next few days were spent relaxing, that is at least when Benjamin was not being interrogated by Angelica. "How long were you planning this, were did you buy the ring, does your mother and father know?" On and on; Benjamin was getting a barrage of questions. But, like a good fiancé he answered every question asked of him with patience.

When it was time to leave they left just as they had come, with Carl driving them to the airport. While they were at the airport, Carl shook Benjamin's hand and congratulated him on his engagement. He then told Benjamin, "Remember what I told you earlier". Carl then took his own hand pointing to his own eyes with two fingers, then back to Benjamin with one finger, letting Benjamin know that he would be watching him. Carl gave his "Little Miss Sunshine" a hug, telling her to be careful. Benjamin found Carl to be a spooky individual, though he did understand it was just Carl's way.

When they arrived back in Leesburg, they had already received a postcard from Benjamin's mother. It appeared that all were having a good time. As for Benjamin, he wanted to go back to the laboratory, back to his research. The first few days back Angelica was distracted with spreading the news of their engagement, but after a few days she settled down and was once again able to concentrate on her work.

The days and weeks went by with Benjamin receiving postcards every few days from his mother. Finally, he began to receive postcards from Israel; this was the last leg of their journey. Israel was Benjamin's mother pick. She had always wanted to go to the "Holy Land". Benjamin himself could not wait for everyone to get home. He wanted to share the news of his engagement. Benjamin knew that his mother of all people would be especially excited to hear the news, but this was news his mother would never hear. Two days before they were to come home, Benjamin's family was visiting a market place in Jerusalem when a car bomb went off. The car bomb killed and wounded many innocent people. Amongst the dead was Benjamin's entire family. It would appear that they were within just a few feet of the car when it exploded. It took only a very short time for before a group of radical Palestinian Muslims took credit for the bombing.

Benjamin made the arrangements for his family members' remains to be brought home. Benjamin was in shock, though he was going through the motions, making funeral arrangements, etc.…Benjamin was just doing that; going through the motions. The funeral would be closed casket for all of Benjamin's family members. It seemed that the entire community turned out for the services. Benjamin's friend Adam Caldwell was in attendance. Even though Benjamin left Harvard University on all but good terms, they sent a large floral arrangement. Everyone was so very sorry and told Benjamin to be strong, things happen for a reason. So many times during the process Benjamin wanted to scream at people for the same stupid and lame clichés that poured out of their mouths with little to no real thought about what they were saying.

Benjamin had for a long time questioned the faith. He was brought up to believe in god but in this moment because of the recent event he was questioning his faith even more. He questioned why the needless taking of human life, taking those who meant so much to Benjamin. This was more than Benjamin could bear, any doubts as to the existence of God he may have had in his mind had been confirmed. To Benjamin; God was a myth, a fable, a crutch to get through the day to day experiences of our otherwise meaningless lives. The whole experience left a dark spot in Benjamin's heart.

(CHAPTER NINE)

Benjamin returned to work, and with constant encouragement given to him by Angelica he was able to once again concentrate on his research. The one noticeable difference in Benjamin's behavior everybody around him had noticed was that he had become consumed by any and all news that he could watch and read about that Middle East and acts of terrorism.

On one occasion Benjamin commented to Angelica that the Arabic Nation as a whole, (as far back as recorded history could take us) have been in conflict for one reason or another. They have been killing each other as well as other people around them because of their particular religious beliefs; millions of lives have been lost because of their belief in the "supposed word of an invisible guy in the sky". The entire concept of a people, that they are killing each other over a book, a book no doubt written by man. A book that's only reason for an existence is to give answers to questions people otherwise cannot answer, and most importantly, to control the population to lead the sheep in the direction you want them to go. In Benjamin's opinion the world would be a better place without religion of any short, and he felt the world would be a better place without the Arabic Nation.

Angelica was the voice of reason for Benjamin and she told him that although she understood his anger toward the terrorists he should not blame an entire group of people for the heinous acts of a few. *The Arabic Nation as a whole was not the problem!* It was but a small group amongst them whom were radical and misguided and that in time as society advances this type behavior will come to an end. Angelica did admit that unfortunately it will more than likely be a long time, many, many years in the future before mankind reaches that point, but you have to believe. Benjamin of course agreed with Angelica, telling her that the comments he had made were those out of anger. He did not really wish for the death of the entire Arabic Nation. He held steadfast to his belief that religion as a whole was a cancer on mankind and though religion did teach many valuable lessons, such as how to live with your fellow man and how to treat others as you would treat yourself. The problem with religion in Benjamin's mind was that different people would interpret their particular religion differently. Some would just believe in their God going about their lives in a peaceful manner. The next person would interrupt things in a completely different manner, leading to divisions in their own religion; some peaceful, some radical, and some dangerous. It did not take a large number of radical people to cause large problems. In the end Benjamin told Angelica that he would agree to try not to fixate on what had happened to his family, but instead he would try to concentrate on the fond memories he had of his family.

Benjamin and Angelica continued their research working diligently as always. They had decided they would be married the following spring. Benjamin for the most part removed himself from the process of planning a wedding; instead he would leave the details to Angelica and her father. The wedding and the reception to follow would be held at Angelica's fathers' mansion.

The months went by, plans were made, and Benjamin's mood seemed to improve. Benjamin always seemed hard at work on his research, research that seemed to have hit a wall, a wall that Benjamin was unable to push through. This was a source of frustration for Benjamin. He often wondered if the research he had vowed to peruse was beyond his own capability, but those types of thoughts would not last long.

Benjamin knew there was an answer to the problem; he just needed to stay on course.

The months continued to pass and it was now time for Benjamin and Angelica to get married. The day was May fifteenth, 1986. Benjamin and Angelica arrived at the airport, and as before they were greeted by Carl. Benjamin himself was completely prepared for Carl to read him the riot act once again just as he had before. Instead, to Benjamin's pleasant surprise, Carl greeted him in a pleasant and civil manner wishing him nothing but good luck on his upcoming wedding day.

When they arrived at the mansion the entire estate was filled with people and vehicles, both coming and going. There were people manicuring the lawn, pruning bushes, and the trees. There were crews of men setting up large tents, tents the size of which you might only expect to see if you were at a circus. The tents were being filled with tables and chairs, crystal chandeliers were being installed in the tents to provide lighting, tapestries were hung from the sides of the tents. The floral arrangements would be extravagant, some of which would tower over twelve feet in height. There were crews of people working the pool area, not because anyone would be swimming, but just because Joseph wanted everything to look perfect. Joseph had a huge gazebo built where the ceremony was to take place. Joseph left nothing to chance. In the event of a rainy day the wedding would be held in the largest of three tents.

When Benjamin entered the mansion it was filed with workers of every sort. The wedding was two days away, yet people had been working to prepare for the wedding day for almost a week already. Just as before, Joseph had Benjamin and Angelica put into two different rooms, after all they were not yet married. The next day would be spent by both Benjamin and Angelica having last minute alterations made to their wedding attire. Angelica's maid of honor was her childhood friend Debbie Mayers. She too came from a privileged family. Her grandfather was the founder of Mayer's clothing stores, a clothing store that was known nationwide. Benjamin's best man would be perhaps the only friend he has ever had, Adam Caldwell. There were four bridesmaids; they were also friends of Angelica from childhood. There also needed to be four groomsmen. The only problem was that Benjamin really had no friends other than Adam Caldwell, Angelica came to the rescue. She had the bridesmaids volunteer their husbands, or boyfriends, whatever the case might have been.

Adam showed up at the mansion around one o'clock the day before the wedding, as did the other members of the wedding party.

Adam was picked up at the airport, and delivered to the mansion in a chauffeur driven limousine. Benjamin greeted him upon his arrival. The first thing Adam said to Benjamin was that he did not realize Benjamin was marrying into royalty. Benjamin laughed and replied, "Angelica's family is not royalty, but as you can see they are somewhat wealthy".

"Somewhat wealthy?" commented Adam.

"Yes, *somewhat* wealthy replied Benjamin". Benjamin showed Adam to his room, telling him that once he was settled in come downstairs and join the rest of the guests. Within the hour the entire wedding party had gathered downstairs. They spent a period of time getting to know each other, or just getting reacquainted. At four o'clock that evening the wedding party gathered at the gazebo. Now at most wedding rehearsals a priest, a pastor, a man of God would be present to conduct the ceremony. Not in this case, the ceremony would be performed by a New York State Supreme Court Judge, who just so happened to be a friend of Joseph's going all the way back to their college days. The rehearsal ceremony went off flawlessly. After the ceremony the wedding party went back into the mansion for a traditional rehearsal dinner. Adam was seated next to Benjamin. He could not help but comment on the size of the table in the mansion's main dining room. Before the evening was over, it seemed that Adam and Angelica's Maid of Honor, Debbie were beginning to have all the ear markings of a couple in the making. This pleased Angelica.

It was now the big day, the day that all the preparations, all the planning, all the excitement was about. The wedding party came together for breakfast, after that careful attention was made to see that the bride and groom would not see each other again until they were being married. The activity at the house had noticeably increased, there were workers everywhere! The catering company was there all day with a staff of almost forty people, all going in different directions. This may seem like a large staff, but preparing and serving dinner for nearly five hundred people was no simple task. There were also workers making last minute preparations in the tents. As for Joseph, he was running from place to place barking orders at the staff. He wanted everything to be *perfect*. Benjamin himself was calm. He showed no signs of being nervous or anxious, just the opposite. Benjamin and Adam spent several hours tossing around mathematical equations for some project Adam was involved with at NASA. Angelica, well she was just the opposite; she was upstairs with her bridesmaids and her maid of honor. The women were helping each other to get ready. Joseph had a staff of hair stylists and make—up artists on site at the mansion that day, once again leaving nothing to chance.

It was now one o'clock, time for Benjamin, Adam, and the rest of the gentlemen to get ready. They had but two and half hours to prepare themselves. In normal male fashion all the men were ready by two thirty either needing less time to prepare or refusing to take more time. The ladies on the other hand would take every minute they could find. Something every man can relate to and something every man finds frustrating from time to time.

The guests had already started to arrive; there was a valet parking service on site to park cars for those who chose to drive themselves. The guest list was nothing less than a list of Who's Who. There were several members of Congress in attendance; the list of CEO's was staggering, numerous Judges representing numerous courts were also in attendance. It would seem that being the CEO of the largest bank in the Unites States gave Joseph access to important people.

The hour was upon us, Benjamin was taken away alone by a member of the wedding planners staff and taken to the gazebo. It would seem the weather was cooperating. There Benjamin stood, alone in front of nearly five hundred people eagerly awaiting a glimpse of his future wife.

Finally, the wedding party started coming out of the mansion towards the gazebo. First Adam and Debbie, then the other four bridesmaid and groomsmen would make their way to the gazebo. Then the moment Benjamin and all guests in attendance had been waiting for, the moment Angelica and her father exited the mansion. At that point the only thing Benjamin saw was an angel coming towards him, *his angel!* Benjamin saw or noticed nothing else, his focus was on Angelica. It seemed to take an eternity for his angel to join him. The ceremony was not too long nor was it too brief, it was just right. When Benjamin was asked to kiss his bride, once again it seems he forgot they were not alone. It was not until he heard Joseph repeatedly clearly his throat, did Benjamin break away from the kiss. The wedding party then took the long walk back to the mansion.

They would not be seen again until all the guests were seated in the main tent. After every one was seated the wedding party started coming into the tent, they were being announced as they came in two by two. When Benjamin and Angelica entered the tent, cameras were flashing as if the paparazzi were snapping photos for a celebrity. Benjamin found this attention to be somewhat uncomfortable, but Angelica was having the time of her life.

When they were approaching the head table Benjamin stopped in his tracks; he could hardly believe what he saw. Angelica leaned over telling him that she hoped he was not angry at what she had done, rather she hoped that it pleased him. Benjamin told Angelica that it was probably the nicest thing anyone could have done for him that day. Before Benjamin stood a picture of his mother, father, sister and his brother—in—law Todd. The picture was seven feet tall by almost twelve feet wide. To Benjamin it was as if though they were there with him. His mother would get to see her son married after all.

As the evening started to wind down, Joseph took Benjamin and Angelica off to the side to present his wedding gift to them. He told them it was not easy trying to get a gift for them, after all Benjamin you are already a wealthy man who is capable of providing Angelica with the finer things in life. So, I thought long and hard about it and I am giving you both a piece of land I acquired through a foreclosure at the bank. I initially bought it for an investment but I would like the two of you to have it to do with it as you wish. Joseph then handed his daughter an envelope, inside the envelope was the deed to five thousand acres of land in Southern Montana. Joseph told them they could sell it, build on it, or simply enjoy it from time to time. Joseph also admitted he had never personally seen the land, but heard it was quite breathtaking. Benjamin and Angelica were quite grateful for having received such a generous gift. As they were thanking Joseph, he told them that he was not done. Your bags are packed, they have been loaded into the limousine, and Carl will take you to the airport where a private jet will take you to St. Thomas Island where you will spend the next two weeks at Peyton's Palace, a resort set aside for people of power and influence, so that they might enjoy themselves away from prying eyes. When you're ready to leave the private jet will be at your disposal. Benjamin and Angelica thanked Joseph for everything that he had done for them, and for the more than generous gifts they had received as their wedding gift.

As they were making their way through the crowd preparing to leave, they would take time out to thank their guests for having attended the wedding. Angelica pointed out to Benjamin that it seemed as if though Adam and Debbie had become very attached to one other, Benjamin just smiled.

Finally, they had made their way through the crowd to the limousine were Carl was waiting. Carl asked them if they were ready. "Yes," replied Angelica.

"In that case it would be my pleasure to personally escort Mr. and Mrs. Benjamin Stone to the airport; your chariot awaits you" replied Carl. He then opened the door to the limousine, allowing Benjamin and Angelica to enter their "chariot". On the way to the airport, Angelica started to cry, Benjamin immediately became alarmed. What could it be, what is wrong, Angelica assured him that nothing was wrong. She was just very happy; to Benjamin this was very odd, why would a person cry because they were happy? Benjamin sat back with a slight smirk on his face remembering something his father had told him. Benjamin's fathers told him too never try to totally figure women out. He said because it cannot be done and to remember, while married you can be happy; or you can be right and it is better to be happy. When Benjamin's father told him of these things; Benjamin did not pay much attention to it, but now it makes sense to him, it was as if though the wisdom of the ages had been passed down, from father to son. This pleased Benjamin; it gave him comfort to know that his father was still with him. It was then that Angelica asked Benjamin, why are you sitting there with that silly smirk on your face? Benjamin told Angelica that he was only smiling because he was also happy. Angelica leaned over to give Benjamin a kiss, then taking his arm and leaning her head onto his shoulder saying nothing, just holding him tight.

A short time later they arrived at the airport. Carl drove the limousine onto the airport tarmac and unloaded the luggage. A member of the staff from the private jet took it and placed it on the jet for them. Before Benjamin and Angelica boarded the jet for their honeymoon to Peyton's Palace on the island of St. Thomas, Carl took Angelica in his arms telling her that his "Little Miss Sunshine" had grown up. Carl then turned to Benjamin with a look of absolute seriousness on his face. Benjamin braced himself for another one of Carl's little talks. Carl told him, "Benjamin I want you to know that I could not have picked a better husband for Angelica if I had done it myself. I am proud to have you marry my "Little Miss Sunshine", Congratulations, good luck, and have fun on your honeymoon." Benjamin thanked Carl, telling him that he knew he was not as mean as he had come across on earlier occasions. Carl let Benjamin know that he should have just said thank you and left, but since you insist on rehashing the past conversation we have had make no mistake; if you *ever* harm Angelica in anyway, I will put you in a shallow grave, giving it little more thought than having buried a family pet. Carl then turned and walked away, Benjamin on the other hand realized that Carl was right; he should have just thanked him leaving it at that. Benjamin had never in his life had someone say the things to him that Carl had, nor was he surer that the words spoken to him by Carl were not those of a threat, but those of fact! Angelica would never be aware of the conversation that Benjamin and Carl had, after all Carl was only trying to protect his "Little Miss Sunshine".

Shortly after Carl left, Benjamin and Angelica boarded the jet, Angelica had been on private jets before, but to Benjamin this was a new experience. They were being treated like royalty. The interior of the jet was quite lavish, on a scale of one to ten the comfort level was most definitely a ten. Benjamin and Angelica were exhausted from the events of the day. They decided to sleep, which they did most of the way to St. Thomas. Early that morning they arrived in St. Thomas. When they exited the private jet they were greeted by a limousine ready to take them to Peyton's Palace.

When they arrived at the resort, which was quite a distance from the other resorts on the island. They were greeted by their own private staff, a staff which had been assigned to them exclusively for the duration of their stay. Their quarters were quite lavish as expected. It would appear once again that Joseph had spared no expense. Peyton's Palace was a very exclusive resort; tailored to the rich and famous. It was a place where people with money and power could be left alone to enjoy themselves away from prying eyes, and enjoy themselves they did. They took advantage of the pampering and they both enjoyed daily massages. They had their choice of eating their meals alone in private, or in one of the restaurants provided for them by the resort. There were plenty of activities to occupy their time. They both enjoyed horseback riding on the beach, more so in the early morning than in the evening. They had a private cabana on the beach, a place to relax to do nothing, something Benjamin was not used to. Benjamin had promised Angelica that he would try not to do any work while on their honeymoon. For Benjamin this was difficult, though he had no computer, pen, or paper. Benjamin was still going over things in his head, which would sometimes explain the blank look on his face. A look Angelica knew all too well, but even Angelica knew she could not shut him down completely.

One evening while enjoying cocktails at the bar, Angelica was pre—occupied talking to a women she had met a few days earlier. Benjamin was seated next to her enjoying his drink, and occupying his mind with thoughts of work. It was then that a gentleman sat down next to Benjamin. He introduce himself as Randal Ashford, but before Benjamin could respond, before he could introduce himself, Mr. Ashford told him that there was no need for an introduction that he was already aware of who Benjamin was and that he was a fan of his work. Benjamin responded by telling Mr. Ashford that he was at a disadvantage because he did not know who Mr. Ashford was or why he knew about Benjamin and his work. Mr. Ashford told Benjamin that perhaps they should start over. He told Benjamin that his name was Mr. Ashford, and that he was the head of the United States Department of Biological Contaminates. He went on to tell Benjamin that not only was he the head of the United States Department of Biological Contaminates but he was also the head of the Center for Disease Control and other agencies that the average American was unaware even existed. Mr. Ashford told Benjamin that he was aware of his past work as well as the project that he was currently involved in. My job is to know who the brightest minds in the world were and to keep track of them and their work. You see Benjamin someday the people I represent may call upon you to possibly do some work for us. When that day comes, and it will most likely come, we would hope that you would be receptive to the idea of working for us. Benjamin was not sure how to respond to what he had just heard. Partially because if he had just heard right the United States Government was keeping track of his work, of his life. After a few seconds Benjamin was able to compose himself enough to muster up a response. "First of all Mr. Ashford, this is my honeymoon and what you call a first contact, I call an intrusion; secondly, I don't care for the idea that my life is being scrutinized by the United States Government and whatever agency you do or do not represent."

"Doctor Stone."

"You can stop there; I am not finished. I also get the feeling that you are not telling me everything Mr. Ashford. That is if Mr. Ashford is your real name, and as if to whether or not I would ever work for the people you represent. That would be for me to determine and it would depend on exactly what the project was. I would defiantly not be willing to work on something that would cause harm to other people, or to help advance the government's military causes around the world. If these are the types of projects that you are considering asking me to help you and the people you represent work on, well then you can now and for always remove my name from your list."

"Doctor Stone if I have offended you I do apologize I was definitely not my intention. It was my intention to inadvertently bump into you, making some small talk, then lead into getting you to know that we were interested in you and your ability to solve problems that others would not begin to try to solve. Once again I apologize; it would seem that my attempt was clumsy at best. Doctor Stone I should have known, after reviewing your file that you are not a man to be trifled with and as far as to whether or not Mr. Ashford is my name, it is indeed my name. As to whether or not I have been completely truthful about the people I represent, no I have not. I do represent the United States Government and the agencies I have mentioned, however, the bigger picture is I not only represent our government, I represent *many* governments from around the world. The organization which we belong to; for *most* people, has no name, it *does not exist*. It is a group of world leaders, a group of the richest, and most powerful, most influential people in the world. This group meets once every four years to decide the direction of the world economy to dictate the very direction of humanity. Contrary to what you might be thinking at this moment, these are not bad people. Of course they make decisions that will benefit them financially, but this has always been the way throughout history. Men of power have always dictated life for the rest of us. Today's difference is that men of power are for the first time able to achieve and use their power in a global theatre. They are also different from those who have come before them because they are also interested in protecting not only the people of the planet, but the renewable and nonrenewable resources, protecting the planet itself."

Once again Benjamin paused considering what he was just told before responding. "Mr. Ashford after hearing what you had to say, coupled with the fact that your organization has no name, or at least no name you care to mention. I am quite sure that I want nothing to do with your group. Furthermore it is my belief that such an organization is filled with aristocrats and power moguls whose only goal is to further their own causes, and line their pockets with the blood and sweat of other people. So I must say to you Mr. Ashford, have a good day." At that Benjamin turned his back on Mr. Ashford, and Mr. Ashford got up from where he was seated slipping away without further commit.

Angelica was so involved in her own conversation that she hardly noticed the conversation that Benjamin had been having. Benjamin felt it was best that Angelica was not aware of the conversation he had with Mr. Ashford. One thing was certain Benjamin did not care for the idea that he was being watched over by some secret organization. Benjamin had never considered himself to be a conspiracy theorist, though he had always suspected that not only the United States government, but all governments operated in the shadows, behind closed doors, away from the prying eyes of the people they were supposed to be representing and always pretending to be above board, putting on a show for their public. A public that for the most part would never be aware of the true nature of those who represented them nor for the most part would they care.

The following days were filled with fun, activities and relaxation. Benjamin pushed the conversation with Mr. Ashford to the back of his mind, trying not to waste energy on things out of his control. Benjamin and Angelica had only a few days left before they were expected back at work so the two of them decided that since they had use of a private jet, they would go to southern Montana to look at the five thousand acres of land that Joseph had given them. Angelica had spoken to her father about going to see the land. He told her that he had hired a gentleman in southern Montana who lived near the land to keep an eye on it. His name was Bart Black, Joseph would have him met the two of them at the airport. Then he could take them to see their property.

When Benjamin and Angelica arrived at the airport, they were greeted by Bart Black just as planned. Now keep in mind that Benjamin and Angelica have been riding on a private jet and being chauffeured in a limousine for the past few weeks. Bart Black on the other hand offered them no such service; instead the transportation he was providing was an old beat up Chevy pick—up truck. The trucks color was red and rusty and the windshield had a large crack running through it. As for Bart himself, he was in his fifties. He wore a pair of cowboy boots, blue jeans, a cowboy hat, and a button up long sleeve blue jean shirt. To complete the look he had a mouth full of chewing tobacco. Bart was what you would call a real authentic western character. When Bart approached them he said, “Hi my name is Bart I suppose you are Mr. and Mrs. Stone?” He then spit a rather large amount of tobacco juice on the ground, as if though no one would notice. “Joseph called me and told me that he had given you two the Twin Falls Ranch and that I should take you out to see your new property, are you ready?” Benjamin and Angelica stood silent for a moment trying to soak up the character of a man that stood before them. Finally Benjamin spoke, “Hello Bart, it is nice to meet you, my name is Benjamin, and this is my wife Angelica. Bart you said you were to take us to the Twin Falls Ranch. Is that what the property is called?”

Yes, the property is called Twin Falls Ranch. On the property there are two waterfalls side by side, I guess they are probably one hundred fifty feet tall maybe more. “We’ll we need to get going, it is over an hour from here, are you ready?” The three of them climbed into the old red and rusty truck. Angelica sat in the middle. As they were driving to their destination Bart rarely stopped talking, telling them about the ranch, about the area and pointing out things along the way he felt they might be interested in. When he did stop talking it was just long enough to spit another mouth full of tobacco juice out the window, and down the side of the truck. Benjamin found Bart to be entertaining, Angelica on the other hand found Bart to be absolutely disgusting, both in his appearance and mannerism. Even though she was put off by Bart's demeanor she never showed it. She sat quietly while Bart and Benjamin talked; only talking when spoken to. All the while Benjamin could tell how she felt. When Bart would do or say something absolutely disgusting Benjamin would give Angelica a little nudge and just smile. To Benjamin the ride to Twin Falls Ranch went by quite fast, after all he was being entertained. To Angelica the ride seemed to last *forever*.

Finally they had arrived. The entrance to the ranch had two gates, chained and locked together. Bart work quickly to unlock the gates. The road leading in was nothing more than a dirt road. Bart told them he could take them back maybe one and a half miles. Beyond that they would need horses or a four wheeler. It was then that Angelica asked her first question "Is there a house on this property?"

"No", responded Bart, "there is a shack were the cowhands used to stay when the previous owner had cattle on the ranch".

Angelica then asked, "How is it that the previous owner lost the ranch".

"The previous owner was a friend of mine; I have known him since we were kids. He lived on the property that joins Twin Falls Ranch. He bought it years ago and was doing well. The cattle he raised was paying for the ranch, all he had to do was set back and leave things alone, but unfortunately he had a taste for the ladies and for gambling. His wife had enough and she left him. When that happened he lost everything, except for Twin Falls Ranch. He moved into the shack your about to see, and no doubt could have made a comeback, if it were not for one thing." "What would that be Bart", asked Angelica.

"He did not learn from his mistakes, he kept chasing after the ladies, gambling, drinking, and in the end the bank took the property back". Angelica commented on how sad it was that someone would throw everything away. Bart told her that if there was no more to the story it would be sad enough. Unfortunately there is more to the story. On the day the sheriff and the bank were coming to evict the previous owner he shot himself in the shack and that's where the sheriff found his body. Angelica told Bart that she was sorry his friend had killed himself. Bart told her there was no reason to be sorry, that his friend was the cause of his own problem and his own death and no one in this truck need feel any guilt.

Just then Bart pointed out the shack, as they came over a hill on the road. The shack was in a large valley at the end of the valley were the twin falls. They were absolutely breathtaking! The falls emptied into a large stream that went on as far as the eye could see until it disappeared into the landscaping. The top of the valley itself was filled with lush grassland as far as you could see. As for the shack; well, that was exactly what it was, a shack.

When Bart stopped the truck they were parked in front of the shack, Benjamin went inside. As for Angelica she could not bring herself to enter, not after knowing that the previous owner had killed himself there. Instead she stayed outside just looking over the scenery.

When Benjamin and Bart came out of the shack they were unable to locate Angelica at first, eventually finding her down at the stream. The stream was filled with smooth round boulders and in the background you could hear the sound of the twin falls emptying into the stream below and the water cascading downstream was very soothing. Angelia asked Benjamin if they could go to the falls to get a better look. Bart told them to follow him, there was a trail leading to the falls. After getting to the falls and enjoying their beauty, Bart told them that if they continued up the trail it would take them to the top of the falls. Benjamin asked aren't you coming with us? Bart told them that the climb was too steep for him, and that he was a little bit "too long in the tooth" to make such a climb. They both laughed at Bart's way of describing things.

Benjamin and Angelica took off up the trail. At one point the trail became very steep, it was then they knew what Bart was talking about. When they reached the top of the trail, and were standing before the head of the falls, on their right while looking straight ahead to see a truly breathe taking view. A view of seemingly endless rolling hills filled with lush grass, and spotted by stands of large pine trees. They both agreed the climb was well worth it. After a few minutes they found a large rock to sit on from which they could see both the falls to the right, the rolling hills in the front, and to the back of them they could see the valley along with the shack and Bart sitting patiently by the stream. As they sat on the rock, Angelica was talking, Benjamin saying almost nothing just letting her talk. It seems that Benjamin had already developed a skill, known to many, if not all husbands, (the ability to pretend that you are listening with the occasional nod or grunt, but in reality hearing little to nothing your wife is saying). It is a survival skill for men, a skill that often gets them in trouble but for now, for today, it seems to be working for Benjamin. So as they sat and as Benjamin pretended to listen, his mind was elsewhere. Benjamin's mind was on his research project, which is where his mind was for the most part, no matter where he was. It was then that it happened, call it total clarity of thought, call it an epiphany, call it what you might, but then and there at that moment he knew he had solved what had occupied his mind for those many years. In a complete and startling, enthusiastic burst of energy. Benjamin shouted out "*I have done it!* I know what causes ageing and how to slow it down. *I have done it!*" Angelica looked at him puzzled, "Benjamin what are you saying?"

"I am saying that right here, just right now I have done it, I have solved our research problem."

"Benjamin, are you sure?"

"I am absolutely sure. I have never been surer of anything in my life. Come on Angelica we have to go. We need to get back to the airport, back to Leesburg, back to the laboratory." Angelica grabbed Benjamin's hand and said, "Well, what are you waiting for, let's go." Benjamin thought that at the speed they were descending down the trail, they might break their necks. When they reached the bottom where Bart was waiting, they told him they were ready to go. They needed to get back to the airport. Bart in his western mannerism told them that judging by the way you two are acting, if I didn't know better I would think you just found gold up there. Benjamin told Bart that gold is exactly what they had found, but not the kind of gold you dig up out of the ground. Bart told them, "I am not sure what you are talking about, but if the airport is where you want to go, then the airport is where I will take you, let's go." On the way back to the airport Benjamin and Angelica were talking about, the human genome, DNA, enzymes, things that Bart could not make any sense of. At one point Bart interrupted their conversation telling them that he had not understood a word they had said for the past forty minutes. So let me ask you something that I am curious about. What is it that the two of you plan to do with the land, neither one of you seem the type to move out to southern Montana and become ranchers. Benjamin told Bart that they have not really discussed it yet, but if he could speak for Angelica and if he could have his way, he would like to keep the land. Whether or not they would ever live there, that would be a question to be answered in the future, but at the very least it would be a place to come from time to time for a visit, just someplace to enjoy. Angelica nodded as if though in agreement. Bart then asked if it would be okay with them if he could raise cattle on their land. He was willing to pay the going rate per acre. Benjamin told him to draw up a contract and send it to him for review, but as far as they were concerned it would be fine with them.

When Bart got them to the airport, they jumped out of the red and rusty Chevy truck barely saying good—bye as they rushed towards their private jet. The conversation they were having in the truck continued all the way to Leesburg. By the time they arrived in Leesburg, Angelica felt that even though she did not fully understand, she had a pretty good picture of what Benjamin was talking about. When they arrived at Leesburg they hit the ground running, not even stopping at their home to unload their luggage.

They went straight to Aspen Pharmaceuticals, straight to the laboratory. The only problem was that it was Sunday and Benjamin had been banned from working on Sunday. No matter how bad Benjamin tried the guard would not let Benjamin have access to the laboratory. Benjamin told the security guard that he needed to call the head of Aspen

Pharmaceuticals at home at once, that it was imperative he gain access to his laboratory. The guard was insistent telling the very man whom Benjamin wanted him to call gave a strict order that under no circumstances was Doctor Stone allowed in his laboratory on Sundays. Benjamin took a deep breath before talking, "Please listen to me very carefully, you have seen me come and go for years, never a cross word have we had, but if you do not make the call and right now I can assure you that come tomorrow you will longer be employed with this company." The guard not knowing what to do made the call. When Mr. Brody, (the CEO of Aspen Pharmaceuticals) answered the phone, he was not happy to have been bothered on a Sunday afternoon. You could hear him scolding the guard over the phone. Then finally, the guard began to speak. He told Mr. Brody how insistent Doctor Stone was about gaining access to his laboratory. The guard then turned to Benjamin telling him that Mr. Brody wanted to speak to him. Benjamin took the phone from the guard, but before Mr. Brody could speak Benjamin began to talk, "*I have done it, and I need immediate access to my laboratory!*"

"Doctor Stone calm down", barked Mr. Brody! "What do you mean, you have done it?"

"I mean I believe I have done it. I have come up with the answer to the research I have been working on."

Mr. Brody asked in a slow calm voice, "Doctor Stone do you mean to tell me that you have solved the ageing issue?"

"That is exactly what I mean to tell you. This cannot wait until tomorrow I need to start running tests to make sure I am right. If I am right, which I believe I am, Aspen Pharmaceuticals will be the wealthiest pharmaceutical company in the world. Your stock will go through the roof."

"Doctor Stone, who else knows about this?"

"No one except my wife, Angelica" Replied Benjamin.

"Alright Doctor Stone, you must not tell anyone about this. Not even your staff is to be made aware of what you have discovered. Once you are certain and only then will we go public with your discovery, do you understand me?"

"Yes, Mr. Brody I completely understand you."

"Alright Doctor Stone put the guard back on the phone" Mr. Brody had a brief conversation with the guard, and then he hung up the phone. The guard looked at Benjamin after he ended his phone call and said, "Doctor Stone I have been told to let you have access to the laboratory and furthermore to give you anything you need. Doctor Stone I would also like to apologize, but you have to understand I have a job to do."

"I likewise apologize to you sir, and I am sorry for threatening you with your job. I had no other choice under the circumstances." Benjamin and Angelica were then taken to the laboratory by the guard, left to start running their tests.

The next morning when the rest of Benjamin's staff showed up, they were quite surprised to see both Benjamin and Angelica at work already. At first the staff members tried to make small talk. How was the wedding, how was the honeymoon? Did you enjoy yourselves? Benjamin made short order of that line of questioning. Within a short period of time and in an orderly fashion Benjamin had every member of his staff working on a series of tests. Benjamin instructed them that they were not to share the results of their individual assignments with each other. They were instead to report to him and him only. It was something Benjamin had never done before, to stop the flow of information in the laboratory was unheard of. The laboratory was abuzz about theories of what was going on, but no one dared to share the results of their individual testing with anyone other than Benjamin. Even if Benjamin was telling them nothing they knew something big was in the making.

Benjamin and Angelica slept at the laboratory Monday night, not going home until Tuesday afternoon, only after Benjamin was secure in the knowledge that his staff's course had been set in the right direction.

The following day both Angelica and Benjamin were right back at it, not wavering nor slowing down. They were exhibiting a passion that the staff members had never seen before. On Tuesday the laboratory was also visited by Mr. Brody, this was not only unusual, it had *never* happened before. Mr. Brody and Benjamin went into Benjamin's office were they spent the better part of two hours. When Mr. Brody left he seemed very pleased with the meeting he just had. Benjamin knew that it would take months of testing before they could go public, but he also knew in his heart that he was right.

After six weeks Benjamin was certain that he had found the trigger in the human body that caused ageing. Now to find away to slow it down, Benjamin was sure that with the right cocktail of enzymes and amino acids he could do just that, Benjamin also knew that he was not supposed to tell anyone and he understood why. Aspen Pharmaceutical did not want a run on their stock; that was until they had positioned themselves and a chosen few were able to reap the vast profits that would no doubt come from such news as a cure for ageing. Benjamin also knew that without him there would be no cure, no profit.

It was decided by Benjamin and Angelica that they tell her father Joseph. Benjamin called Joseph telling him to buy Aspen Pharmaceutical stock, and that if he could somehow hide the purchase, making it difficult to trace directly to him it would be best. Joseph wanted to know why he should by Aspen Pharmaceutical stock, and exactly what was going on? “Sorry Joseph, but I cannot tell you”. Benjamin could only tell him to buy as much as he could hide, and don’t tell another human being. He told him to trust in what he had just been told. Joseph took Benjamin’s advice and through varies methods bought Aspen Pharmaceutical stock.

The work continued, Benjamin was getting closer by the day. Then it happened, he and his team had done it. Benjamin was able to put together enough information from his team to solve the problem. Now the process of testing on live subjects needed to begin. The problem Benjamin now had was to either get Mr. Brody to go public with the information or allow Benjamin to confide in his team. In order to conduct further studies, he would have to let the entire team in on exactly what they had collectively done. It was decided then by Mr. Brody to proceed with the clinical trials, to let Benjamin tell his staff. The following day Mr. Brody came to Benjamin’s laboratory along with one of the company’s lawyer. Benjamin explained to his staff what they had done. The room erupted in shouts of joy, people were hugging! Some were brought to tears, all shared in the excitement.

When things settled down, the lawyer Mr. Valex took over, he explained to everyone that they were all not to speak to anyone outside of the people in this room about what they had discovered. Furthermore everyone was given a legal document to sign. The document stated that if you were to talk to anyone else about this project, that Aspen

Pharmaceuticals would prosecute you to the fullest extent of the law. In addition they would lose their job and not share in any profit from the discovery. Even Benjamin and Angelica were asked to sign a contract. This did not bother Benjamin even though he had told Joseph, because he had told Joseph *prior* to signing the contract. Besides that, Joseph was a cautious man, and would not have acquired the position in life that he had by being a careless person.

Aspen Pharmaceutical provided Benjamin with people who for a fee would take part in the clinical study. Benjamin insisted that he have some patients with terminal diseases. None of the subjects were to be told what they were taking or what to expect. Instead they were to report any changes in the way they felt, all the subjects were to come in once a week for blood work, and to fill out a questionnaire. Now Benjamin being Benjamin felt it only right that he subject himself to the same clinical testing as the rest of his subjects. Within the first few weeks it was apparent to Benjamin that his body was going through noticeable changes. His fingernail and toenails were growing much slower; he went from shaving everyday to shaving only every fourth day. The same results were being reported by the other test subjects. It was still too early to claim total victory.

The months passed, it appeared that other than the hair and nail growth being reported by the other patients there were no noticeable changes. That is in everybody except for the terminal patients. For them, their particular disease had slowed its advance on their bodies. According to all their blood work their condition was being slowed down three to four times. This was not a cure, but it would definitely give them a longer life. Still Benjamin was not completely satisfied; he wanted the testing to go on for at least one year before he would agree to go public.

Again months went by and after one year with no noticeable side effects, it would seem that Benjamin's data was solid. He and his team had truly done it. They have developed a method by which the human ageing process could be slowed down three to four times its normal rate depending upon the person.

Benjamin had a meeting with Mr. Brody and the full board of directors from Aspen Pharmaceuticals. The information that needed to be exchanged was so vast that several meetings were to be held over a ten day period. To Benjamin this was far more painful than the research itself.

The final stage was set; a press conference was arranged by Aspen Pharmaceuticals. There would be people from every corner of the planet at this conference. All were wondering if the great Doctor Stone had actually done it, or if it was just publicity by Aspen Pharmaceuticals. In any event, all who were invited were in attendance. No one wanted to be the person who did not show up just in case.

According to Mr. Brody just the announcement of a press conference, concerning Benjamin caused Aspen Pharmaceutical stock to go up eighteen percent. Benjamin smiled to himself, thinking how pleased Joseph must be right now.

The date was January 17th, 1987; the conference room was completely packed. Mr. Brody, Angelica, and others were either very nervous or very excited, it was hard to tell. The process was different for Benjamin; he was trying to talk to Mr. Brody about the next research project that he wanted to work on. It was as if Benjamin had already moved on. The fact that he was about to give the world the news of possibly the greatest medical breakthrough in history did not seem to excite him in the least.

It was time; Mr. Brody approached the podium and began, "I would like to thank everyone for being here today. Today is a day of celebration, not only for Aspen Pharmaceuticals, but for the whole of humanity. Ladies and gentleman I would now like to present a man who needs no introduction, but never the less I give you Doctor Benjamin Stone". As Benjamin walked across the stage towards the podium, you could have heard a pin drop. A room with over fifteen hundred people in it, and not a sound. Benjamin stood at the podium looking the crowd over, still not a sound. "Good Morning, I would like to thank everyone for being here today. I know that there has been a great deal of speculation as to why Aspen Pharmaceuticals has called on everyone to be here today. I would like to announce that the research I and my team have been working on since January of 1980 is completed; we have solved the problem. We can now slow the aging process down by three to four times. Before I answer any questions, I would like to say a few things. I would like to give thanks to Aspen Pharmaceuticals without their support I could not have done this. I would also like to thank my team; they were instrumental in many ways to my research. I would like to give a special thanks to my wife, Doctor Angelica Stone who had to put up with me during the process." That comment caused a bit of laughter from the crowd. It also seems as the person responsible for the research I have the honor of giving a name to what we have done, I have decided to call it *Nathanial's cure, The De Leon factor*. Nathanial's cure after my brother who died from Leukemia many years ago, and the De Leon factor after Ponce De Leon who came to America in search for the fountain of youth. I thank you for your patience. I will now try to answer any questions you may have."

Benjamin's first pick was a gentleman in the front room. "Doctor Stone how long before the product goes public and what will be the cost?"

"Questions of this nature will not be handled by me. Those type of questions are best handled by Mr. Brody."

Mr. Brody told the reporter that first there would be the drawn out process of getting approval from the Food and Drug Administration. This could take several years as for the cost that has yet to be determined.

Benjamin's next pick was a gentleman from the middle of the group. "Doctor Stone, besides the obvious benefit of living longer, what other benefits do you see?"

"As I stated earlier, my brother Nathanial died of Leukemia. So if you have a terminal disease you can expect to live longer, perhaps giving science more time to find a cure."

Next Benjamin picked a gentleman from the back row. "Dr. Stone, do you see any other benefits?"

"Yes, I do. To me the next obvious step in this field is to speed up the aging process. You may all wonder why a person would want to speed up the process of aging. Consider this someday to be able to clone an organ, or heart, a lung, a liver, or kidney, then to be able to accelerate the growth of the organ perhaps by a ratio of twenty to one. To be able to get an organ that is your own, one that your body will not reject. Not to die while you are stuck on a waiting list for years. This is most definitely the direction I see this research going."

Benjamin's next pick was a gentleman from the middle of the audience. "Doctor Stone do you see a negative side to you research?"

"Yes, I do. To me the negative side of my research would be with people living longer. The planet may become overpopulated straining the use of our natural resources, both renewable and un—renewable. However that is a question for mankind and our various governments to deal with. How to control the earth's population is not a debate I care to have here today."

Next Benjamin picked a woman who was seated four rows from the front. "Doctor Stone, I am here representing the Christian Science Magazine." Benjamin knew right then and there he had called on the wrong person. This line of questioning would not be pleasant for him. "I would like to ask you, do you feel on some level that you are playing God, or do you feel that God has somehow empowered you to do this type of research?"

"What I believe is that I am a scientist, and that my research is purely scientific."

"Doctor Stone you are avoiding my questions. Who do you give credit to for your research, for your very being?"

"I give credit to myself, my staff and Aspen Pharmaceuticals". Benjamin cut the woman off, and moved on to the next person.

This time he would pick another person from the back of the crowd. "Doctor Stone I am afraid I cannot ask the question I had in mind. That is until you answer the last question asked of you. Simple enough do you are do you not believe in God?"

Benjamin could have said yes, kept his opinion to himself and moved on, but no not Benjamin, he could not do just that. He had to be truthful. "Ladies and gentlemen it seems I have reached an impasse in the questioning. By a show of hands how many people feel it is important that I answer that question?" Much to Benjamin's surprise, an overwhelming number of people raised their hands. This angered Benjamin. Why could people not just accept his research for its pure scientific value? Why did it matter how he felt personally about an issue like God one way or another? It was then that Mr. Brody got up from his seat and charged the podium. "Ladies and gentlemen we are not here to talk about Doctor Stone's personal beliefs. I believe we need to redirect our line of questioning." This angered Benjamin even more, who was Mr. Brody to believe he could brush Benjamin away from the podium to answer a question directed towards him! Benjamin spoke abruptly and with a sense of anger in his voice. "Ladies and Gentlemen do you want me to answer the question or would you rather have Mr. Brody continue to employ damage control?" Shouts erupted from the crowd, "Answer the question!" Benjamin looked at Mr. Brody telling him that he could reseat himself. Then Benjamin leaned into the podium, "Ladies and Gentlemen I will answer the question you desire so much. It will also be the last question I will answer. Mr. Brody was at the edge of his seat not knowing from moment to moment what Benjamin might say. We have gathered here today to discuss a scientific accomplishment but unfortunately for many that is not enough. Ignorance appears to be the rule of the day. I personally believe that each individual person in this room has the right to believe what *they* want, that includes *me*. As for myself I do not believe in a higher power. I believe in Science. If you chose to believe in your particular brand of religion or your particular God that is your business, no one else." Now as if Benjamin had not done enough damage, he felt compelled to elaborate on his belief. “To me a person looking in on the religious community and not being a part of it, it would appear that throughout history, mankind has killed, murdered, and maimed in the name of their brand of religion. Throughout history mankind had argued that their “invisible guy” in the sky knows more than the other guy’s invisible guy in the sky. The whole thing is ludicrous. Today as we speak the newest threat to our world is that of the Islamic terrorists. In the end all they stand for is pushing their own particular brand of religion and if you do not agree then you must die. I know this personally having lost four family members to Islamic terrorist. It is my opinion that religion developed as a means of population control. If I can give you the answers to that which you do not have and try to convince you that my information comes from God, it would most definitely be to my advantage if I were trying to control a large number of people. Throughout history religion has evolved. Tt has changed to keep pace with human evolution, to keep pace with the human experience. It is nothing more than a security blanket. Having said all that, religion can often be a good thing. It teaches us how to treat your fellow man, how to exist in society, but if left to open interpretation as it most often is, and then there will always be those who read into it what they want to read into it. As long as that goes on, the world will always be in constant turmoil.”

Benjamin then turned away from the podium. As he was walking off the stage he passed Mr. Brody, who had a look of complete desperation and panic on his face. Mr. Brody was headed for the podium to make an attempt at damage control. When Benjamin got to the back of the stage, Angelica was waiting for him. Angelica told Benjamin that she would ask him why he did what he did, but she already knew the answer. Benjamin, you have never fully understood people and society and how they work, I understand this and I do accept it. I do not even blame you for being yourself. After all, you are what you are; but for my own sake of mind I have to say I wish you had not done that. Benjamin told Angelica that he understood if she were mad at him, however he was just tired of people trying discount his work, his efforts, and instead giving his credit to something that does not exist. Angelica took Benjamin by the hand letting him know that she understood and that things would be okay. She then told him she wanted to go home; there will be plenty of time to deal with this.

When they arrived at their home, Angelica went around the house unplugging phones. She decided it would be best to keep a low profile for the evening; that is until several hours later, when Mr. Brody showed up at the front door. “Hello Angelica is Benjamin home?”

“Yes he is, won’t you please come in”. Angelica led Mr. Brody into the den, offered him a drink, which he declined then she went to retrieve Benjamin. When Benjamin entered the den, Mr. Brody smiled at him saying, “Benjamin I don’t know what to do with you.” Benjamin stood there saying nothing. “Benjamin after you left I did what I could to employ “damage control” as you put it. With any luck your views on religion will only be a side bar to the real story.” Benjamin commented, “Perhaps it is a bigger deal to you Mr. Brody than it is to the press.”

“Perhaps” replied Mr. Brody, “perhaps, but for now I need you and Angelica to take a few days off, let things settle down. Turning your phones off was probably a good idea. I will come by in the next few days to touch base. Until then keep a low profile, Okay?!” They both agreed to keep a low profile, and wait for Mr. Brody to contact them.

Well, just as promised Benjamin and Angelica keep a low profile, talking to no one and as promised Mr. Brody came by to see them. He told Benjamin that on the following day at ten a.m. he was to come to the board room of Aspen Pharmaceuticals. Benjamin commented, “If you are going to fire me, why not do it right here?”

“No one wants you to leave Aspen Pharmaceutical Benjamin especially me. After all you are the goose who laid the golden egg. Just be there at ten o’clock Benjamin and if you want, bring Angelica with you. Don’t worry I believe I have a solution that will make all parties happy.” Mr. Brody then excused himself going as he had came. The next day as planned both Benjamin and Angelica showed up at the board room promptly at ten o’clock a.m. When they entered the board room all the members were in attendance. At the head of the table was Mr. Brody and to his right was their lawyer Mr. Valex. Mr. Brody began by saying, “I appreciate everyone being here today. Instead of calling you both Doctor Stone, with your permission I would like to call you by your first names today. Benjamin and Angelica agreed. Benjamin I do not know if you have been following the news, *but we most certainly have*. It would seem that your religious views are getting almost as much attention as your research. We can hope that it will eventually die down, but then today’s paper claims that the Christian Community is calling for a boycott of our products. They are calling you “Doctor Devil” in the papers. Not to flattering is it Benjamin?”

“No, Mr. Brody it is not very flattering.”

“So Benjamin I believe it is easy enough for you to see that we are in the middle of a *public relations nightmare*! I believe I may have a solution though; I have prepared a statement that we want you to sign. A statement we can release to the press. The statement will basically say that you said the things you said out of frustration due to the line of questionings, and that you were under a great deal of pressure. You had been working to long without a break, that you were exhausted. If you will sign the prepared statement then follow it up with a personal appearance in a few weeks, and then I believe we can in time put this behind us. What do you say Benjamin, can I count on you?"

"Mr. Brody, Aspen Pharmaceuticals has always been able to count on me. Today is no special occasion. You can count on me to be true to myself just as I have always been. I will *not* sign any such letter nor will I publicly apologize for what I believe. All I have ever wanted to do is be true to my research, be true to science. Why do people concern themselves with my personal feelings and my personal beliefs?" Mr. Brody started to speak, but before he got very far, he was interrupted by Mr. Shepherd, the chairman of the board. "Doctor Stone, you know who I am we have met on many occasions. Now, let me be true to myself, let me speak my mind. I understand the outrage being felt by the religious communities. I understand it, because I am a part of it. *I am a deeply religious man*; I hold my relationship with the Lord near and dear to my heart. I, Doctor Stone am very offended by your attack on religion; I also speak for the board when I tell you if you do not do what we ask, Aspen Pharmaceuticals will sever *all* relationships with you. Doctor Stone you may think you know our minds, you may think that we would tolerate anything because of the money you have made for us, but you couldn't be more wrong; we *cannot and will not* tolerate your slandering religion. You see Doctor Stone even money whoring, soulless bastards like us have our limits! Now, Doctor Stone what will it be?"

"Mr. Shepherd my answer is still no".

"In that case I will now turn the meeting over to Mr. Valex." Benjamin knew that the legal maneuvering was about to begin, after all Mr. Valex was not there to keep anybody company. "Doctor Stone, as you know I represent Aspen Pharmaceuticals. If we cannot sway you to do what we want, you must be removed from the company. You do understand don't you?"

Benjamin did not like Mr. Valex's condescending tone. "Mr. Valex considering that my IQ dwarfs yours, yes I believe it would be safe to say that I do understand you."

Mr. Valex then turned to Angelica asking her if he could get any help from her or was she going to watch her husband throw their careers away? Angelica looked at Benjamin and smiled then turned to Mr. Valex telling him that her place was with her husband, and as far as his career, people will be standing in line to offer my husband work if he wants it. "Alright", commented Mr. Valex, "alright Doctor Stone Aspen Pharmaceuticals would like to offer you a buyout. They would like to make you an offer of two hundred and fifty million dollars to buy your contract. Considering that as of yesterday, you already hold one hundred and eighty million dollars of Aspen Pharmaceutical stock you could leave us a very wealthy man."

"Mr. Valex your offer sound intriguing, but as you put it I already have one hundred and eighty million in Aspen Pharmaceuticals stock, that already makes me very wealthy. My answer is still no." Before Mr. Valex could speak, Benjamin cut him off telling him that he was not quite finished. "Mr. Valex, Mr. Brody, members of the board. I have a counter offer for you. As we all know my current contract gives me thirty percent of any profits derived from my research, also if you think you are going to take me to court on some sort of moral issue, please keep in mind I was never asked to sign a contract with a morale clause. Something I am sure that Mr. Valex now regrets. We all know how much money you are already making from the psoriasis cream, as well as the wrinkle cream. That amount of money is *nothing* compared to what will be made from Nathanial's cure. *No,* you will not buy me out for the meager sum of two hundred and fifty million dollars. You will give me *two point five billion dollars* in Aspen Pharmaceuticals stock, based on yesterday's price. In addition, you will call the aging compound Nathanial's Cure, the De Leon factor by Doctor Benjamin Stone. In return I will give up any rights to my research and will agree to do no further research in the area of aging. This is my offer, if you choose to buy me out. If not Aspen Pharmaceuticals can pay me my thirty percent for the reminder of my life and beyond to whomever I have willed it to. As they say Mr. Valex, the ball is in your court. Now, do *you* understand?"

Mr. Valex paused looking at Benjamin, not in a look of anger, but more in a look that you might give to someone who you know had just got the best of you. "Doctor Stone could you and your wife go into the other room for a moment, so that Mr. Brody, the board, and myself might discuss your offer." Benjamin knew then and there that he had them! They would have no choice but to meet his demands. Benjamin stood up reaching out, taking Angelica by the hand. He turned to Mr. Valex and told him, "we will be waiting in the other room for your answer, but there is one more thing you should know; *I will not* accept any counter offer." With that Benjamin and Angelica left the room.

As they entered the room adjacent to the board room, Angelica looked at Benjamin and said, "Do you really believe they are going to give you two point five billion dollars, Benjamin?"

"Yes I do, because if they don't it will cost them more much more in the long run, and they will lose their high moral ground that they cherish so much. Either way Angel my dear, we will know shortly. One thing is for sure, I guarantee that they are having quite a heated debate in there."

Benjamin was absolutely right; the conversation was quite heated to start off, Mr. Shepherd commented that there was no way Aspen Pharmaceuticals was going to pay that arrogant son—of—a—bitch two point five billion dollars in stock. Mr. Brody along with the rest of the board members agreed. They all turned to Mr. Valex for confirmation that there was some way out of his mess. Instead Mr. Valex couldn't tell them what they wanted; he could only tell them what they needed to hear. I know tempers are high, and there are things we can do. We could refuse his offer; let him take us to court. We could hold our ground on moral issues. The only problem is Doctor Stone had no moral clause in his contract, but for the average person you could tie them up in court for years, and they will settle for less money because of the financial and emotional strain. The problem with Doctor Stone is that he is already a wealthy man. Plus Doctor Stone could find a job very easily with a handsome salary. If that weren't enough, his father—in—law Joseph Webb is an extremely wealthy man. With connections some could say lead all the way to the White House itself. I personally believe that Doctor Stone would take us to court, not caring if it took ten years to settle. I agree with everyone in this room, Doctor Stone is an arrogant son—of—a—bitch, unfortunately as they say, he has us by the balls. If you don't pay him the two point five billion dollars, he is asking for, then you will eventually pay him the thirty percent his contract calls for and most likely you will pay it with interest. As Doctor Stone has previously stated, you will pay him for life and beyond. As much as it pains me to say so, I believe it would be in the best interest of Aspen Pharmaceuticals to pay Doctor Stone the two point five billion dollars he has asked for."

Mr. Shepherd was sitting in the background mumbling to himself. Mr. Valex continued, "if we do buy him out, we can claim that he no longer works for Aspen Pharmaceuticals because he does not represent the values we hold near and dear to our hearts. If you do this then the public relations nightmare that you are having will go away. We can represent ourselves as the company who cares more about principal than profit. After a few more minutes of discussion, they all agreed to pay Doctor Stone two point five billion dollars in stock." This would be the largest buyout ever for a personal contract. Mr. Valex went into the next room to retrieve Benjamin and Angelica. When they entered to room, everyone had been seated; Mr. Valex informed Benjamin that they would meet his demands, and that a contract would be drawn up in the next few days for his approval. As Benjamin and Angelica was leaving the room, Mr. Shepherd could not resist making a harsh comment. "Doctor Stone I want you to know that I hope you enjoy your blood money" Benjamin looked at Mr. Shepherd smiling, then he told him "Thank you, just as I hope you enjoy yours." Just as promised Benjamin had a copy of the contract in his hands in three days. He forwarded the contract to a law firm in New York, one that had been recommended by Joseph. After careful scrutiny, the law firm agreed that everything Benjamin had asked for was in the contract. There had been no play on words, no slide of hands, no loop holes. A lawyer from the New York firm flew down to Leesburg to oversee the signing of the contract.

Less than ten days had passed since Benjamin's initial meeting, but since the number was based on the price of day prior to the meeting, coupled with the fact that the stock was still rising. Two point five billion dollars was now two point eight billion.

The law firm Benjamin had used to approve his contract, was Jacobs and Morton, they also had a tax attorney in their firm. Benjamin quickly set a meeting with the tax attorneys at Jacob and Morton. Their attorneys offered to come to Leesburg, but Benjamin and Angelica thought it would be a good opportunity to visit Joseph.

While in New York they stayed in Joseph's penthouse apartment. This would work out well, because they could visit with Joseph in the evening, and then spend time with the tax attorneys during the day. The tax attorney's were very informative and helpful. They explained to Benjamin that the average person pays around twenty to twenty—five percent of their income in the form of income tax. Now for you, Doctor Stone, we should be able to get your tax obligation down to three, maybe five percent. Benjamin wanted to know how it was possible to have so much money, but yet pay so little in taxes. The tax attorneys explained it as simply as they knew how. As they explained it, Congress passes laws for the Internal Revenue Service. These laws on the surface seem to have substance and meaning, and they are intended to raise money to operate the Government. That is on the surface what they intend them to mean. The reality of it is that the members of Congress for the most part are wealthy when they get to Congress. If not they are almost always wealthy when they leave Congress. They also enjoy campaign contributions from wealthy people. For that reason the Internal Revenue Service tax code is riddled with loop holes that allow people of wealth to pass through the system relatively unscathed. Meanwhile, Congress can talk tough about the new laws they have passed and all the while knowing that the only people affected are those that can't afford to be affected. Doctor Stone we propose moving your money around by year end into a variety of tax shelters that will allow you to avoid taxes. Benjamin agreed with what the tax attorney's wanted, though Benjamin told them he wanted to wait until he was satisfied that Aspen Pharmaceuticals stock had topped out.

Benjamin waited for three more months until he was satisfied. When he sold his stock, the two point eight billion dollars in stock was now worth to whopping three point seven billion dollars. The day Benjamin sold his stock; because of the volume of shares he owned the price of Aspen Pharmaceuticals stock dropped fifteen percent. Benjamin had literally flooded the market.

With their financial future secure; they could now do anything they wanted. For Benjamin that was a problem, what to do, and who to do it for. After some considerable discussion, and after some considerable persuasion on Benjamin's part, they decided or Benjamin talked Angelica into it; whatever the case may be into moving to Southern Montana.

They decided to tear the shack down and in its place build a truly magnificent home, a home with a laboratory of their own; where they could work on whatever project they wanted to work on. Benjamin was much more enthusiastic with the prospect of moving to Southern Montana than Angelica. To Benjamin the idea of living out in the middle of nowhere, to be alone, to not be bothered by people was very appealing. It was no secret that Benjamin did not understand or care for most people. As for Benjamin, nobody understood him completely, not even Angelica. Though she did understand him more than anyone else, there were places his mind would go that she could not follow. Benjamin had once told Angelica that every person on the planet living, dead, and even those who aren't even born will live their lives alone, no matter where they were, no matter how many people surrounded them, they would all have to live their lives within the confines of their minds. For the average person being in a crowded room, full of people gives them comfort, for they do not feel alone. For Benjamin whether the room was full or empty he always felt alone. Angelica felt sad when Benjamin told her this, but Benjamin was not looking for pity, he was just was stating a fact. Because of his intellect, which was by all accounts was the highest ever documented by man. Benjamin was never able to make the social connections with other people that most of us take for granted.

(CHAPTER TEN)

Benjamin and Angelica waited till spring to get their project off the ground. Between February and May 1987, the two of them had several meetings with architects to determine exactly what they wanted. Benjamin let it be known that money was not a problem and that he wanted his home started by late spring or early summer at the latest; and that it was to be done *before* the worst of Montana's winter sets in; no matter what the cost would be. That meant the building of The Stone's new home went into hyper drive. The workers were to be on site twelve hours a day, seven days a week. The schedule was staggering. The number of workers some days were too numerous to count.

During this period Angelica's stayed at her childhood home in New York. Benjamin on the other hand felt overwhelmingly compelled to be on the jobsite every day making sure things were being done to his liking. Benjamin bought a large double wide mobile home; he had it placed on the property where he stayed the entire time. Benjamin would be up to greet the worker's and was always there to thank them at the end of day. On several occasions Benjamin had lunch catered in; this was no easy prospect considering the closest town was forty miles away. The men seemed to appreciate Benjamin's gesture. For Benjamin it was his way of making it up to them for *constantly* changing his mind. It was not unusual for the men to spend days on a portion of the project, just to have Benjamin make them tear it down, because he had changed his vision of the home he had seen in his mind.

The final cost for the two story log cabin home ended up an astonishing thirty—two million dollars. Each floor of the home was eleven thousand square feet. The house had a full basement; there was even an elevator that ran from the basement to the second floor. The interior of the house was nothing less than *magnificent!* The floors were a combination of oak and the finest marble money could buy. The main floor had twelve foot ceilings throughout. All the doors in the house were eight feet tall; the stair case leading to the second floor was beyond description. There were large ornate lighting fixtures that hung in many of the rooms. The bathrooms were large and spacious, *no expense had been spared*. The outside of the house had a large porch that wrapped around three sides. The front of the porch was covered by smooth stones of various sizes, all of which were taken from the stream located on the property. To the right of the house was a six car garage that was attached by a covered walkway and deep enough to park cars two deep. When you walked around the porch, finally getting to the back, the view was *breathtaking*! There before you stood the twin falls just three hundred feet from the back of the house. The sound of the water *crashing* onto the rocks below and cascading down the stream was very soothing. The basement of the house was to be Benjamin and Angelica's laboratory. Of the eleven thousand square feet that the basement provided, nine thousand square feet would be set aside for laboratory space. This laboratory would indeed rival the laboratory that Benjamin had worked in at Aspen Pharmaceuticals.

Angelica did come to Montana from time to time during the construction phase. After all, it was to be her home as well. Benjamin left the interior decorating to Angelica. Angelica hired an interior decorating firm from Montana. She as well as Benjamin felt that the home should be decorated in a style suitable for the type house they had built and the region they were living in. Benjamin told Angelica that she had no budget restrictions. Now keep in mind when a man tell his wife that she has no budget restrictions, then a man can only brace himself and prepare for what will come. In Benjamin's case it was no surprise that Angelica spent over six million dollars on the interior. The money did not matter to Benjamin, what mattered to Benjamin, was Angelica's happiness.

(CHAPTER ELEVEN)

It was now November and Benjamin and Angelica were moving into their new home at Twin Falls ranch. Angelica wanted to wait until spring to have a house warming party, something Benjamin could not understand. The concept of having a house warming party was to invite people to your new home, just to show off what you have seemed very strange to Benjamin; but as always, Benjamin just smiled and let Angelica have her way.

During the long cold winter months there was not much to do, Bart would come by from time to time. He and Benjamin would talk for hours about the ranch and about the cattle Bart was raising on the ranch. Benjamin began to learn more and more about cattle with each visit from Bart. Benjamin told Bart that he had been looking for some sort of project to work on. He then informed Bart that he had done some research on varies breeds of cattle. Reading whatever documents he could find. It was then determined by Benjamin after several months of researching various cattle breeds, that he could genetically alter cattle with the hopeful results of producing cattle that were easy to manage, and cattle that would produce more muscle mass. Bart sat and listened to Benjamin saying nothing. When Benjamin finished Bart told him, "Perhaps you could put wings on them while you are at it. That way they could fly to the market by themselves." Bart then broke out laughing almost choking on his own tobacco juice. Benjamin smiled knowing Bart did not understand what he wanted to do, nor did Bart understand what Benjamin was capable of when he puts himself to a task.

It was late January 1988; Benjamin had decided to throw himself into trying to genetically alter cattle. This was a project that surprised even Angelica, and she was not easily surprised. Benjamin decided to work on the Black Angus breed. This was a breed of cattle considered by many to already be the "cattle of choice". For Angelica and Benjamin there would be another surprise come spring. It would seem that the flowers would not be the only things to bloom in the spring. Angelica told Benjamin on February the tenth that she was pregnant. He chuckled when she told him that the long Montana winter proved productive after all. After going to the doctor Angelica found out that she would give birth to *twins,* in August.

Angelica decided not to tell anyone, she wanted to surprise everyone when she had her house warming party in May. Angelica immediately began to redecorate a room upstairs next to hers and Benjamin. This room would become the nursery. Angelica also started the process of interviewing for a nanny. They already had a housekeeper, a woman by the name of Pam Leach. She was not much to look at, not much at all. Angelica made sure of that. She did not need her husband distracted by a young and beautiful woman. Young and beautiful Pam was not; she was tall, thin, and her hair was course and grey. Her skin was tough and thick like leather with deep wrinkles, but as far as housekeeping she did an excellent job keeping the place neat and tidy. She did not speak much and when she did if often made little sense. Angelica did notice something about Pam, a "quirk" if you will. If you were to move a flower pot, a coaster, or anything for that matter just ever so slightly she would notice it *immediately* was out of place and have an overwhelming need to re—adjust the item at once. There were times when Benjamin would enter a room, move one or more items just to sit and wait for Pam to walk through the room to see if she would notice. She *always* noticed, and she *always* fixed the item. Benjamin attributed it to some form of OCD.

After two months of searching, Angelica found the nanny she had been looking for. The woman Angelica hired was from Maine, and she came with a long list of recommendations from some very prominent families. Her name was Theresa St. John; she was a pleasant, kind older person. Theresa had never married, nor did she have any children of her own. Helping others to raise children is what she enjoyed doing. Angelica hired her and had her move into the house in April, even though the twins were not expected until August. Angelica did not want to chance losing Theresa. Angelica and Theresa would become friends and this relationship, this friendship would make it easier on both Benjamin and Angelica to entrust their children to someone they both liked.

During this period Benjamin would throw himself into his new project. The first thing Benjamin did was buy a sample of semen from the owner of a prize winning Black Angus bull named Mr. Atlas. Mr. Atlas had won more blue ribbons, and sired more champions than any other bull on record. The semen sample cost Benjamin eight thousand dollars. If he could improve on the genes that Mr. Atlas already carried, this would be an accomplishment.

When Benjamin told Bart about the sample he had bought, how much he had paid, and what bull it had came from. Bart just looked at Benjamin and smiled. He spit a mouthful of tobacco juice over the railing on the back porch and replied, "If mine was worth that much an ounce I could have been worth a million in my younger days. Hell, if it were worth that much an ounce, I guess I wasted a million just experimenting by myself in my younger days." Bart found his commits to be much funnier then Benjamin did, but this was usually the case.

You would not think that someone like Benjamin could be friends with someone like Bart, but somehow the two of them had made a connection. A connection that Angelica could or would never understood.

Benjamin kept to himself for the most part working on his project. Angelica along with Theresa decorated the nursery planning for the arrival of the twins. They were also planning the housewarming party that Angelica had threatened Benjamin with the previous year. Before Benjamin knew it the time was here, time for the house warming party. To Benjamin the party meant he had to stop working on his project and be an attentive husband, and the gracious host. Something he was not looking forward to, but if it made Angelica happy then it made Benjamin happy.

Angelica had invited the entire wedding party; she had also made arrangements for their travel. They were all to be flown in on private jets, and then picked up at the airport by limousine. This was quite the event for the local inhabitants. They were not used to seeing private jets or limousines for that matter. Joseph was also invited, he did not need help with his travel arrangements, and he already had his own private jet. Joseph brought Carl with him; he thought Carl would enjoy seeing his “Little Miss. Sunshine”. Angelica did have a limousine pick up Carl and her father. Carl commented on how the limousine ride seemed better from the back.

In all there were twelve people coming to the Stone’s housewarming party. The guest started to arrive around one in the afternoon. Once everyone had arrived and were all gathered in one room, Angelica would make her entrance.

However, only when the time was right, after Benjamin had been asked at least *a dozen times* where Angelica was. Just then the elevator door opened and Angelica entered the room. It was apparent to everyone that Angelica was expecting. The women immediately rushed to her, they were all giddy with excitement. Joseph slowly walked across the room; it was not in his nature to get overly excited. When Joseph finally stood in front of his daughter, he congratulated her, hugged her then he asked the obvious question that *everyone* wanted to know. "When do you expect the baby will arrive?" Angelica told everybody that the babies will be here sometime in August. Without missing a beat her father replied, "That is wonderful; I will be a grandpa in August." Almost as fast as he started talking, he stopped; looking at his daughter he said, "Did you say babies Angelica?"

"Yes, I did father."

"Oh my, that is even better I will have *two* grandchildren in August. Do you know what you are having?"

"Yes we are having twin girls."

Joseph *shouted*, "I am going to be a grandpa!" The women were already giddy; the news of twins put them over the top.

Now as for the men they congratulated both Benjamin and Angelica, but seemed to show no need to display the type emotion that Joseph and the women were displaying. Carl did not show much emotion, but when he was congratulating his "Little Miss. Sunshine", you could see that he was holding back the tears. This surprised Benjamin; perhaps there was a human being inside his steel armor demeanor after all.

Benjamin was especially glad to see his old friend Adam. They rarely called one another, a year or more could pass without either one of them picking up the phone. But it mattered not, for what they have shared in the past would bind them together for a lifetime to come.

Benjamin told Adam that he could not help but notice that Adam and Deborah had become an item since the wedding and that if his sources were correct the two of them were getting pretty serious. “Do I hear wedding bells in your future Adam?”

“I don’t know Benjamin, what does your source tell you?”

Benjamin laughed; and replied, “My source would be speculation at this point.” Well, Benjamin only time will tell, and that is all you are going to get out of me. After that Benjamin and the rest of the men went outside and sat on the deck at the back of the house. They enjoyed drinks, some light conversation, and the magnificent view of the twin falls.

The week seemed to fly by, a good time was had by all, and even Benjamin seemed to be enjoying himself. One of the high points for everyone was meeting Bart. He did not let them down; he was everything they heard he was, *and more*.

The day had come for everybody to start saying their farewells, the week had ended. It was time for the guests to go home, there were three limousines parked in the front of the house. Benjamin periodically thanked everyone for coming one person at a time. The last person he would thank was Carl, after thanking him, Carl told Benjamin that he had really enjoyed himself. Carl also told Benjamin that Angelica seemed very happy. Carl then gripped Benjamin’s hand in a firm, but familiar manner, leaned in and whispered into his ear, “It looks like I may not have to kill you after all Benjamin." Carl then looked Benjamin in the eyes and smiled, Benjamin did the same. By now Benjamin had grown accustom to Carl and his odd ways.

After all the good—byes had been exchanged, the last guest was in the limo and headed towards the airport, this just left Benjamin and Angelica standing on the front porch. Angelica took Benjamin by the arm, gave him a peck on the check, and told him thank you.

She then went inside leaving Benjamin on the front porch by himself. Benjamin walked around the back, took a seat, watching the twin falls, contemplating the week he had just enjoyed. For Benjamin it was time to get back to his research. For Angelica it was time to prepare for the coming of the twins, and relax as much as possible.

(CHAPTER TWELVE)

The weeks past and Benjamin continued to do research for his project. Then, in July Benjamin felt he was ready to impregnate a Herford with Mr. Atlas's semen. Benjamin had Bart find him the best example of a Black Angus Herford that money could buy. Benjamin then had the veterinarian come to the ranch to artificially inseminate the Herford. Benjamin knew that he had done his best and now only time would tell. The calf would not be born until spring. The twins on the other hand would be here anytime.

With Benjamin's focus off his project for now, he was able to concentrate more on Angelica and the twins. They have been discussing names for months. They finally settled on Christine and Abigail, Christine after Benjamin's mother and Abigail after Angelica's mother. When Angelica told Joseph what the names they had settled on, he was speechless.

The time had come; it was three a.m. when Angelica woke Benjamin up, giving him a nudge. "Benjamin wake up it is time, we need to go." Benjamin was not very responsive at first, but once he realized what was going on, he flew out of bed. Benjamin was running around the room in a wild and haphazard manner. It took a few minutes for Angelica to calm him down. Once Benjamin calmed down they both got dressed, Benjamin grabbed the suitcase that Angelica had already packed. Benjamin had also woken Theresa, who he had called the hospital and the doctor to let them know that they were on their way. The three of them headed for the hospital. Angelica thought it would be best to have Theresa drive, considering how nervous Benjamin was. Benjamin sat in the back of the car with Angelica.

Every time Angelica had a contraction, Benjamin had a small panic attack. It took thirty minutes to get to the hospital. When they pulled up to the emergency room entrance they were greeted by the hospital staff as well as Angelica's doctor. Angelica looked at the doctor saying "Thank God you are here Doctor Barrett. I am not sure who needs your attention more right now, me or Benjamin." Doctor Barrett smiled and then laughed; he told Angelica that he was capable of handling both patients at the same time. Angelica they are going to take you to the delivery room, Benjamin and I will join you there in a moment. As they took Angelica away Doctor Barrett turned to Benjamin telling him that everything was going to be okay, and that Benjamin needed to be calm for Angelica's sake. "All you need to do is be strong and remember your Lamaze training. Angelica is going to do most of the work, you and I are there to assist her, and support her. Do you understand me Benjamin?"

"Yes I understand you Doctor Barrett. It is just that I am nervous and worried."

"Benjamin there is no need to worry. As for being nervous, that is normal. Now are you ready to go to Angelica and become a father?"

"More than anything in my life Doctor Barrett, more than anything in my life, then let's go". Benjamin and Doctor Barrett headed for the delivery room when they arrived Benjamin was put into a cap and gown and a pair of booties. The doctor also prepared himself for the delivery. The nurses had already prepared Angelica and were making her as comfortable as conditions would allow. Benjamin sat by her side holding her hand, and coaching her with her breathing. He also tried to help her through her ever more increasing labor pains. It had gotten to the point that the contraction were accruing every two to three minutes. Doctor Barrett told Angelica, "It is time; you need to give me a big push when I tell you. Are you ready?"

"*Yes!*"

"Alright," Angelica, push!" Angelica pushed as hard as she could. "Again Angelica, push", once again Angelica pushed this went on for almost five minutes. Then Doctor Barrett announced, "I see her head, one more time, Angelica push". Angelica pushed with all her might, the sound of Benjamin's knuckles cracking could be heard, because of the grip Angelica had on his hand.

Then it happened, the sound of a baby crying, Angelica was crying, Benjamin started to cry. The nurses and the doctor were smiling. Doctor Barrett handed the baby girl to the nurse and then looked at Angelica telling her that it would be time to celebrate when her other daughter was here. Angelica I need you to push again. With that the process started over.

The doctor was coaching, Angelica was pushing and Benjamin looked as if he was in shock. After several more minutes there was again the sound of a baby girl crying. Their first daughter arrived at 5:31a.m., August twenty—sixth 1988. She was named Abigail. The second daughter arrived at 5:36a.m., she was named Christine. Both daughters were presented to Angelica. Doctor Barrett told her now you can celebrate. Both Benjamin and Angelica sat and starred at the miracle they had both just encountered the miracle of birth. After a few minutes the nurses took both Abigail and Christine. Benjamin was emotionally exhausted; Angelica was both emotionally exhausted *and* physically exhausted.

Benjamin left Angelica and his twin daughters in the hands of the nursing staff and went into the waiting room to tell Theresa that Angelica and the twins were fine. Benjamin then went to a telephone; he needed to call Joseph, Debbie Mayers, his friend Adam, and his friend Bart. Joseph received his good news at 6:15a.m. By 12:45p.m. Joseph was at the hospital along with Carl. By now Angelica was feeling somewhat better. Everyone was able to see the twins and everyone had an opportunity to hold them. Joseph had a glow about him, not a more proud grandparent would you see.

After three days Angelica and the twins were allowed to come home. Joseph and Carl returned to New York. Now it was just Benjamin, Angelica, the twins, and Theresa. The house was filled with the sounds of babies crying. Everyone seemed to adjust to things rather quickly, especially with the help of Theresa. Benjamin remained very attentive, at least for the first few weeks. After that it was time for Benjamin to get back to his laboratory.

During the time Benjamin was helping with Angelica and the children and not his laboratory, he realized that he had overlooked something while working on his Black Angus project. Benjamin knew that the calf to be born in the spring sired by Mr. Atlas, altered by Benjamin would indeed be an improvement on the breed. But at the same time Benjamin realized he could do better. Over the next few months, Benjamin worked on his project, at the same time the twins seemed to be growing by the day.

In early April 1989, Bart came to the house, he needed to let Benjamin know that Lady Diane was giving birth, that's right Lady Diane. Bart felt a Herford of her stature needed a proper name. Benjamin allowed Bart to name her and Bart named her Lady Diane. Bart had already called for the veterinarian. When he arrived Lady Diane was already in labor. Benjamin stood to the side while the veterinarian, who was being assisted by Bart, delivered the calf. The calf was a male, a young bull. It was more apparent to the veterinarian and Bart that this was a fine specimen of a Black Angus calf. Bart looked at Benjamin and said "Looks like your experiment might have worked; only time will tell. Have you thought about a name for your young bull?"

Benjamin replied, "Yes since it is a young bull I will name him Hercules, born of Lady Diane, sired by Mr. Atlas." The veterinarian commented to both Benjamin and Bart, "I hoped he lives up to his name."

The months past, the young bull grew stronger by the weeks. Late that same summer the veterinarian artificially impregnated Lady Diane with the newly improved semen of Mr. Atlas. The calf would not be born until early spring. In the mean time Hercules was being watched carefully. For his age, he was already bigger than other Black Angus bulls of similar age. To be exact he was fourteen percent larger. This proved to both Benjamin and Bart that Benjamin's research was successful.

As predicted early spring of the following year Lady Diane gave birth once again. As luck would have it she gave birth to another young bull. Bart asked "Well Benjamin, do you have you a name for this young bull?"

"Absolutely he is to be called Zeus." Once again Bart half laughed and half choked on his tobacco juice. At first Zeus did not appear to be much different than Hercules, but by late summer it was easy to tell the difference. Zeus for his age was twenty—two percent larger than a normal Black Angus bull of that age. Benjamin was *excited*; he knew he could do it! Bart was excited as well, the prospect of having the finest Black Angus herd in the world made Bart very happy.

The following spring when Hercules was two years old, Benjamin and Bart took him to auction. It was May 1990. The auction of Hercules was advertised around the world. Hercules was fifteen percent larger than the largest two year old Black Angus on record. Hercules in his appearance was flawless. Cattle buyer's came from everywhere, even those who could not afford to buy; they just wanted to see Hercules. He was billed as "Stones Black Angus Bull, Hercules".

The bidding started at twenty thousand dollars. By the time the bidding had ended, a gentleman from Wyoming had paid the unheard of price of *sixty five thousand dollars* for Stones Black Angus bull Hercules! Benjamin had accomplished what he set out to do. More meat on the animal means more profit for the rancher.

Now as for Zeus, he was twenty—two percent larger than other Black Angus bulls and eight percent larger than Hercules. Bart would eventually have the finest herd of Black Angus in the world. The only thing Benjamin asked was that any cattle sold for breeding stock, the proceeds would be divided eighty percent to Benjamin and twenty percent to Bart. As far as Bart was concerned that was not a problem. Not only would he have the finest herd of Black Angus in the world, he would make money off Benjamin's research, Bart was very happy, *very happy indeed.*

The following summer Zeus was a healthy two year old bull, doing what bulls do best. As predicted, Zeus was working diligently; and with any luck, by the spring of 1992, would be the beginning of the finest Black Angus herd known to man. But for now that was only hopeful speculation, only time would tell for sure.

Other things were in the air that summer for example Adam and Debbie had announced their engagement. It was to be a fall wedding. Other than that, the summer had come and gone without much event. The twins were growing bigger and smarter with each passing month. In August, they celebrated their second birthday. Joseph and Carl came down for the twins' birthday, as they had done the previous year. Bart also attended the birthday party. The twins' seemed to have a particular fondness for Bart. He had started calling himself "Uncle Bart."

The summer had passed, and it was now time for Benjamin and Angelica to go to New York, for Adam and Debbie's wedding. Benjamin was to be the best man, and Angelica was to be the maid of honor. Benjamin chartered a private jet for the trip to New York. While they were gone the twins' were left in the hands of Theresa. Benjamin and Angelica would stay with Joseph while they were in New York.

Adam and Debbie's wedding was just as lavish and expensive as Benjamin and Angelica's. There was to be no expense spared, no detail left unattended. The night before the wedding, a customary the rehearsal dinner was held. The rehearsal was held at St. Thomas Cathedral. This was the most lavish Cathedral in the state of New York, if not the entire Eastern Seaboard. The rehearsal went off without a hitch. After the rehearsal, the wedding party was taken by limousine to Sparks Steak House. This was a place known for its fine food. Although anybody could go to Sparks Steak House for dinner, most people could not afford to eat there; the average meal cost two hundred dollars per person.

During the dinner Benjamin was seated next to Adam and Angelica was seated next to Debbie. This way everyone catch up on current and past events in their lives. Benjamin and Adam talked about a little bit of everything, then from nowhere, from left field I suppose, Benjamin was engaged in a conversation that he could not have seen coming.

Adam said he understood that Benjamin had received a visitor while on his honeymoon, a Mr. Ashford. With that comment Benjamin leaned back in his chair, looking at Adam in a very inquisitive nature. He told Adam, there is only one way you could have possibly known that and that is because Mr. Ashford has spoken to you as well. Are you part of what ever organization he belongs too? Because I *never* told Angelica about Mr. Ashford, so Angelica could not have told Debbie therefore Debbie could not have told you. For that matter I have never told *anyone* about my encounter with Mr. Ashford. So Adam, please enlighten me as to where you came by that information. Adam looked at Benjamin with a smile and told him, "You are absolutely right; there were only one or two ways I could have known about your meeting with Mr. Ashford. I have spoken to Mr. Ashford personally, and *yes* I am part of the same organization he belongs to. Before you say anything Benjamin hear me out. I as well as Mr. Ashford along with *many other people* belong to this organization. This is an organization that is ran by the most powerful and influenced people in the world. They are host to some of the most talented and intellectual people in the world. These men have only one purpose and one common goal, to make the world a better place to live. Sure along the way there is money to be made and power to be gained but these were mere side effects of the true purpose, the true nature of the organization."

Adam paused just long enough for Benjamin to speak, "Adam if what you say is true, they why do you continually refer to them as "The organization", and why do they not have names?"

"Of course they do Benjamin, they are known as the Bilderberg Group. The Bilderberg Group has been around for many, many, years Benjamin. Adam I have heard of your organization, the Bilderberg Group. If what I think I know is true. Your group does not operate in the open. Instead they choose to operate behind closed doors. To operate in the shadow and Adam no matter how well intended a group of people are if they hide their activities behind closed doors and they conduct themselves on the fringes of the law and society, then at some point no true good will come from what they are doing. If everything they were doing was as well intended as you say, then they would operate in the open, in the light of day for the whole world to see."

"Benjamin these are not evil men, they are not bad men, and they are men who know how the government works. They are men who know how the world and the world's economy works. They are the men who can and do control both. The only reason I brought this topic up tonight Benjamin is because I was asked to make contact with you. They had hoped that because you and I know each other that I might be able to convince you to join us. There is room in the Billionberger Group for a man of your talent and stature."

"Adam as I told Mr. Ashford, I will also tell you; I am not interested in belonging to such an organization. I have chosen my path Adam, and it is a path that I will walk alone."

"I hope you are not mad at me, and I hope you understand I had to try. I also hope that with more time to consider you might change your mind."

"Adam I am not mad at you, I do understand, but as for needing more time to consider, no more time is needed on my part." Benjamin could not be mad at Adam for having tried; he even understood why Adam would want to belong to the Bilderberg Group. The lure of being part of the most influential group of men in the world would be hard for the average person to resist. But in Benjamin's case he was anything but average, he was even more than above average. Benjamin and Adam spoke no more of the matter; instead they went back to their normal conversations, at least normal for them.

The following day Adam and Debbie were married, the wedding was flawless; the reception to follow was spectacular! After the reception Adam and Debbie were whisked away on a private jet. They honeymooned in Europe, seeing three countries in two weeks, Benjamin and Angelica headed back to Twin Falls Ranch the following day.

On the ride from the airport to Twin Falls Ranch, Angelica commented on the road conditions, Angelica told Benjamin that the only thing she did not like about living in Southern Montana was the winters and the bad roads. Angelica told Benjamin that it was not so much the winters as it was the constant snow and ice on the roads. She wished that someone could come up with a product that could keep the roads clear. And with that comment Angelica had set of light off in Benjamin's head. As you may have gathered by now, once Benjamin had locked onto an idea, it was hard to budge him. Benjamin looked at Angelica and thanked her. "Why on earth are you thanking me Benjamin?"

"I am thanking you for have given me a wonderful idea for my next research project."

"Is that right, and what might that be?"

"I believe what you said is true; someone needs to come up with a product that will keep the roads clear."

"Benjamin if it keeps you busy, and makes you happy then you go ahead and create a product that does just that." Benjamin was excited at the prospect of having something to work on. Not just anything, but something that may be *impossible* to do. These were the types of project that Benjamin truly loved. Within a few days of returning to the ranch, Benjamin threw himself into his new project. Benjamin knew right away he would need radical ideas for the difficult solution. He knew that everyone else was concentrating on making products that could be applied to the roads causing ice and snow to melt or at the very least to keep ice from forming on the roads.

Early on Benjamin knew that he needed to take his research in a different direction. Benjamin felt it would be better if you could put an additive in concrete or asphalt during construction. That would work from within to keep roads clear. Benjamin would never say that he was the first person to think of such a thing, but he most certainly would tell you he was the first person to take the idea seriously.

Benjamin spent months researching various properties of all known concrete compounds. He already knew that certain chemicals when introduced to each other would heat up. He also knew that those chemicals would not maintain heat for long periods.

This was a challenge for Benjamin. Time meant nothing to him, for he had *nothing* but time. Benjamin would spend a good deal of time in the laboratory every day, all the while making sure to spend time with Christine and Abigail each day.

(CHAPTER THIRTEEN)

The girls were now four years old and they sure had their mother's looks, this pleased Benjamin. He had long believed that Angelica was the most beautiful women he had *ever* known. The girls were equally as beautiful as their mother. The twins were identical in almost every way you could think of. They both had blue eyes, blonde hair, both were slightly freckled faced, and they always wanted to dress the same. The girls enjoyed the same games, and they watched the same cartoons. Their differences were very subtle, only someone very close would know the difference. Abigail liked corn, but most definitely hated green beans. Christine liked green beans, but most definitely hated corn. Even though this may have been their biggest difference, Angelica and Benjamin could *always* tell them apart. It was everyone else who seemed to have problems telling them apart.

Bart sometimes had problems telling the girls apart, until he bought the girls each a pony. That's right, Bart bought them ponies. He felt it was important that the girls learn to ride. Angelica was not fond of the idea at first, but eventually she learned to live with the idea. Now Benjamin on the other hand thought it was a wonderful idea from the beginning. Bart told him he would supply the ponies and free lessons twice a week to the girls. Benjamin's part was to have a stable built to keep the ponies in.

Now back to Bart being able to tell the girls apart. They may have looked the same, talked to same, dressed the same, and even may have had the same mannerisms, but they did not fit the saddle the same. The girls had distinct differences in their riding styles. Bart could always tell the difference in the girls when they were riding. By the time the girls were seven years old, they were riding like professionals. Bart always showed every Wednesday and Saturday to give the girls their lesson, always at the same time never late, never early.

On Wednesday, Angelica would work around their riding lessons, since the girls were being home schooled. Angelica had hired a private teacher to educate the girls. It wasn't that Angelica and Benjamin weren't capable (because they certainly were), it was just that they both felt it would be best to have an outside source help in the girl's education. Both Benjamin and Angelica were involved in helping to educate the girls. It came as no surprise to anyone that the girls were above average in intelligence. At age seven years they should have been doing second grade studies, however, they were both doing work at the fourth grade level.

Abigail was showing a high degree of understanding in mathematics, while Christine was showing more of an interest in science. Benjamin and Angelica could not have been happier. As always, when Benjamin was not watching the girls take their riding lessons or helping with their education he could be found in his laboratory working.

While working in the laboratory in July of 1996 Benjamin was mixing aluminum with a combination of other chemicals. Aluminum was just one of the many metals being mixed in small portions with other chemical compounds. He was trying to create a bonding agent on a molecular level, what he ended up with however was a type of aluminum that was half the weight of known aluminum and three times as strong. In science many times great discoveries are made while doing research for something else. Benjamin would be no exception to that rule.

After testing and retesting Benjamin was sure he had stumbled on something extraordinary. The first thing he did was to hire a patent attorney. After Benjamin had acquired the patent on his newly found aluminum, he began to negotiate with varies aluminum manufactures from around the world through his attorney.

After several months of negotiating Benjamin signed a contract with Allied Aluminum Manufactures. Their plant was located in Granite City, Illinois. Benjamin did not sell the patent outright, which is what Allied Aluminum wanted. Instead Benjamin and Allied Aluminum agreed to a sixty/forty split of all profits, sixty percent for Benjamin and forty percent for Allied Aluminums. The only way Benjamin was able to get such a large share of the profits was due to the fact that Allied Aluminum knew that forty percent of such a discovery was worth billions and billions of dollars.

Allied Aluminum assured Benjamin that his aluminum would be available on the market in less than one year. As for Benjamin, this would no doubt make him one of the wealthiest men in the world! Benjamin also insisted that he and he alone be able to name the newly discovered aluminum. He decided to call it Stoneium. After the deal had been made, and the entire legal contract had been signed, Stoneium went public; the scientific community was absolutely taken aback.

Benjamin was the lead story of every major news channel in the world, they all reported on what he had done. Benjamin was on the cover of several magazines, including Life Magazine as well as the cover of Scientific Journal. The cover of Life magazine read, "The Great Doctor Benjamin Stone has done it again." The cover of Scientific Journal called Benjamin "The greatest scientists of this and any other century".

The implications of Benjamin discovery were almost endless. Imagine aluminum at half the weight we are used to, but three times stronger. Cars would be safer but lighter; airplanes would weigh less allowing them to burn far less fuel. Everything from soda cans to the space shuttle would be affected by what Benjamin had discovered. For Benjamin the excitement lasted only a short period of time, in his normal fashion Benjamin did not give things as much thought as everyone else did, he simply moved on.

He went back to his laboratory and back to work on a de—icing product. Not long after Benjamin's discovery was announced he was informed that he was to receive the Nobel Peace Prize. Benjamin had often wondered if he would ever be given such a prestigious award as the Nobel Peace Prize.

Benjamin would from time to time think of such things, but not dwell on them. Even when Benjamin tried to hide his excitement, Angelica knew how much it meant to him. For Benjamin winning the Nobel Peace Prize meant recognition for all the work he had done, for all the discoveries he had made.

Benjamin had become somewhat of a recluse, when he was asked to go to Stockholm to receive the award, he declined. The Nobel Peace Prize committee for the first time ever agreed to present the award to Benjamin at his home. The committee felt that Benjamin's work was important in its nature, revolutionary in its implications. If Benjamin wouldn't go to them, they would come to him.

Benjamin agreed to let them come to his home for the ceremony. This would be a massive media event. Angelica worked closely with the committee, with the media, and with all parties involved. As for Benjamin, he did what he always did. He went to his laboratory leaving others to deal with things he felt were boring in nature.

On the day of the big event, the media people along with their trucks and equipment started showing up around nine o'clock in the morning. The actual awarding of the Nobel Peace Prize would not happen until two that afternoon.

Angelica had hired extra help to care for the over one hundred people who would be in attendance; all of this was in addition to the catering company she hired to feed everyone.

What may have been most important, but given less thought than the other arrangements was security. At the insistence of Angelica's father Joseph, security would be provided for the day's events. Joseph told Angelica that *he* would take care of the security (all she needed to do is pay the bill).

Joseph employed a security company that he had used numerous times during his career. There would be eight security personnel in all at the event. These men were trained to blend in at all times and to be as inconspicuous as possible. The security personnel showed up one full day before the event, giving them plenty of time to make whatever arrangements they needed and to get a feel for the layout of the property. With security in place, extra workers, the caterer, the news media showing up, and the committee members on their way, Angelica felt that everything had been taken care of; now to find Benjamin. Angelica first thought was to check the laboratory, but to her surprise Benjamin was not there. After looking around the house, Angelica finally found Benjamin. He was on the back porch talking to Bart. "Benjamin it is almost time, are you ready?"

"Yes, Angel I am ready, just come get me when they are ready". Angelica smiled and she then went about checking on all the last minute details. Bart and Benjamin stayed on the back porch talking about many things, but oddly enough the Nobel Peace Prize was *not* amongst them. At one point Bart asked Benjamin if the man who was standing fifteen feet from them, (one of the security personnel), really had to be there. Before Benjamin could answer the man told Bart I am here for the protection of Doctor Stone and his guest. With that Bart peeled his jacket back to reveal the shoulder holster and pistol he was carrying. Bart then told the security agent, "This is one guest that does not need your protection." Immediately the agent stepped forward, and in a *loud commanding voice*, barked, "Sir, I need you to give me your weapon." Bart had no intention of giving up his pistol and told the agent, "It looks like you and I are having a good old Mexican standoff because not you or anybody else is going to be taking my pistol *today* or any other day." Benjamin spoke up telling the agent to leave Bart alone. If Bart wanted to harm me or my family he could have done it a thousand times over. The agent reluctantly backed down. A few minutes later Angelica came to get Benjamin telling him that everyone was there and they were all ready. "Ok Angel, let's go Bart are you coming?" Bart told him he wouldn't miss it for anything.

When Benjamin came around to the front of the house, what he saw was a host of cameras, waiting for him. Because of the large number of people in attendance the event was being held on the front lawn where Angelica had a podium and stage erected. Benjamin was led to the podium where he would be presented with the Nobel Peace Prize award. Angelica and the twins were also on the stage with Benjamin. The twins were eight years old and not too sure of exactly what was going on, but they could tell it was a big deal to both their parents.

Bart had made his way to the front of the stage or at least as close as he could get with all the cameramen in the way. As Benjamin was being awarded the Nobel Peace Prize a shot rang out loudly, then another shot, then a third shot. After the first shot, Bart spotted the man doing the shooting; he was only fifteen feet away without thought. Without consideration if he should or should not do what he was preparing to do Bart once again, peeled back his jacket to reveal his pistol. This time it was not for show; but rather for business. In a single *effortless* flow, Bart drew the colt revolver from its holster (It was reminiscence of an old west shootout.) placing a round in the chest of the man doing the shooting. He then took a few steps forward placing two more rounds, in the man's chest. Bart was not at all concerned with right or wrong, he simply wanted to make sure the man was *not* going to shoot again. Bart did all of this before any of the security agents could react.

Once the smoke form the gun fire had settled, everyone turned their focus to the stage. Bart could hear Angelica screaming "*No, No, Oh my God!*" Benjamin had been shot, struck once in the shoulder apparently with the first shot. The second shot missed altogether, hitting nothing or no one. The third shot fired by the gunman was to be the most devastating shot; it hit Abigail in the head.

The crowd was in frenzy, in short order Benjamin and Abigail were taken by helicopter to the nearest hospital. Benjamin's wounds though serious would heal causing him no long term damage. For Abigail however, it would be different, the shot to the head would leave her with partial paralysis on her right side and permanently blind in her left eye.

The Stone's spared no expense; they employed only the best doctors in their fields from around the world. They would come to realize that no amount of money could repair the damage that had been done. The blessing in disguise for Benjamin and Angelica was that Abigail had no permanent brain damage, she would still be Abigail; and most of all she was still with them, for that they were thankful.

The police investigated the man who did the shooting; they discovered his name was Lance Baker. When the police went through his belongings, they found a diary and in it he had written, "If Doctor Benjamin Stone gives no credit to God where credit is due then Doctor Benjamin Stone must be giving credit to Lucifer. For no man, on his own could possibly have done as much as he has. Since I do believe in God, and do consider myself a soldier of the Lord, it is my duty to send Doctor Benjamin Stone to hell where he belongs." The entry was made on the day of the shooting.

There were rumors that Bart might be prosecuted for having killed Lance Baker that day. Benjamin personally went to see the prosecutor handling the case and let him know that if they decided to prosecute Bart the amount of money Benjamin and Angelica were prepared to spend was *endless*. The prosecutor firmly let Benjamin, know that his office would not be swayed by the great Doctor Stones money *nor* his fame. The only thing that matters are the facts in Bart's case and the facts of the case would make it impossible to get a conviction for what he had done. Maybe someplace else in this great country of ours could they get a conviction, but not in Southern Montana. Just the opposite in fact; it seemed that throughout the state Bart has become a folk hero. No charges would be pressed, Benjamin was thankful for what Bart had done, and equally thankful for Bart not being prosecuted.

Life for Benjamin, Angelica, and the twins would never be the same. There would always be religious nuts out there, if not that, then someone who was mentally unbalanced, someone who wanted to be famous at Benjamin expense.

From that day forward Benjamin employed a full time security staff twenty—four hours a day. Benjamin would never allow Angelica or the twins to go *anywhere* without security that was if he would even agree to let them go at all. Benjamin who has always been somewhat of a recluse has now become an absolute recluse. He *never* left the ranch. He stayed there working in his laboratory where the only people he had contact with were Bart, his wife, his children, and his staff. There might be an occasional visit from Joseph and Carl, or maybe Adam and Debbie. Other than that Benjamin conducted his business over the phone or through his computer.

The years went by and Benjamin kept at his projects, Angelica and the girls, well they had become prisoners in their own home. They were swept up in Benjamin's constant paranoia. In July of 2000, Benjamin had the breakthrough he had been looking for; he had discovered a product that would generate heat once it was subjected to a temperate of forty degrees or less. Above forty degrees the product would stop generating heat. Once the temperature dipped below forty degrees it would start heating up again, the process seemed endless. Benjamin believed that the product he had come up with could be mixed with concrete or asphalt during the construction process and if Benjamin was right the concrete and the asphalt would heat up once the temperature dipped below forty degrees melting the snow or ice.

Benjamin had Bart get him a bag of premix concrete to test his theory. He made several test samples then placed each of them in the freezer after placing water on top of them to see if they would freeze. Some froze; some of them had slush on the top, but *one* of them remained as a liquid. This was the one Benjamin would use to get the right ratio of concrete per yard to chemical per ounce to make the product work.

In September 2000 Benjamin hired a contractor to pour a ten foot by ten foot concrete pad on the property for a test study to see if the concrete would remain free of snow all winter. When the concrete truck showed up Benjamin gave the driver a container with the right amount of chemicals in it to pour into the mixture. The driver refused not knowing what it was or what is might do the mixer. Benjamin called the concrete plant tried to explain without giving them very much information at all. They were also very reluctant to let Benjamin put some sort of unknown chemical concoction in their mixer. Benjamin did the only thing he could, he told the plant to bill him in full for the cost of the truck. With that they agreed and Benjamin poured his concrete that day.

In the following days Benjamin's attorneys were busy getting a patent for his discovery. Benjamin named it "Stone's Ice Off". That winter just as any winter in Southern Montana was *harsh*. The ground was covered by eighteen inches of snow at one point, but Benjamin's ten foot by ten foot concrete pad was snow free all winter. When the snow would fall on Benjamin's pad it would melt. If there was snow on the pad it was more like slush than snow or ice, then it would melt. The product worked perfectly.

Benjamin had spent the winter calculating the life span of the product, this was very important. What Benjamin finally concluded was that the product had a shelf life of one hundred years plus or minus just five years.

Once Benjamin allowed his attorneys to go public with his newest discovery, the scientific community once again all but bowed down to Benjamin. One notable scientist interviewed about Benjamin was Doctor Robert Ricco. When asked about Benjamin he commented, “A man like Doctor Benjamin Stone cannot be explained nor should you even try. Whether Doctor Stone will admit it or not his hand is being guided by a higher power than that of man.” As always these types of comments infuriated Benjamin, but as always he knew he could not control other people’s beliefs.

Benjamin himself refused all request to be interviewed. He told Angelica, “let them think what they want too, let them believe what they want too. My work speaks for itself.”

In May 2000, Benjamin’s attorneys settled on a contract for him giving the rights to distribute and manufacture his product solely to Vision Chemical Corp. This agreement would make Benjamin the richest man in the world. Every place on the planet that experienced snow and ice would no doubt want to use Benjamin’s product in their new construction projects. Image if you will, never having to shovel snow from your sidewalks or driveways again and never having to worry about bad roads. Just consider the lives that would be saved from accidents on ice and snow covered highways. Not to mention the injuries that would be prevented from the shoveling of snow. The product would cause the cost of highway construction to go up by around nine percent, but the cost in savings of not having people and equipment removing the snow and treating the roads for ice would far outweigh the cost of Stones Ice Off. For Benjamin the excitement seemed to last for just a short period of time as always. For Benjamin it was the pursuit of a discovery that was more exhilarating than the actual discovery.

It did not take Benjamin long to find something to occupy his time. He wanted to work on creating an artificial human body, an android. Benjamin felt that for those in the world who had a body that no longer worked if such an android could be built then perhaps their brain could be transferred to the android body giving them back the part of the life they had lost. Now to the average person hearing such a thing would appear to be science fiction, but as always science fiction can sometimes become scientific reality. Benjamin knew that he would probably spend the rest of his life on this project and that he may never finish what he had set out to do. He also knew that at the very least his research would lay the ground work for future generations of scientists to continue on the path he had set.

Benjamin poured himself into his work as always spending increasingly less time with his family and more time in his laboratory. It was August 2001, Angelica and Benjamin had grown more and more distant as the months and years past. Angelica informed Benjamin that she and the girls were going to New York to visit her father. Benjamin was against anyone going anywhere but Angelica would not take no for an answer, not this time! Angelica had not been to New York in years, and the girls had *never* been to New York. Despite Benjamin's best attempts, Angelica could not be swayed, her mind was set. Benjamin had never seen so much conviction on Angelica's part. Even though he did not want them to go, he did finally agree. It was the end of August when Angelica, Abigail, Christine, and Theresa left to go on trip to New York. Angelica promised to be back in a few weeks, and to call every day. Benjamin arranged for a private jet, he also made sure that Angelica was traveling with a full entourage of body guards (Something Angelica found irritating, but knew that it was necessary) As they were leaving Benjamin gave the girls hugs and kisses, then shared a long embrace with Angelica.

As always when they arrived in New York, they were met by Carl, but with so many people this time Carl had to employ the services of another limousine and driver. Carl told Angelica that her father was still at work and was not able to get away. Angelica instructed Carl to take her and the girls to Joseph's office. She thought it might be a pleasant surprise for her father. Angelica thought that the girls might also enjoy being in one of the two largest building in New York City.

Just as Angelica thought, her father was very surprised and the girls were having a good time. Christine asked if they could call their father. Joseph dialed the phone, putting it on speaker mode. When Benjamin finally answered the phone the girls were laughing and giggling having a grand ole' time, Abigail told her father that she could see the whole city from pa—pa's office. The mood for everyone was one of excitement. Then Benjamin heard Christine in the background say, "Mommy look at the airplane". Benjamin then heard Angelica's voice scream, "*Oh My God*", then nothing; just silence, the phone went dead. Benjamin did not know it then but he would soon discover that he would never hear the voice of his angel again nor would he hear the laughter of his children *ever* again.

Benjamin thought the way the phone conversation ended was odd, but gave it little thought. He had no reason to believe his wife or children were in any danger. Benjamin just looked at the phone in a curious manner, hung up, and went back to work. It would be several hours before Benjamin would find out the fate of his family.

When Bart heard of the attack on the twin towers in New York he was in Benjamin's stable tending to Abigail and Christine's horses with the radio on. Bart stopped at once going to the house to let Benjamin know. Bart had no idea if Angelica and the girls were in harm's way. But he did find the fact that they were in New York when this happened to be somewhat alarming. Bart found Benjamin where he could almost always be found; in his laboratory. "What are you doing here", asked Benjamin?

"Have you been listening to the news Benjamin?"

"No, I haven't, why?" Bart told Benjamin to turn on the television, turn it to any channel it doesn't matter which one. "Why Bart?" asked Benjamin.

"*Benjamin, just do it!*"

Benjamin walked over to where he kept a television in the laboratory (mainly for Abigail and Christine). It gave them something to do when they came down to Benjamin's laboratory for a visit. When Benjamin turned the television on, the first thing he saw was a picture of one of the twin towers on fire. What happened, I don't understand? Benjamin just kept watching. It was then they showed a picture of an airplane going through one of the twin towers. With that Benjamin fell to the floor. He began weeping and then he began to scream "*no, no, tell me it is not true, please Bart tell me it is not true!*" Bart told Benjamin we don't know for certain Benjamin, maybe they got out.

Benjamin called the airport to charter a private jet, it was then he found out that all flights throughout the country had been grounded. There was not a single aircraft in the sky within a few hours. By the time Benjamin had gotten off the telephone the second tower had been struck by another airplane. Benjamin and Bart stayed glued to the television. They sat hour after hour watching the news for any new developments. Benjamin called Joseph's house to see if Carl or anybody else could tell him something. He called Adam and Debbie to see if they knew anything more than what the news had reported.

As the hours went by Benjamin knew in his heart that his wife and children were gone, if not Angelica would have called him by now. Then at 7p.m. that evening Carl called. Carl told Benjamin that Angelica wanted to go to her father's office before going to the house to surprise him. Carl had stayed downstairs with the limousines. When the planes hit the towers Carl tried his best to get to the floor where Joseph's office was located, but the only way there was up the stairs, and people were pouring out of the building through those stairwells.

Carl talked to many people, all telling the same story; the floor Joseph's office was on took a direct hit from the airplane. No one Carl spoke to had made it out of the building from above the floor or for several floors below. "I am sorry Benjamin, I am truly sorry." Benjamin dropped the phone, walked over to the couch and just sat there starring at the television.

Bart picked the phone up and he talked to Carl for a few minutes then joined Benjamin in front of the television. Neither one of them spoke; they just sat and starred at that damn television.

Bart stayed with Benjamin until the early morning hours when Benjamin finally fell asleep. Bart left the television on then headed home, he needed to rest as well.

The next day Bart returned as early as he could. When Bart arrived Benjamin was preparing to leave. “Where are you going Benjamin?”

“I am going to New York; I have to see for myself.”

“I thought all planes were grounded?”

“They are that is except for military aircrafts.”

“I don’t understand Benjamin; you’re not in the military.”

“No I am not, but I have made some rather large campaign contributions to Senator Lexus Bode of the great State of Montana. She had made arrangements for me to catch a ride on a military aircraft. They will be waiting for me when I get to the airport. Bart I have to leave, watch over things for me while I am gone.”

“I will Benjamin, and you be careful, good luck friend.” Benjamin jumped into his limousine which was being chauffeured by one of the body guards he had with him. Benjamin had no less than four body guards with him. When they arrived at the airport, as promised by Senator Lexus Bode, there was a military aircraft waiting for Benjamin and his entourage. The flight to New York seemed to last forever; the plane provided was large and sluggish. As slow as it went there were times when Benjamin wondered how it stayed afloat.

The captain sent one of the crew members back to let Benjamin know that if he looked out the window he could see what was left of the twin towers. Benjamin cast his eyes out the window and down to what was left; his heart sank into his stomach. Benjamin said nothing; he just starred at the pile of rubble which used to be the world famous twin towers. He had to see it for himself, Benjamin stood amongst the rubble. Knowing then and there that his three angels were gone, there was no more room for denial.

Benjamin asked to be taken to Joseph's house. The ride from the city to Joseph's mansion used to be a pleasant one, but not today. The mood today was somber and lonely.

When Benjamin arrived at the mansion, he was greeted by Carl, who immediately started to apologize. Benjamin let Carl carry on far a few minutes then he abruptly stopped him. "Carl you need to stop apologizing, it is not your fault, you did nothing wrong."

"Yes I did Benjamin, Joseph told me to pick Angelica up at the airport and bring her here. Instead I let her talk me into taking her to the office and if I only had done what Joseph had asked of me. It's just that I have never been able to say no to my "Little Miss Sunshine" Why, Why, Benjamin did I not do as Joseph asked of me?"

"Carl that is enough, you cannot blame yourself for what Angelica asked you to do. It is not your fault. After all Carl it was me who let her come to New York. I also had a hard time telling Angelica no"

"Benjamin, please don't blame yourself there was no way to know that something of this nature could happen."

"Carl, I know that, but it doesn't ease the pain. I had come to New York to see for myself, I needed to know without a doubt and now I know without a doubt that my wife and my daughters are gone. I offered whatever financial assistance the city of New York might need to the Mayor less than two hours ago. The only hope I have left is that they are able to find my family, so I might give them a proper burial. The reason I have came to see you Carl is not to place blame on you, but to see if there is anything I can do for you. Are you going to be alright?"

"I will be fine Benjamin, but thank you for asking."

"Carl I have to leave now, there is a plane waiting for me I am going back home. It is the only place I know, the only thing I have left. If you ever need anything, and I do mean *anything* call me, it is yours. Angelica would have wanted it that way." Carl took Benjamin's hand, thanked him, and then reassured him that he needed nothing. At that Benjamin looked at Carl, nodded turned and walked away.

(CHAPTER FOURTEEN)

Back at Twin Falls Ranch nothing had changed; everything was just as Benjamin had left it. That is except for the void that had been left in his home, the void that had been left in his heart. No more would Benjamin be interrupted by the girls while in the middle of something or would he hear the sound of the girls running through the house. No more would Benjamin hear their laughter. So much has changed in such a short period. When Benjamin rolled over at night to reach for Angelica, she would no longer be there. Everywhere Benjamin went in the house he saw constant reminders of his family, constant reminders of what *was,* of what could have been.

Bart came by everyday to visit with Benjamin, they could always be found doing the same thing watching the news for any new developments. Benjamin often commented on why anyone would believe that killing innocent people would somehow serve their cause. This group or that group would take credit it did not really matter. Benjamin knew what had killed his wife and family, he knew where the ultimate blame went. It went to religion; in this case radical Islamic terrorist where the culprits.

As time went by Benjamin began to *hate* Islam or anything connected to it. Bart told Benjamin in life we all must face losses, and with any luck our losses will make us stronger and better people. Benjamin did not think much of that idea not much at all.

In time Benjamin was informed that his family had not been recovered and more than likely would not be. Yet another blow for Benjamin, a blow he needed not. Benjamin had made arrangements for headstones to be made and to have them placed next to his mother, father, sister, and brother—in—laws headstones at the head of the Twin Falls. Benjamin would visit the site daily. No matter how bad the weather was, Benjamin would go to them. No one knows for sure what Benjamin did up there, what he thought, or what he said. Benjamin always went alone, he never *allowed* anyone to go with him, not even once.

Adam called from time to time to talk to Benjamin to try to get him interested in some sort of project. But for Benjamin, his desire to research something was gone, he just could not focus. Benjamin made a few attempts to go back to work on his android project, but they were not long lived.

Doctor Benjamin Stone was without a doubt once the greatest scientific mind in the world, but without his passion he was no more. For now Benjamin was content doing nothing. He would spend his days reading and visiting with Bart.

The only problem with Benjamin spending his days reading is that he reads nothing other than books on Islam. On their culture, on their way of life, on the history of their people, Benjamin even read the Qur'an and when he was finished he spat on it and then ceremoniously burned it.

Benjamin found the Qur'an to be filled with nothing but lose interpretation of its teaching. He saw the Qur'an as a source of evil; and believed that those who followed it were nothing more than misguided fools.

Benjamin had become consumed with hatred. He blamed the Islamic people as a whole for the events that happened on September 11th. He knew that only a select few where causing the problem, but Benjamin felt that these select few where able to operate as they do because of the tolerance of the rest of the Islamic community. They were intertwined, good and evil both living in the same house, the house of Islam, but in the case of Islam, evil seemed to be ruling the day. Bart constantly reminded Benjamin that people were *both* good and bad everywhere in the world, and he would be better off if he concentrated on the positive in people not the negative. At least that is what Bart kept telling Benjamin; if Benjamin heard him or not was another matter.

Spring of 2002, Benjamin received a phone call from his attorney in New York; it was to inform him that if had Joseph lived, he would have been broke in less than one year. Benjamin could hardly believe what he had just heard. Joseph going broke, there must be some sort of mistake exclaimed Benjamin! "No, Doctor Stone there has been no mistake. Joseph made some very risky and very questionable business investments over the past several years. He borrowed as much as he could, enough money just in time to prevent bankruptcy." Benjamin could scarcely believe what he was hearing. How could it have been possible that a man like Joseph, a man schooled in the world of finance would go broke? Benjamin told his attorney that had Joseph lived he would have never gone broke, that is unless I also ran out of money. "Benjamin there is no doubt in my mind that you would have taken care of Joseph."

Suddenly as if from out of nowhere Benjamin's voice changed, he became excited speaking about taking care of people. "Do you know what will happen to Carl?"

"Benjamin that I do not know, but the one thing I do know is that the house, as well as all of its contents will be auctioned off June fifteen. Carl and the rest of the staff will have to be gone before that." Benjamin thanked his attorney for the information and asked him to call if he had anymore updates on the situation. Soon after hanging up the telephone, Benjamin called Carl. It took several attempts to get through to him, when Benjamin finally did get Carl on the phone; he let him know how hard it was getting a hold of him. "Carl, I am glad you finally decided to return my call; I have been trying to get you on the phone for days. I am sorry Benjamin I have been a little busy lately. I know Carl, I heard about Joseph. I still find it hard to believe, the reason I am calling is";

"*Stop Benjamin,* I know why you have been calling; you want to give me money or something of that nature. That is the reason I have not returned your calls Benjamin. I am not completely broke, I can manage if I rent a small apartment somewhere, and watch how I spend my money."

"I hope you are done Carl, because giving you money is *not* the reason I called, not at all. The reason I called is to see about hiring you for myself. I know that you are probably looking for a job. Believe me, I am not offering to *give* you anything."

"Well I suppose that would be a different matter. I am sorry; I assumed I knew what you wanted."

"Apology accepted; now how do you feel about working for me?"

"What would I be doing for you Benjamin?"

"The same things you did for Joseph, driving people around, running some light errands, whatever."

"Benjamin, I do not want the job if it is a charity".

"Carl you can call it whatever you want. Angelica would want it this way, this is also the way *I* want it Carl. So what do you say? I am asking you to share my home."

"Alright, Benjamin I will take you up on your offer, when do I begin?"

"You can begin just as soon as you're ready for me to send a jet to get you."

"I need a few more days to put things right here Benjamin, then I will be ready."

Four days later Carl was on a jet headed for Twin Falls. Carl had taken this flight before, the difference this time is he would not be coming back to New York; this was a one way trip.

When the jet landed, Carl was greeted by Bart, now these two men had met several times in the past and not only did they get along but they seemed to be cut from the same stone. Perhaps opposite ends, but the same stone nonetheless.

When they arrived at Twin Falls, Benjamin greeted Carl at the front door. Not as his employer, but as his friend. Carl immediately felt welcomed in his new home. Benjamin personally took Carl to the room he was to occupy. He helped Carl get his things into his room and told him to get himself situated and make himself at home. This is now your home also Carl, you are the newest member of Twin Falls; I know you will like it here. Carl walked Benjamin to the door as Benjamin was leaving Carl stopped him; Benjamin I would like you to know something also. Benjamin leaned in close as if he were prepared to cling to every word Carl was about to speak. "Benjamin I want you to know that I am glad I never had to kill you." Carl then smiled and shut the door in Benjamin's face. Benjamin could only smile back, shaking his head from side to side as he walked down the hall towards the elevator. Carl would *never* change; perhaps that is why Benjamin liked him. Benjamin no longer had Angelica in his life. She would always be the one to tell Benjamin what he needed to hear, not what he wanted to hear. Benjamin could always count on Adam, Bart, and Carl to do the same.

(CHAPTER FIFTEEN)

In the spring of 2002, Adam came for a visit. It was totally unexpected but was never the less a welcome visit. Adam told Benjamin that his wife Debbie was going to Europe with her mother and father for a month or so, so he thought it would be a good time to visit. After all, I knew that you would be here. Benjamin smiled, and said "here is where I will stay". Benjamin knew that Adam's visit would probably lead to being more than a social visit, but Benjamin was also fine with that.

Benjamin, Adam and Carl would spend a large portion of the day just sitting and talking. They would always sit outside as much as possible watching the Twin Falls. For the most part the only time Benjamin would wonder off on his own; was to visit the graves of family. Adam asked Carl if he goes up there often. Carl remarked "everyday no matter what the weather is", Adam just sat watching his friend climb the stairs next to the Twin Falls thinking here is a man who has more money than he could ever spend, a man who is no doubt the smartest man alive, but yet he is a prisoner of his own life, and mind. Adam felt sorry for Benjamin.

The next day Bart joined the three of them for some light conversation, that is until Carl told Benjamin I know you do not like to talk about what happened to Angelica and the girls, but Benjamin I have often wanted to ask a question or perhaps more to put a thought in your head. "Alright Carl let us get this over with what is on your mind?"

"Benjamin I am not a smart man, not like you and Adam, but if I were like you Benjamin, if I were the smartest man on the planet. I would try to find a way to kill all of them."

Benjamin did not quite understand what Carl was saying. "What do you mean Carl?"

"I mean kill them all, all the people of Islam. Old Testament Benjamin says an eye for an eye, a tooth for a tooth; wipe their seed from the planet." Adam jumped into their conversation, "*stop it, stop it now!* Carl don't ever say such a thing again. It would be wrong to even give thought to such an idea. Benjamin I know you are in pain, everyone can see that, but to even consider such a thing."

"That is right exclaimed Bart. You cannot blame an entire group of people the misdeeds of a few." Benjamin sat looking at the three of them; he knew they were waiting for a response. "Carl they are right, as much as I hate those who took my family I cannot blame everybody." Carl told the three of them, he knew what he said was wrong, but he cannot help the way he feels, and there was nothing the three of them could say to change that. Carl then stood up and said, "Gentlemen I think I am going to take a walk." He then turned and walked away without further comment. Bart looked around and said," It looks like the mood has turned sour around here; I think I am going to check on the cattle." Before they knew it Adam and Benjamin were alone. Benjamin commented what an awkward moment. "So, Adam what else is new with you?"

"It is funny you should ask Benjamin. I am afraid I must confess, the real reason I came to see you is to try one more time; try to get you to help us on a project."

"By us Adam, do you mean NASA; or do you mean your friends the Bilderberg Group?"

"The Bilderberg Group, Benjamin."

"I have told you in the past Adam; I am *not* interested."

"Benjamin this time it is different."

"How so," Adam?

"Even *I* do not have all the facts Benjamin. I just know that people at the highest levels in government and society have sent me to ask for your help or at the very least a meeting so that they may explain themselves to you."

"Adam I have to admire your persistence, but I once again will respectfully decline." Now in no uncertain terms as far as the conversation about the Bilderberg Group; well, it is over. Adam stayed at Twin Falls for a few more days and he honored Benjamin wishes speaking no more of the Bilderberg Group.

Once Adam was gone Benjamin's life went back to the normal, mundane, familiar pattern it was stuck in. A few months after Adam had visited, Benjamin was visited again, but this time the visit was by none other than Senator Lexus Bode.

When Benjamin was told who had come to see him, he thought about what she might want. Benjamin figured she was looking for a hand out or as she might put it, "a contribution." When it came to politicians no matter what party they belonged to Benjamin gave and he gave often. Benjamin felt it was better to have the politicians in his pocket, than on his back. Benjamin told Carl to bring the Senator out back where he was sitting in his usual spot. "Senator Bode what brings you all the way out here, all the way to Twin Falls? You could have simply called; I do not believe I have ever denied a reasonable request for a contribution."

“Doctor Stone I am not here today to ask for a contribution, I am here today on the behalf of the President of the United States.”

“Is that right? Can you tell me exactly what the President of United States wants with me?”

“Doctor Stone this is information I do not have. All I know is that through various channels I have been asked to talk to you about a possible meeting between yourself and the President. Doctor Stone this is highly irregular, I do know that; and that alone tells me how important this must be. Can I tell the President that you have agreed to meet with him?”

“You can tell the President whatever you want, but the reality will always be the same, the answer is *no*.”

“Doctor Stone, do you mean to tell me you are turning down the President of the United States?”

“Senator Bode that is *exactly* what I am telling you.”

“Doctor Stone, I wish you would reconsider.”

“Senator Bode; I have already given my answer yet you do not seem to understand; so I also have a wish, I wish for you to leave my home now, good day. With that Senator Lexus Bode excused herself from Benjamin’s home. No doubt the Senator was in a hurry to make a report. Even if Senator Bode did not know what the President wanted with Benjamin, Benjamin himself was pretty sure of what the President wanted. He gave it little thought; assuming the entire matter would go away. At least that is what Benjamin thought.

Two days after Senator Bode came to the house Benjamin found himself as he could almost always be found on the back porch watching the Twin Falls, passing time reading a book on Islam. It was then that Benjamin started to hear a dull roar; the noise became increasingly louder by the moment. Then, from nowhere five helicopters appeared. At first they hovered over the house, and then they came to rest on Benjamin's front lawn. Benjamin walked around the porch to the front of the house to see what was going on. He was met at the front of the house by Carl and his housekeeper Pam, along with his two bodyguards. Not one of them said a word, considering one of the helicopters belonged to the President. The others were military helicopters. A larger number of Marines came pouring out of the helicopters. They seemed to be running in all directions securing the area, once they were in place, three secret service agents came out of the Presidents helicopter. They approached the front porch where Benjamin and everyone else were standing. The first thing they did was relieve the bodyguards of their weapons; they then asked Benjamin if anybody else was in the house. Benjamin told them other than the two Marines he saw going into his home no, there was nobody else. One of the secret service agents spoke into his mouth piece for a few moments then another secret service agent exited the Presidents helicopter along with the President. The President came onto the front porch where Benjamin was standing. "Doctor Stone I assume you know who I am?"

"I know who you are. Is there something I can do for you?"

"Doctor Stone I hope you are not angry because of my unannounced visit, but it seemed to be the only way I could talk to you." Benjamin stood silent for a moment, then said,

"If you need I can repeat myself, is there something I can do for you?"

"Doctor Stone most men would be very impressed that the President of the United States had just landed a helicopter in their front lawn. But not you Doctor Stone, you do not seem the least bit impressed."

"With all due respect Mr. President, right now I am focused on how much damage your helicopters are doing to my lawn. Do you have any idea how hard it is to maintain a decent lawn in Southern Montana?"

"No, Doctor Stone I do not, and for that I apologize. You are *exactly* as they told me you would be. You appear to be a man who has chosen his path in life and on that path you walk alone." Benjamin said nothing even though the President was clearly waiting for a response. This caused an awkward moment, not for Benjamin, but for the President. The President quickly moved on, "Doctor Stone the reason I am here is because your country needs you, and beyond that humanity *needs you*. It seems that all the normal channels of contact have been exhausted. That is the reason I am here today, the reason there are five helicopters on your front lawn, and once again I do apologize."

Benjamin looked at the President and then told him, "I have *heard* every word you have said, but yet just as all politicians do, you have spoke without having said *anything*. Why don't you do us both a favor, and just say what you mean?"

"To the point Doctor Stone", the President then gave one of the secret service agents a nod, the agent spoke into his mouth piece, and at that moment two men exited one of the military helicopters. Benjamin immediately recognized one of them as Mr. Ashford, (he was the one who approached Benjamin while on his honeymoon) as for the other man, Benjamin did not recognize him. Both men approached the front porch where Benjamin and the President were standing. Mr. Ashford greeted Benjamin by saying, "Doctor Stone it is a pleasure to see you again." The other man introduced himself as Doctor Gage Lexor. Benjamin was aware of who Doctor Gage Lexor was, he was after all the foremost expert in the world when it came to viruses. Benjamin wondered what it was they wanted from him; his curiosity was beginning to peak. The President spoke saying, "Now that everyone knows who everyone else is what I need from you, Doctor Stone is to have you agree to spend a few minutes with these gentlemen. They can explain what this is all about much more clearly than I can. So Doctor Stone can you grant me this favor?" If for no other reason other than curiosity Benjamin wanted to know what they wanted from him. What was so important that they needed to involve the President of the United States? "All right Mr. President, as a favor to you I will grant a few minutes of my time to Mr. Ashford and Doctor Lexor."

"Doctor Stone I thank you; and someday humanity will thank you. Gentleman I have places to be, one of the helicopters will stay behind for the two of you." With that the President, his secret service agents, and all but one of the military helicopters along with most of the marines left just as they had came.

This left Benjamin, Mr. Ashford, and Doctor Gage Lexor standing alone on the front porch. Benjamin asked the men to join him on the back porch where they could get more comfortable. Once all the men were seated, Benjamin started the conversation by saying, "Mr. Ashford you very well may be the most persistent man in the world. You have obviously gone to great lengths to have this meeting. So I suggest that you think very carefully about your presentation, because you will have only this one chance."

"Doctor Stone I would like to thank you for allowing me to speak to you today. I am sure that you are aware of the carrying capacity when it comes to the human population and the planet, correct?"

"Yes", replied Benjamin, "It is simply the number of people this planet can support based on the renewable and non—renewable resources of the planet. Most experts agree that we will have reached our limits around nine to ten billion people, which I believe will occur somewhere between 2050 and 2070. Does that sound about right?"

"Yes, Doctor Stone that is exactly right and that is why we are here today. It has been decided that something must be done to reduce the world's population. We are currently in the neighborhood of seven billion people."

"I agree that something's must be done, what is it you propose?"

"Doctor Lexor and a team of the finest minds in the world are currently working on a virus that will cause sterilization, as well as an anti—virus. We can infect the world's population with the virus, thus slowly reducing the number of people on the planet in a humane and efficient way. The anti—virus will be given to enough people so a good breeding population will exist." The look Benjamin had was one of disbelief, as well as one of understanding. "I am with you so far Mr. Ashford, please continue."

"Doctor Stone to be honest with you, we are stuck! Doctor Lexor and his team have hit a wall with their research. They have made no headway in months. We were hoping that you might find it within yourself to assist us."

Benjamin looked at Mr. Ashford for a moment and then with a smirk replied, "You mean save you, *not* assist you?" Mr. Ashford knew that honesty was the only thing that would work on Benjamin. "Yes, Doctor Stone, save us is *exactly* what I meant."

"How do you plan on delivering the virus Dr Lexor?

"Ideally we want the virus to be airborne, easily transmitted from person to person."

"How do you plan on explaining to the world that they have just been sterilized?"

Mr. Ashford spoke up, "we will create a false pandemic. The Center for Disease Control in the United States and it counterparts from around the world will release statements saying that a new strain of the flu has been discovered. They will then *urge* people to get vaccinated. The vaccine itself will deliver the virus. As for the people who do not get vaccinated; well, they will be infected by those who do once the virus goes airborne."

Benjamin thought for a moment and then spoke, "While I do sympathize with your problem Mr. Ashford and I do agree that something needs to be done, I am afraid I will have to say no." Mr. Ashford went into a pleading mode, trying his best to change Benjamin's mind. At first Benjamin heard everything Mr. Ashford was saying, and then suddenly Benjamin was struck with an idea. At that point Mr. Ashford voice was but a distant buzzing sound in the background. It had occurred to Benjamin that he could use the virus they were trying to create to his advantage.

Since the comment Carl made a few months earlier about, "killing them, kill them all", Benjamin had become fixated on the thought of what Carl had suggested just might be possible. Benjamin knew as much if not more about the human genome than anybody else. He knew that the human race had breeds and sub—breeds, and that the Arabic breed was but one of four major breeds. If Benjamin could design a virus that would cause flu like symptoms leaving the victim sterile and at the same time install a virus within the virus that would attach itself to only persons of Arabic decent then he might have something; something indeed.

The secondary virus would have to be designed to have a much longer incubation period than the initial sterilization virus; perhaps up to six months. He needed to be sure that the piggy back virus would be a total killer, that no person of Arabic decent could escape it. Benjamin also knew that the piggy back virus had to be undetectable. All of this ran through Benjamin's mind in just a matter of moments. After Benjamin had finished his thought he could hear Mr. Ashford's voice once again. Benjamin let him carry on for a few more minutes before stopping him. He broke in, "Mr. Ashford, I have changed my mind, I will help you design your virus."

"Doctor Stone, we could not be more pleased. Could I ask you why you changed your mind, committed Doctor Lexor?"

"I have several reasons; if you *must* know, first of all you are *both* right, something needs to be done. Beyond that boredom I suppose. I see this as a challenge and I need something to occupy my time, besides that you and your team do not seem to be capable of solving the problem." Doctor Lexor did not like that comment, it was obvious with the rebuttal statement he made. "It remains to be seen if *you* can solve this problem Doctor Stone; but if anybody can then perhaps you are the one."

Benjamin told Doctor Lexor that he would need all the information he had on the virus they were trying to design as well as needing access to a sample of all known influenza viruses. "Doctor Stone, you cannot possibly be thinking of doing the research here!"

"That is exactly what I am planning to do", remarked Benjamin. Doctor Stone we have a state of the art research facility with access to *everything* you might need. Your laboratory *cannot* possibly be equipped to handle such research." Benjamin gave Doctor Lexor a stern look, Mr. Ashford, Doctor Lexor please come with me.

Benjamin led them to the elevator which took them to the basement of his home; this is where his laboratory was located. Benjamin had to enter a code in order to get the elevator to go to his laboratory, a code which only Benjamin and Bart had. When the elevator doors opened Mr. Ashford may not have been impressed, but I can assure you that Doctor Lexor was *most certainly impressed*. Before him was a state of the art research laboratory. It was filled with the best equipment from around the world, the best that money could buy. Benjamin spared no expense, anytime a better or more updated piece of equipment came along he would upgrade.

Doctor Lexor wondered around Benjamin's laboratory for a while looking at every inch of it. Finally he spoke; "alright Doctor Stone this will do. When do we start?"

"By *we*, you must mean when do I start."

"No, Doctor Stone by we, I mean you *and* I. It is my plan to assist you in your research." At this point Benjamin became visibly irritated. "Doctor Lexor I work *alone*, with assistance from no one."

"Doctor Stone that will not work for me, I *must* have access to your research."

"You will, remarked Benjamin. I will keep you updated as to my progress." Doctor Lexor looked at Mr. Ashford telling him that there was no way that any of this is going to happen unless they work *together*. The thought of having someone working by his side all day was almost more than Benjamin could handle, but at the same time Benjamin needed to design their virus in order to install the virus he wanted to release. Benjamin also knew that having Doctor Lexor breathing down his neck would make it even more difficult to do what he intended to do. As much as Benjamin tried he could not get Doctor Lexor to agree to anything *except* being part of the research on a daily basis.

After a heated argument Benjamin got Doctor Lexor to agree that he would only be at Benjamin's laboratory on Fridays and Fridays only. Doctor Lexor did not like the newly formed arrangement, but with a little coxing from Mr. Ashford he finally agreed. Benjamin could not have been more excited. No one knows for sure whether he was excited because he had something to work on or because he was preparing to seek revenge.

The following day Doctor Lexor came back to see Benjamin and to bring him all the information his team had collected on the virus. Doctor Lexor arrived by helicopter and this would be the way he would always come unless the weather would not permit it.

Benjamin had always had a fascination with helicopters. From the first time Doctor Lexor came to Twin Falls by himself Benjamin went out to meet the pilot and to talk about the helicopter itself. Every time the helicopter would bring Doctor Lexor he always had the same pilot. Benjamin and the pilot had struck up some sort of friendship. Benjamin would always bring the pilot a cup of coffee to take with him each time he left. It made Benjamin feel good and the pilot seemed to enjoy it as well. This is the way it went for week after week after week. Benjamin would work alone and Doctor Lexor would come by on Fridays to review Benjamin's progress; if any.

(CHAPTER SIXTEEN)

Benjamin worked nonstop resting very little. Then in May 2004, Benjamin had a breakthrough. He had finally done it! He had engineered a virus that would mimic flu like symptoms, not killing the person infected; but only causing the desired sterilization.

Benjamin kept this information from Doctor Lexor; he was by no means prepared for anybody to find out that he had solved the problem. Now he needed to design a piggy back virus one that could blend in with the initial virus, but would remain undetected by prying eyes.

This virus would prove to be much harder than the initial virus. Benjamin gave everything of himself; everything he had, but to no avail. Benjamin had hit a brick wall, what was he overlooking? What was he doing wrong? He knew the answer was in front of him, he just could not see it. Yet he stayed on course, never wavering from the belief that he could do it, nor from the belief that the people of Islam where bad. Whenever Benjamin thought he could go no further, he would think of all the loved ones he had lost. From that he would gain enough strength to go on, and that is exactly what he did.

Not only had weeks passed, but months as well as years had gone by. It was midsummer 2006 when Benjamin was in his laboratory as always he received a call from upstairs. It was Pam the housekeeper, she was in a panic letting him know that It seemed Carl may have just suffered a heart attack. Benjamin scrambled to get upstairs; Carl was lying on the floor of the back porch clutching his chest. Benjamin ran to where Carl was, "Carl you hang on, a helicopter is on the way!" Carl could not speak; he just lay there clutching his chest; he was having difficulty breaking as well. It seemed to take forever for the helicopter to get to Twin Falls. They finally arrived and not a moment too soon; Carl would not have lasted much longer without medical attention. As the helicopter was preparing to leave Benjamin asked if he could go with them. They told Benjamin that it was not allowed. Benjamin looked at them and said he would give everyone in the helicopter one million dollars each if they would allow him to ride along. (Apparently for the sum of one million dollars each there was suddenly an open seat in the helicopter.) As they had predicted, the four man crew lost their jobs. And just as promised, Benjamin gave each of the four a check for one million dollars.

Once at the hospital and after Carl had been stabilized Benjamin was finally able to talk to the doctor. The doctor told Benjamin that Carl had suffered a Massive Myocardial Infarction. He told Benjamin that that his heart muscle was severely damaged and that the only way Carl would survive would be to have a heart transplant. Benjamin could not and *would not* accept this answer. Benjamin had the foremost cardiologist in the world flown in from Belgium.

Less than forty eight hours from his initial diagnosis, Doctor Van Braun told Benjamin that his college was right. Without a heart transplant Carl would not live. Benjamin told Doctor Van Braun to make the necessary arrangements. "I wish I could Doctor Stone, I really wish I could, but there is a waiting list for transplants. Carl's case is even tougher; he has a rare blood type. I am afraid all we can do is make him comfortable."

"*No* Doctor Van Braun you are wrong, we *will* find a heart for Carl, at any cost." Benjamin *immediately* contacted Mr. Ashford explaining to him what the problem was. Within a few hours Mr. Ashford was at the hospital meeting with Benjamin and Doctor Van Braun. Mr. Ashford looked at Doctor Van Braun and asked, "If the United States Government can locate a heart will you do the surgery?"

"Why yes; of course I will, but how are you going to do that?"

"Leave that to me Doctor Van Braun, I want both of you to know that at a moment's notice you need to be prepared to leave. Benjamin asked, "leave to go where?"

"If we can find the heart we need, the operation will be performed at a military hospital."

"Why a military facility asked Doctor Van Braun?"

"Because what we are doing is throwing away all rules and regulations in order to get Carl a new heart. We do not want the media to get ahold of this, and make a big deal out of it. Doctor Stone has done many great things for his country as well as mankind and we are sure that many more wonderful things will come from Doctor Stone. So, if saving Carl will help Doctor Stone stay focused then saving Carl is what we will do."

Two days later Benjamin received the phone call they had been waiting for. Both men were picked up by military helicopters and taken to Mead Air Force Base. When they arrived Carl was already there. He was being prepared for surgery even before Doctor Van Braun arrived. Both Doctor Van Braun and Benjamin were greeted by Mr. Ashford. He took Benjamin to the waiting area; he then led Doctor Van Braun to the surgery room. Everyone was ready, the only thing they needed was Carl's new heart. Mr. Ashford said the heart was in route and should be here in a few minutes. Just as Mr. Ashford had predicted the heart showed up about thirty minutes after Benjamin and Doctor Van Braun arrived. The surgery itself would last for several hours; Benjamin could do nothing except wait. He was being kept company by Mr. Ashford.

Benjamin asked Mr. Ashford, "Where did you get the heart?"

"You need not to worry about such things Doctor Stone, all that matters is that Carl pulls out of this in good shape."

"Mr. Ashford, I may not *need* to know where Carl's new heart came from, but I *want* to know. Now will you please tell me?"

"Alright Benjamin if you insist. Carl's new heart came from a prisoner in the United States Department of Corrections from Texas to be exact."

"What were the circumstances that allowed his heart to become available?"

"The prisoner was on death row, and exactly two hours and fifteen minutes ago his execution was carried out. His heart was removed and rushed here to save Carl's life. Does that somehow bother you Doctor Stone?"

"No, not in the least bit commented Benjamin." Doctor Stone this may not be the proper time or place to ask. But how is your research going. Have you made any progress? Benjamin paused for a moment, knowing that he could not tell all. Mr. Ashford all I can tell you is that I truly believe I am getting close to what you need. "Doctor Stone when you say "getting close", how close would you say you are?"

"Mr. Ashford close means close, when I am there you will be one of the first people to know. Right now I do not feel like talking about my research, I am too busy thinking about Carl."

"I apologize, Doctor Stone, I do understand." After the heart surgery had been completed Doctor Van Braun came to see Benjamin and Mr. Ashford. He told Benjamin that because of Carl's weakened state physically; he *personally* did not feel Carl would pull through. He told Benjamin that Carl would more than likely only live for a few more days.

Once they had Carl in his room, Benjamin went to sit with him. Carl was in and out of consciousness, not saying much for the most part. After more than a day had passed, Carl became more alert. To Benjamin it seemed as if though Carl might be getting better, but that was not the case. Many times when a person is dying they will experience a short period of clarity and calm. This often gave false hope to those who witness it. At one point Carl told Benjamin that he appreciated all that had been done to save him. Even though he knew he was dying. Benjamin told him not to think or talk that way. "Benjamin I am an old man, my time has come, it is ok." Benjamin and Carl talked for a few hours, and then Carl told Benjamin, "The time is near Benjamin, I can feel it." Benjamin leaned in close, and said, "Carl do you remember the conversation we had several years ago when you asked me why you can't do something to kill them, to kill them all? Do you remember?"

"Yes, Benjamin I remember and I still wish you could do it."

"Carl before you die I want you to know that I am very close to having created a virus that will do just that. If I am right every person of Arabic decent in the world will die." Carl looked at Benjamin and smiled saying "Kill them, kill them all Benjamin. Wipe their seed from the face of the earth down to the last seed." After that Carl said very little; his breathing became shallow, and then he slipped away.

Benjamin was now in a bad way, it was as if he just lost Angelica all over again. Perhaps because the connection between Carl and Angelica was so deep losing Carl brought up bad feelings. Benjamin had Carl's body buried at the head of Twin Falls with the rest of his family. He thought that Angelica might like it that way.

For Benjamin it was time to get back to work. He was so close, so back to the laboratory, and back to the weekly visits by Doctor Lexor. This pattern would remain unchanged for months.

Then on January 3rd, 2008, Benjamin had the breakthrough he had been looking for. Benjamin threw his hands in the air saying, "*Angelica I have done it, I have done it!* I will make right, the wrong you and girls have suffered. I will make them pay, and pay they will." It was almost as if Benjamin was waiting for Angelica to reply.

It had become clear that Benjamin was losing control; he was no longer in touch with reality. On that Friday when Doctor Lexor came for his visit, Benjamin would present him with the news he had been waiting for. "Good morning Doctor Stone, how are things going today?"

"Well Doctor Lexor, I would like to say that things are going just fine, that things are normal, but that is *not* the case."

"What is wrong Doctor Stone? I will tell you what is wrong; I am embarrassed that it took me as long to solve this problem as it did."

"Doctor Stone, are you saying what I think you are saying?"

"I am saying exactly what you think I am saying. I have your virus." Doctor Lexor became very excited. Benjamin allowed Doctor Lexor to take his research papers with him, along with a sample of the virus. Doctor Lexor wanted to go back to the Center for Disease Control where he and his team could study Benjamin's findings.

Now, for Benjamin this was the moment of truth. He had spent six years working on two viruses that he had combined to look as if though it were only one virus. Would they discover what he had done? Benjamin felt confident that the piggyback virus was well hidden within the sterilization virus, only time would tell. Benjamin waited for a phone call from Doctor Lexor, but no such call came.

The days turned into weeks, the weeks into months. Then finally the call Benjamin had been waiting for came. It was Doctor Lexor, "Doctor Stone we can find nothing wrong with your virus, least nothing we can detect. I am calling to let you know that we plan to have a controlled trial run of your virus. I will keep you updated as to the results."

"How and whom are who planning on testing the virus."

"Doctor Stone, do not concern yourself about that, I called you out of professional courtesy, and out of professional courtesy I will update you when the controlled trial run of your virus has been completed." What Benjamin did not know is that his virus was going to be given to a group of twenty—five men. These men would be checked to make sure they were fertile before the virus was given to them. After the virus had ran its course they would be checked again to see if they remained fertile. If they were no longer fertile then the virus would be hailed a success.

The men that were chosen for the experiment would be taken from a captive audience; all twenty—five men were prisoners in a military prison. They were told that if they volunteer to take part in a new flu vaccine trial their sentence would be cut in half. Doctor Lexor had no shortage of volunteers.

The men were put into a sterile environment, free from exposure to the outside world. Within seventy—two hours of having been introduced to the virus the men started to exhibit flu like symptoms. They ran a high fever, had the chills, experienced a loss of appetite, as well as a fierce case of diarrhea. The infection lasted anywhere from a short period of three days to as long as ten days. However the results were the same for all twenty—five men, they were all sterile after the infection had run its course. Benjamin's virus was hailed a success by Doctor Lexor and his team. When Benjamin received the call he could not have been happier. Not only did it work, but most importantly the piggyback virus remained undiscovered.

Doctor Lexor did a second testing of the virus. This time all the subjects were female. The results where exactly the same, on the surface the virus appeared to be doing exactly what everyone wanted. The entire testing group was released from the controlled environment in which they had been held. This only after testing to make sure they were free from the virus. Doctor Lexor did not want anyone to spread the virus until everything was in place. At least that is what Doctor Lexor thought, Benjamin knew that his anti—virus would not kill the piggyback virus it would remain in the host's body infecting others along the way during its lengthy incubation period.

The next step was to manufacture large quantities of the virus along with the antivirus for worldwide distribution. This took only a few months. The manufacturing and distribution would be done under the watchful eye of the Center of Disease Control, supervised by the Bilderberg Group.

The time was near, Doctor Lexor had already signed off on the virus, and production was near completion. Then Doctor Lexor came to see Benjamin as he still often did, (not every Friday as before, but still on a rather regular basis). Benjamin knew as soon as he saw Doctor Lexor that this visit would not be like the rest. Something was wrong, something was different Doctor Lexor was acting peculiar. Benjamin waited, but Doctor Lexor said nothing. Finally Benjamin couldn't wait any longer, "Doctor Lexor there seems to be something on your mind, what is it?"

"Doctor Stone, I have studied your virus for months, I have tested it on both men and women with success in getting the results I have been looking for."

"So far I do not see a problem", remarked Benjamin.

"The problem is that there is one marker on the virus that I cannot figure out." Benjamin's heart leapt into his throat, "I am sure the marker is only a left over signature of the parent viruses that it was derived from."

"That is what I thought at first, Doctor Stone, but now I am not too sure."

"Let's look at the virus under the microscope, you show me what marker you are concerned with Doctor Lexor." Benjamin was trying his best to remain calm. Benjamin put a specimen of the virus under a microscope. Sure enough when Doctor Lexor pointed out the marker, there it was, it was the piggyback virus. Doctor Lexor had found it, he did not know yet what he had found, but he knew it did not belong. Benjamin did his best to satisfy Doctor Lexor telling him it was nothing to be concerned with that he had also noticed the same marker long ago and determined it to be harmless. There was no satisfying Doctor Lexor he told Benjamin that as soon as he gets back to the Center of Disease Control, he was going to put a stop to the distribution of the virus until that marker could positively be identified and whether or not it posses any unknown threat. Benjamin asked Doctor Lexor, "How many people are even aware of the marker?"

"Other than you and I, Doctor Stone no one. I was hoping you could explain it to me. Look, Doctor Stone we have come so far, and have worked so hard. I just feel we need to be one hundred percent sure. And if that means a few more months or even years we as scientists must not act out of hast."

"You are absolutely right Doctor Lexor commented Benjamin. It is just that we are so close, and I do believe in the end of the marker will prove to be nothing."

"You are probably right Doctor Stone, but let's make sure." While Doctor Lexor was putting some papers together, preparing to leave Benjamin went to his coffee pot and began making a cup of coffee to go for the helicopter pilot. While he was mixing in just the right amount of sugar cream he had a thought that made his heart race, there was a way to protect his virus, but it would mean killing two people, the helicopter pilot and Doctor Lexor. Benjamin determined in an instant that if he was prepared to kill hundreds of millions of people that two more were nothing more than collateral damage. Benjamin knew that Doctor Lexor would only be busy for a few more minutes. If he were to act, he must act now. With no more thought he remembered he had in his laboratory the secretion off the belly of the tree frog from South America. The frog when feeling threatened would produce a slimy substance through glands in its belly. The substance was a powerful toxin that would cause someone to be paralyzed in just a few minutes after ingesting it. The locals have known for years about the toxin that the frog produces. They would coat their arrows with it while hunting, Benjamin coated the rim of the coffee cup with it, and just in time, because Doctor Lexor announced what he was ready to leave.

Benjamin walked with Doctor Lexor to the helicopter. Along the way Benjamin could have dropped the coffee by accident, but instead Benjamin was extra careful with his "death potion." Benjamin gave the coffee to the pilot, and said to him, "Be careful the coffee is extra hot today, so you may want to give it a few minutes before you try to drink it." Benjamin then turned to Doctor Lexor, "I know your right about wanting to know for sure about the marker."

"Like you said Doctor Stone it will probably turn out to be nothing." With that Benjamin walked away from the helicopter, he stood silent watching it disappear over the hills. There was no turning back now not for Benjamin. He was fully vested in seeing that the virus was released.

Later that night Benjamin received a call from Mr. Ashford, telling him of the bad news, "Apparently the helicopter crashed in the hills of Southern Montana less than ten minutes after it had left your house. There were no survivors." Naturally Benjamin acted surprised at the loss, so much so to the point that he almost convinced himself. Benjamin did not attend the funerals, but did send flowers along with a healthy cash donation to the families telling them he hoped it helped during their time of need. Benjamin played the part to perfection, no one was suspicious. The crash would later be ruled pilot error.

Mr. Ashford told Benjamin that they must carry on *with or without* Doctor Lexor, no one man is more important than the project. Mr. Ashford told Benjamin that the virus was scheduled to be released in the fall of 2009. Benjamin was told that the virus would be called H1N1; all the governments involved would create a false pandemic reporting large numbers of infections and deaths. This would create a panic for people to get vaccinated. The vaccine itself would in reality be the virus. It was felt that if you vaccinated enough people, the ones who were not vaccinated would be infected by those who were.

It was estimated that a worldwide infection could be possible by spring of 2010. The day was here and the government via the media started their campaign. In just a matter of a few days the media went from calling it the H1N1 virus to calling it the "Swine Flu." People were in a panic, to make matters worse, the government pretended to have a shortage of the vaccine. They were telling people it was a first come first served basis. They would only be able to vaccinate people until the supply ran out, which of course they never did.

The rate of infection was staggering, only twenty percent of the world's population remained uninfected. These were the *chosen* ones; they had been given the antivirus, some with consent, and some without. The wealthy people, the important people, the power mongers were safe along with enough "worker bees" to keep their society running.

By midsummer of 2010 the flu virus had run its course and was hailed a success by those knew of its true intention. Benjamin knew that the first cases of the secondary infection would start showing up shortly. Benjamin gave a great deal of thought to what was about to happen, in his estimation within thirty days or less "it" would start. Benjamin decided to do something that was out of character. He decided to throw a bone to the United States Government, the only government he had ever lived under.

Benjamin chartered a private jet to Washington D.C. Once he was in town he looked up an old friend, Senator Lexus Bode. Benjamin knew if he were to get what he wanted he would need help. With just one phone call Benjamin was granted an appointment with Senator Bode. Benjamin wasted no time getting to the Senator's office. "Hello Doctor Stone, what takes you off Twin Falls Ranch and brings you to Washington D.C.?"

"I have a favor to ask of you Senator."

"What might that be Doctor Stone? I want you to arrange a meeting between myself and the President of the United States."

"May I ask why, Doctor Stone?"

"Of course you may ask, but I am not so inclined to answer." The Senator looked at Benjamin with a slight look of disapproval, and then told him, "What you are asking is highly unusual and to be quite honest; without knowing what you want of the President, I am afraid I will probably have difficulty arranging the meeting." Benjamin took control of the situation, "are you telling me you cannot help me?"

"I have always been there for you Doctor Stone, what I am trying to say is that I will have to call in most of my favors to get this done, and to do that without knowing why? I am sorry Doctor Stone; I do not think I can help you."

"Senator Bode, you are coming up for re—election in the fall, if you arrange this meeting for me I will see to it that financially you want for nothing. *Do I make myself perfectly clear?*"

"Yes, Doctor Stone you have made yourself *perfectly* clear. I will use all my power, influence, and favors if need be to arrange a meeting between yourself and the President. I will contact you as soon as it can be arranged."

"Senator Bode I do not think you understand I wish to see the President today; *now* if possible."

"Doctor Stone let us be realistic, that is just *not* going to happen."

"Start making your phone calls Senator, I will wait in the other room." At that Benjamin stood up and walked out of the room. Senator Bode was stunned by his arrogance. "Today; is he serious?" The Senator sat for a few minutes giving thought to Doctor Stone's endless supply of money. It did not take much for her to talk herself into trying to make it happen. The Senator figured she had everything to gain and very little to lose.

Senator Bode went straight to the top; she called the head of the Democratic National Committee trying her best to explain her current situation with Doctor Stone without revealing anything about the financial offer. This would be an extremely hard deal to make under any circumstances, but since Senator Bode was a Republican, it was making it almost *impossible*. In the end the Senator had to agree to vote anyway the Democratic Party wanted her to vote on the next three bills they would try to pass. The Senator had made a deal with the "devil;" *both politically and personally*.

The President was a very busy man, but arrangements were made to meet in the Oval Office between twelve—fifteen and twelve—thirty. This was all the time the President could spare. Benjamin was escorted to the Oval Office by Senator Bode. When they arrived they were greeted by the President's chief of staff; Robert Maxwell. He and the Senator exchanged a few words, and then the Senator told Benjamin, "good luck with your meeting" then excused herself from the room. Robert Maxwell then turned his attention to Benjamin. He began to tell Benjamin that such a meeting on such a short notice was all but unheard of, and if you do not mind could you tell me what is so important. Benjamin found Robert Maxwell to be an unpleasant man, not caring much for his mannerism. "I know that such a meeting is unusual and I do appreciate the time I have been given, as to what I wish to speak to the President about, well that is between me and the President." Mr. Maxwell looked at Benjamin in a distasteful manner not commenting on what Benjamin had just said. He just said, "I will see if the President is ready to see you." He walked into the Oval Office, he then came back to retrieve Benjamin. When they entered the Oval Office the President was not alone; he was surrounded by four of his staff members. Benjamin and Mr. Maxwell stood just a few feet from the President waiting for him to acknowledge Benjamin's presence. It may have been a minute or less before that happened, but to Benjamin it seemed much longer. The President then stood up from his desk walked around to where Benjamin and Mr. Maxwell were standing, "I am sorry for having kept you waiting Doctor Stone, but things are a little bit crazy here today. I am leaving for Camp David in a few minutes for a meeting with some other world leaders. Before we started I wanted to apologize for being able to give you very little time. I would also like to add that you need no introduction, your body of work and your reputation precedes you. Having said that Doctor Stone, what is it you need from me?"

Benjamin told him that what he had to say needed to be said in private. The President told Benjamin, "You seem very nervous about *whatever* it is that is one your mind." He then looked at Robert Maxwell telling him to get everyone out of the room. He ordered the four staff members to leave the room; he shut the door to the Oval Office behind them, but he did not excuse himself. The President looked at Benjamin telling him, "Alright we are alone." Benjamin told him they were not completely alone, Mr. Maxwell was still there. "Doctor Stone, Mr. Maxwell is my Chief of Staff, if he does not hear it first hand; he will here if from me anyway, so feel free to speak." Just then the sound of a helicopter could be heard, it was the President's helicopter ready to take him to Camp David. Before the President or Benjamin could continue, Mr. Maxwell blurted out "Mr. President we must go time is of the essence, we cannot be late to greet out guests." the President looked at Benjamin, "Doctor Stone there is precious little time left if there is something I can do for you then you must tell me now." Even though Benjamin was talking to the President of the United States, Benjamin was not a man who was used to being rushed through a conversation. Benjamin had become irritated by the way he was being rushed. If the President could not give Benjamin the fifteen minutes that has been promised but instead giving him just a few moments, then Benjamin would give the President a very shortened version of the events that were about to unfold.

Benjamin looked at the President, "Mr. President it is obvious to me that you do not have time for this meeting, and have only taken it out of political pressure. Since you are in such a hurry the shortened version of what I want to tell you is that I have designed a virus that has already infected every person on the planet and in thirty days give or take people will start dying. According to my calculations about one point eight to two point three billion people will be dead in the next sixty days. Alright Mr. President, you can leave now; I'm done." The President's face was a blank showing no emotion of any kind, saying nothing, Mr. Maxwell had a similar look. Benjamin looked at the President, "what are you waiting for you can leave now. I said what needed to be said." The President finally regained his ability to speak, "What did you just say Doctor Stone, because there is no way I could have heard you right"

"You heard me right, genocide; an ethnic cleansing is upon us, one that cannot be stopped." Robert Maxwell interrupted, "Mr. President the helicopter is waiting." The President snapped at Mr. Maxwell, "Maxwell would you just shut up for one damn minute! Doctor Stone is what you're telling me the truth?"

"Yes, answered Benjamin." The President told Mr. Maxwell to cancel the helicopter and the committee meeting. "Tell everyone I have become ill, that I am currently unavailable for anything other than rest, do you understand me? Maxwell." Mr. Maxwell was always the obedient servant, "Yes, Mr. President I understand." Benjamin began to speak, when he was cut off by the President. "Doctor Stone before we go any further, I would like Mr. Maxwell present, so let us wait just a few minutes." The two men sat and starred at each other saying nothing; just exchanging looks which conveyed the emotions they were both feeling.

Just as promised within a few minutes Mr. Maxwell returned to the Oval Office. "Alright Mr. President I have canceled every appointment for the next few days. Now, someone needs to tell me what the hell is going on!"

The President looked at Benjamin; "Doctor Stone tell us *everything*, do *not* leave one detail unattended." Now that Benjamin had their full attention, he would tell them a story that not only would they never forgot, but find all but impossible to believe. "To begin with Mr. President, have you heard of the Bilderberg Group?"

"Yes, I have. But I think of them more as a group of powerful men who control their own financial destiny than as a group of men who control the world stage as the conspiracy theorist would have us believe."

"Alright Mr. President, to begin with you are wrong; they *do* control the world stage, and they *are* in control of every government in one way or another. I have been approached by these men from time to time in my life wanting me to work for them, I always declined. That is until the last time they came to see me."

"What made the last time different from the other times Doctor Stone?" The last time was when I was approached by your predecessor. He landed the very helicopter that you were about to leave on in my front lawn along with four military helicopters. He wanted me to take a meeting with Doctor Gage Lexor and Mr. Ashford. Both of these men work for the United States Government in Viral and Biologic research. I had turned down their attempts to make contact with me on several occasions." Mr. Maxwell wanted to know why the previous President of the United States would be involved. Benjamin told him, "It is my belief that the previous President was either part of the Bilderberg Group, or at the very least, working on their behalf. I agreed to the meeting and it was then that Doctor Gage Lexor and Mr. Ashford were presented to me. They had been waiting in one of the helicopters. The previous President excused himself from the meeting leaving the three of us alone to proceed without him."

"Exactly what was it these men wanted from you, Doctor Stone?"

"They had been trying to design a virus that would mimic flu like symptoms that would at the same time not kill anyone but instead, leave them sterile." Mr. Maxwell asked, "Why would anyone want such a virus?"

"There's a specific number of people that can be supported by our planet based on renewable and nonrenewable resources; it is called the carrying capacity. Most experts agree we will reach the limits of our ability to support ourselves around nine to ten billion people, which will occur in the next fifty years. The thought was that a virus that caused sterilization would be the most humane way to reduce the population over a period of time. There was also to be an antivirus. I am sure it would be given to the rich, the powerful, and the power mongers of the world, along with enough workers bees to keep society running." The President wanted to know two things, "How was the virus delivered and who determined what people received the antivirus?"

Benjamin told them, "The virus was delivered through a manmade pandemic. In this case, the H1N1 flu virus, or if you prefer the swine flu, people were told to get the vaccine protecting them from the deadly affects of the flu. The vaccine itself was nothing more than the flu virus. Once a person was infected they could spread the virus to others. Guaranteeing every man, women, and child would eventually be infected." The President informed Benjamin that he and his family had been given the vaccine, and they did experience some flu like symptoms, as well as did all the Presidents staff members and families. “Does this mean we have all been sterilized?”

“Mr. President I do not know if you are sterile or not, I do know that if you did not receive the antivirus you are most certainly sterile, as far as to who received the antivirus and who did not, perhaps Mr. Ashford could tell you, that information I do not have.” Mr. Maxwell wanted to know if Benjamin received the antivirus. “Yes I did receive the antivirus; not because I plan on breeding, but simply because I did not want to suffer through the flu.”

“Do you have any idea how arrogant that statement sounded Doctor Stone, exclaimed the President!”

“To me it was a factual statement, *not* one of arrogance.”

“Doctor Stone you mean to tell me that I, my wife, and my children could have been sterilized?”

“There is that possibility Mr. President.”

“Alright Doctor Stone you still have not explained the part were billions of people die, you said earlier that the virus would not cause death.”

“That is right Mr. President; the initial sterilization virus will not cause death. It is the secondary virus that will cause people to die.”

“Why is there a secondary virus Doctor Stone, asked Mr. Maxwell? The secondary virus is the reason I took the project to begin with. I knew that if I could design a virus to cause sterilization that I could probably design a piggyback virus that would ride on the initial virus. A piggyback virus if you will, this is the virus *I* wanted to design, the virus *I* wanted to release. The Bilderberg Group gave me the method in which I could release my intended virus. I do not know if either one of you is aware of it or not but I lost my mother, father, sister, and brother—in—law in a market bombing in Israel in July of 1985 by the hand of Islamic terrorists. Then in September 2001, I lost my wife, my twin daughters, and father—in—law to the hands of Islamic terrorists when the first plan hit the World Trade Center Tower. I have tried to find understanding in these events; someway of comforting myself. Instead after researching Islam, Mohammed, and his teachings in the Qur'an the only thing *I am sure of*; is that Mohamed was a *false* prophet, a conman who through his ability to be a great speaker convinced millions of people that he spoke directly for God. Today the millions have turned to billions, and the Qur'an is full of versus that can be interpreted in a number of ways. Even if Mohamed was "just a man fighting for a just cause", the people of today have strayed from his original path. They kill innocent people, and then claim it to be a "Jihad", a "holy war" in the name of their God. The Arabic nation as a whole is either involved in it or they are tolerating it. If a Jihad is what the Arabic nation wants than a Jihad is what they will receive. If their religion teaches hate and death to those who are not a part of it, then their religion will bring needless death to them. They are about to enter into the Jihad of all Jihad's; one in which there is no escape. The secondary virus which is my true virus will take effect in the next thirty days more or less. There is no place on the planet the Arabic community can hide and I did not create an anti—virus. The virus will attach itself to the very genome of a person of Arabic decent. If you have more than thirty—five to forty percent of the Arabic genome in you, well then you will die. *Nothing* can be done to stop it, not Mohamed, not the Qur'an, not the belief in a "magical being" who lives in the sky, *nothing*."

"Doctor Stone I pray that what you are telling me is not true, and that for whatever reason you have simply lost control of your mind and that you are delusional. Because the thought that you could be right is almost unbearable; Mr. Maxwell, have the secret service take Doctor Stone someplace and make him comfortable. Then get the top people in the proper fields and put them into contact with Doctor Stone. We need to know if he is right or if my prayers are being answered and Doctor Stone is simply misguided. Also find Doctor Gage Luxor and Mr. Ashford, I need to speak to both of them."

Benjamin spoke up, "First of all, I am *not* delusional *or* misguided. Secondary, Doctor Gage Luxor died in a helicopter crash."

"Mr. Maxwell, check that out; and for God sake, do what else I have asked of you. Also no one is to know of this. Do you understand me Mr. Maxwell?"

"Yes sir, Mr. President." Benjamin was escorted to a secure area in the White House where he could be watched, but yet be comfortable. Mr. Maxwell was busy assembling a team of Scientists to verify *or* discount Benjamin's statement.

The President of the United States summoned his personal doctor with orders to give him a fertility test. The next day the President received word that he was *indeed sterile*. This infuriated the President! "Who were those men, The Bilderberg Group?" They felt they and they alone controlled mankind's destiny.

That same day the team of scientists that Mr. Maxwell had assembled was fast at work trying to decipher Benjamin's viruses. All the while Benjamin was explaining to them how it was engineered, how it worked.

Mr. Ashford was also located; and had been brought to the Oval Office along with the Director of the CIA. Until such time as the President began to speak, Mr. Ashford and the CIA director did not know why they had been summoned. The President started by telling Mr. Ashford that he was aware of the sterilizing virus that Doctor Stone had engineered under the supervision of the Bilderberg group.

“Now, Mr. Ashford; before you deny any involvement in this matter, I think you should know that if you lie to me I will enter an executive order to terminate your life as an enemy and a direct threat to the United States of America. I have that authority and Mr. Nash can verify that for you.” Mr. Nash told Mr. Ashford that the President was correct, though seldom used, but he does have the authority to issue the executive order. “So Mr. Ashford, are you going to tell me what you know or are you going to lie to me?” Mr. Ashford sat silently considering his response also wondering how the President knew what he knew.

“No, Mr. President, I am not going to lie to you, I am fully aware of the sterilization virus.”

“Alright, the President said, tell me everything you know.” Mr. Ashford spoke for fifteen minutes straight uninterrupted by all. When he had finished the President knew that Benjamin was also telling the truth. This angered him as well as sickened him. The President had the secret service take charge of Mr. Ashford for the time being, leaving Mr. Nash and the President alone.

“Mr. Nash you have not said much of anything what are your thoughts on this matter?”

"Mr. President I can hardly believe what I heard, how could such a thing be possible, how could such a thing happen?"

"It could only happen with the cooperation of a group such as the Bilderberg Group. Mr. Nash, are you aware of these men?"

"Yes sir, Mr. President, the CIA is fully aware of these men and their members."

"Mr. Nash, would you agree that the Bilderberg Group is a threat to our national security?"

"Yes sir Mr. President, I would agree."

"Alright I am going to give you an executive order signed by me to hunt down and terminate all known Bilderberg members from around the world effective immediately!"

"Does that include Doctor Stone and Mr. Ashford, sir?"

"Mr. Ashford most definitely, as for Doctor Stone not yet, we may need that sick son—of—a—bitch."

"Yes sir, Mr. President, I will start cleaning house immediately." The President was left alone in the Oval Office knowing he had just sign the death warrant for every member of the Bilderberg Group. This was one burden that this President could live with.

The following day, the President met with Doctor Stone and a team of scientists assigned to verify the virus. When the President entered the room everyone stood up, but social graces were not the order of the day. The President blurted out, "*Everyone sit down we are not here today to beg, bow and kiss ass, we are here to find out if Doctor Stone is right! Now, someone start talking.*"

"Mr. President my name is Doctor English; I will speak for the team"

"Then speak Doctor English, I am not in the mood for delays."

"Without a great deal of time to study what Doctor Stone has shown us, it would appear that his virus will attach itself to the genome of a person of Arabic decent and *indeed* cause their death." With that the President jumped out of his chair slamming his hand on the desk! He looked right at Doctor Stone and said, "You sick son—of—a—bitch, and do you realize what you have done?"

"Yes, Mr. President I do realize what I have done, I have opened Pandora's Box, and it will *never* be closed." Mr. Nash interrupted, "gentlemen please be seated, Mr. President this behavior will settle nothing." The President and Benjamin both seemed to calm down. The President continued to question Doctor English. "How will they die, or do we even know?"

"Mr. President, I and the other team members feel that the early stages of the virus will cause headaches so bad that a person will experience a loss of equilibrium, finally they will be bed ridden. They will then experience blood loss through the eyes, ears, and their nose. This is because the virus will attach itself to the brain causing it to liquefy. Death should occur within seventy—two hours of the first symptoms." The President looked at Benjamin with a look of absolute disgust and contempt. The President then turned his attention to Doctor English and his team. "Doctor English I would like to thank you and your team for what you have done, I would also like to know if it is possible to create an anti—virus on such short notice perhaps saving some of the people infected." Doctor English told the President that in his opinion, there was no time to create an anti—virus because of the complex nature of the virus. By the time an anti—virus could be completed the initial virus would have already ran its course, and there would be no one left to save. "Are you sure, asked the President?"

"I am absolutely sure Mr. President answered Doctor English."

"Alright Doctor English, again; I want to thank you for your help in this matter, I will now ask you to go into the next room and wait for a member of the CIA to debrief you to let you know how to handle the information you have." Doctor English and his team went into the other room; as they were ask to do leaving the President, Mr. Nash, and Doctor Stone alone. The President looked at Benjamin and began to speak, "Doctor Stone I have to ask, did you thoroughly think through what you were doing and how it would affect the world, not just the people you *wish* to kill; but the rest of the world? Do you realize that there will be a worldwide economic meltdown before this is over?"

"Mr. President I thought of nothing but how this would play out, it consumed my life day and night for a number of years before I actually created the virus. I assumed the world would be in chaos for a number of years before it settled down. I assumed that a number of innocent people would die because of what I did, because of rioting, because of food shortages, because of a lack of basic essentials. So yes, Mr. President I have given it careful consideration. If you are wondering can I live with myself, the answer is yes. I know that I am the cause of the largest mass die off of human beings since the dawn of time, and *I am okay with that.* Mr. President you sit in judgment of me for what I have done and I am also okay with that. You and men like you have been directly responsible for the deaths of your fellow man throughout history, but somehow men like you always find a way to "justify" what you do, and by justifying what you do, you can live with yourself. You can sleep at night; I am also ok with that. Yes Mr. President I am fully aware of what I have done and what will come."

"Doctor Stone men like me try to make the world a better place, sometimes in order to make the world safer blood *must* be spilled, but you Doctor Stone, what you have done is nothing short of genocide; the wholesale slaughter of an entire race of people. A race of people who have been around for as long as recorded history and beyond, a group of people for all their shortcomings have a rich and diverse culture, who have contributed to mankind throughout history. No, Doctor Stone we are *nothing alike; nothing at all*." Benjamin sat saying nothing, just listening to what the President had to say. There was something else the President wanted to know, "Doctor Stone when you say the Arabic nation exactly who do you mean?"

"Mr. President, when I say the Arabic nation I am referring to anyone of Arabic decent. The countries of Saudi Arabia, Sudan, Eritrea, Yemen, India, Egypt, Jordan, Syria, Iraq, United Arab, Emirates, Omen, Turkey, Turkmenistan, Armenia, Libya, Afghanistan, Pakistan, Italy, Greece, and the country of Israel." The President stood silent for a moment; he looked at Mr. Nash then at Benjamin. He then cast his eyes down at the floor before once again looking at Benjamin, "Words escape me Doctor Stone. I simply cannot find the right words to express my contempt for you at this time."

There was a moment of silence then Mr. Nash spoke, "Doctor Stone something has been bothering me, I want to know why did you tell what you have done. If you remained silent chances are that no one would have ever know it was you, so why tell?"

"I will answer your question Mr. Nash", remarked Benjamin. "You are right; I could have kept silent and probably have remained undiscovered. The reason I chose to come to Washington D.C. was to give the United States the opportunity to remain the world leader. There is nothing that can be done to save the Arabic nations, but, there is time to take steps for the control of the vast territory in the Middle East that will soon be up for grabs. Steps need to be taken for control of the unattended dams and nuclear power plants, not to mention the most precious natural resources we have; "oil".

"So, Doctor Stone you would have the President and myself believe that you are some kind of patriot?"

"On some level Mr. Nash I *do* believe that I am a patriot."

"I will not speak for the President, Doctor Stone, but as for myself I don't believe you to be a patriot. I believe you to be a mad man, and as for the reason you came to Washington, I believe you wanted credit for your virus. The thought that you created a virus that could be considered "a perfect killing machine." The thought that no one would knew *you* created it was too much for your ego. This is what I think Doctor Stone." Benjamin said nothing, he did not disagree nor did he agree, instead he chose to say nothing. The President had enough time to compose himself and decided to continue with the questioning. "Doctor Stone you mentioned many countries that would be affected, but what about people from around the world from all countries who are descendants of the Arabic race, they will die as well won't they?"

"Mr. President I do not know how many times or how many ways I have to say to you that *all people of Arabic decent will die.* Their geographic location will not matter. *Every* country in the world will be affected in one way or another."

The President's facial expression was one of pure anger. He could not believe the manner in which Benjamin had just spoken to him. "Doctor Stone you are exactly as I have always heard you were. You are a very self righteous, self centered, arrogant man. Now let me make myself clear, for what you have done their will be no trial, the last thing the United States wants or needs is to appear to of had any involvement in the design of a virus of this nature. *I* will be your judge and jury, and by Presidential decree I will put you in a small dark cell for the rest of your natural life. There will be no contact with the outside world, no newspapers to read, no television to watch, not so much as a magazine, or a book. Doctor Stone you will spend your days starring at the walls and ceiling with nothing to occupy your time except the burden of guilt that you will carry in this lifetime and beyond. Now do you understand me Doctor Stone?" Benjamin waited for a moment, and then he told the President, "Before you proclaim your "Presidential decree" locking me up for life without a trial and throwing away the key you may want to consider the rest of the story concerning the virus."

The President raised his eyebrow and leaned back in his chair, "what more could their possibly be Doctor Stone?"

"There are three breeds of human beings left after the Arabic breed is gone. There is the Asian, Caucasian, and Negroid."

"What did you just say", exclaimed the President!

"It is a scientific term, let us move one. What you need to ask yourself is if and when the Chinese (Asian race) figures out what has been done; and they will, it may take five years or it may take twenty—five years, but eventually they *will* figure out how such a virus works. And when they do I am sure they would love to create a virus to eradicate the Caucasian and Negroid breeds from the planet leaving only one, theirs. But as for today, for right now, *I* am the only person who *really* knows how it works. I think it is important that you understand I know how to create a virus for the Asian breed. For that matter any of the breeds that are going to be left I can create the same virus. Now, ask yourself when that day comes (and it will come) what will you do? If you have the information that *I* can provide then you can pull the trigger first, because no matter how you may feel "personally", one day in the near future that decision will have to be made. Is the United States strong enough to make such a decision? I believe in the name of self preservation (no matter how distasteful), the United States would be willing to kill billions of Asians in order to survive. And if given enough time I do truly believe that I can design viruses that are even more selective. For example a virus that would kill only selective groups of people within a particular breed perhaps a virus that would kill only the Asian populations. If any group of any one breed is separated long enough they become a sub—breed slightly different from the original breed. That slight difference is all I need to design a virus for them and them alone. So you see Mr. President, I do not plan to spend the rest of life locked away in some dark hole. If you wish for me to help design the viruses you need along with the anti—virus that should accompany each and every virus; *I plan to spend the rest of my life at Twin Falls Ranch,* working for and on behalf of the United States Government; of course under the watchful eye of my government. What do you say Mr.

President, are you going are you going to lock me away in some dark hole and throw the key away as you stated, or will you consider me a "necessary evil" using me for your own purposes?"The President looked Benjamin then to Mr. Nash, "Doctor Stone I need you to go into the other room for a moment and be seated, the secret service will keep you company while I talk to Mr. Nash."

Benjamin stood up not saying a word as he left the room. The President looked at Mr. Nash who drew a deep breath before he began to speak. "Mr. President as distasteful as I *personally* find Doctor Stone *he is right*. He is right and he knows it, we *need* him. Someday one of our enemies will try to duplicate what Doctor Stone has done, and if they are successful, *God help us*, because they *will* use it. That is a fact you cannot deny, and you need to make your decision based on what is best for the country."

"Mr. Nash I also do not care for Doctor Stone on a personal level. I consider him to be a *lunatic*; a genius that has been led astray. Doctor Stone has done so much for the human race it is almost ironic that he who had done so much may also be the one who destroys the human race. I cannot disagree with you, because you are right, we do need him. I insist that Doctor Stone *never* leave Twin Falls and that Doctor Stone be under the watchful eye of the secret service seven days a week twenty—four hours a day for the rest of his miserable life! I furthermore *insist* that Doctor Stone never be allowed in his laboratory without the supervision of someone like Doctor English, these things not only do I insist on *I demand*. There will be no room for negotiations in this matter by Doctor Stone. If Doctor Stone doesn't care for what I propose then we will lock him away."

"Yes sir Mr. President I could not agree more exclaimed Mr. Nash! Shall I bring Doctor Stone back into the room Mr. President?"

"No, Mr. Nash you shall not, I do not care to ever see the face of Doctor Stone again. You Mr. Nash can take it from here. You know what needs to be done, make it happen." Mr. Nash stood up "Yes sir" Mr. President, and then excused himself to the other room where Benjamin was waiting. That would be the last time Benjamin saw or talked to the President of the United States

Mr. Nash and some of the men who work for Mr. Nash took Benjamin to a separate room far removed from the Oval Office and the President. "Doctor Stone is there anything I can get for you, do you need something to drink or eat." Benjamin told Mr. Nash that he was just fine. "Alright Dr. Stone, I am not one who dances around an issue. I have spoken to the President, your choices are go back to Twin Falls under government protection, only being allowed into your laboratory if Doctor English or someone like him is with you watching your every move, or you can be locked away for whatever time you have left and that time could be cut short if we do so decide. Now, Doctor Stone what do you say, Twin Falls and research or prison and an almost certain short life?" Benjamin smiled at Mr. Nash (it was more of a smirk than a smile). He knew that they had no choice. "Mr. Nash both offers sound inviting, but I believe I will go with the Twin Falls option if it is all the same to you."

"Wise choice" answered Mr. Nash, *"Very wise indeed."* Benjamin was escorted from the White House directly to Twin Falls. He was accompanied by enough secret service agents to keep watch over him twenty—four hours a day.

(CHAPTER SEVENTEEN)

Once Benjamin was home, the only restrictions he had were that he would not be allowed in the laboratory without supervision from Doctor English,(if Doctor English chose to take the job) or someone like Doctor English. Also from this date forward Benjamin's phone would be monitored along with his mail.

It would not take much getting used to having the secret service around, considering that Benjamin already had his own team of security people for some time now. As for Benjamin's security people he had to let them all go, they were no longer needed by Benjamin nor were they *wanted* by the secret service.

It would be a few weeks before the Government assigned Benjamin a laboratory watch dog, until then Benjamin would do as he had always done, read a little, sit and watch the Twin Falls, and make his daily trip to visit his loved ones.

Bart showed up a few days after Benjamin had come back home the secret service escorted him to the back of the house were Benjamin was sitting reading a book. When Bart saw Benjamin the first thing he asked was, "*Who the hell are these people; I thought they were going to look up my ass for weapons!* And what the hell happened to the old security you had?"

Benjamin told Bart that the new security people worked for the Government, they were members of the secret service, and that they would be providing protection for him from now on. Bart wanted to know why the government would be providing security for Benjamin; "You are not in some sort of fix are you?"

"No Bart," answered Benjamin. I am not in "some sort of fix." I have agreed to do some work for the government. They just want to make sure nothing happens to me, that's all; Bart. Do not worry about me I will be fine."

"I am sure you will be fine, but I am not sure about myself. "I tell ya, that search they gave me was close to being rape. I don't like the new set up Benjamin, not at all!"

"Bart you need to calm down, you will get used to them and in time they *might* get used to you. I say *might* because getting used to you may require more patience then they have" Bart and Benjamin both laughed at Benjamin's comment.

For Benjamin life seemed to be the same with little to no changes. Ironic isn't it that Benjamin's life is the same, but the rest of the world is about to experience genocide on a scale never before known to man along with the financial collapse of most world governments? The government allowed Benjamin to conduct his financial affairs without interruption, knowing what was about to happen. Benjamin converted most of his wealth to precious metals, gold, silver, and copper. These would keep him financially sound during the rebuilding phase of the world's economy.

After a few weeks had past Benjamin was informed by Mr. Nash that Doctor English had agreed to work with Benjamin in his laboratory. Just as Doctor Lexor had done, so would Doctor English. He would arrive every day, five days a week within a few minutes of the same time each day by helicopter. The only difference this time is Benjamin would be denied contact with the helicopter pilot. The first day Doctor English came to Benjamin's laboratory, he commented to Benjamin about the state of the art equipment the laboratory was filled with. Then Doctor English committed to Benjamin on a personal level, "Doctor Stone I want you to know that your work at least up until now is known worldwide. I consider it a privilege to be here working with a scientist of your caliber. *I do not* by any means agree with what you have done, but to be able to learn from you may be the most educating experience of my life." Benjamin thanked Doctor English, and then told him, "Now, let's get to work."

The two men rarely had conversations that were on a personal level; their arrangement was very businesslike.

Not long after Benjamin and Doctor English started working together, *it happened!* The first case of the virus causing death began. It started in the United States, and then spread to Europe, the Middle East and so on. Just as Benjamin had predicted death came within seventy—two hours, more or less. The newspaper and the media called the virus the "Arabic death" because it seemed to affect only, or mostly Arabic people. In the United States there were nearly seventy million deaths in a three month period before the virus had run its course. Not a country in the world was left unaffected by the virus, but the Middle East, the heartland of the Arabic nation was destroyed. You could go hundreds of miles and find just one or two people still living. The deaths were almost that of a biblical proportion.

The Christians of course put their own spin on it, they claimed that the hand of God himself had destroyed the Arabic community because of the way they were living their lives, because of the religion that they were practicing. When the "Arabic death" hit the Middle East, people died by the millions on a daily basis. They prayed to their God, they cried out to Mohamed, but he heard them not. They wanted a Jihad and a Jihad is what Benjamin gave them.

In the end when the virus had run its course, the number of deaths was staggering! The total count was *two point eight billion*, a number larger than Benjamin had anticipated.

As expected the world economy was affected greatly. This would cause the deaths of millions of more people from rioting and the loss of basic essential needs. But in time, the flow of money and goods would be reconnected. Also, just as Benjamin had thought the United States took control of vast areas of the Middle East. In order to keep world peace China, Russia, and a few European countries also took control of parts of the Middle East. The United States of course had seized a lion's share for itself.

The United States was now without question, even for those who may have felt differently, "the number one super power on the planet." The United States coming out on top was the only good thing that happened because of the virus. For Benjamin personally, he had to live with knowing that he caused the death of his long time friend Adam's wife. Though her family were devout practicing Catholics, they were of Arabic decent. The death of Adam's wife crushed Adam, and sickened Benjamin.

If that was not bad enough, Bart came to Benjamin begging him to do something that would save his two children whom had fallen ill. Until the very moment Bart made the announcement to Benjamin, he had no idea that Bart was married in his earlier years, and had children. It seemed Bart keep that information a secret. Benjamin was deeply saddened had to tell Bart that there was nothing he could do. Bart continued begging and pleading, "*Please Benjamin; please*, you are the smartest man alive *please*, can't you do something?" Once again Benjamin had to tell him nothing can be done.

Burying his only two children was a hard thing for Bart to take; and Benjamin knew what it was like to bury two of your children. He also knew what it was like to bury a wife; Benjamin was sickened by what he had done. If only he knew Adam's wife was of Arabic decent. If only he knew that Bart's ex—wife was of Greek decent. I did not take long for Benjamin to snap back to reality and admit to himself that he was wrong. Benjamin gave a great deal of thought to what he had done. That is on the inside, on the outside Benjamin showed no signs of remorse. He could not because he knew it would change nothing.

After four months had passed the virus was winding down and only a few pockets of the planet were still being affected. No doubt there were the last few pockets to be infected; Benjamin had accomplished what he wanted. But like so many things in life, ***you should be careful for what you wish; because what you wish may not be what you want***.

This seemed to be the case for Benjamin; he was no exception to the rule. Benjamin tried to forget what he had done; spending his days with Doctor English working in the laboratory would be Benjamin's "Life sentence."

As time went by Benjamin found it harder and harder to sleep at night. He had taken to using sleeping pills in order to get through the night. On one particular night Benjamin wanted to sleep through the night so instead of taking the two pills he had been accustomed to he took four pills. It took very little time for Benjamin to slip into a *deep, deep sleep*. Later that night Benjamin was awakened by one of the secret service agents. "Wake up Doctor Stone, wake up!" Benjamin was in a deep dream, the words were barely coming through, "wake up Doctor Stone", again and again. Finally, Benjamin awoke from the deep slumber he had been in. "I am awake, alright you can stop yelling. What are you doing in my room what do you want?"

"Doctor Stone, Mr. Nash is on the phone, we have been ordered to get you up and on the phone with him at all cost. Doctor Stone are you awake? Can you take the call now or do you need more time?"

"Give me a minute; let me splash some water on my face." Benjamin stumbled to the bathroom, turning the water on cold; he then splashed his face several times. It seemed to help a little, but Benjamin could still feel the effects of the *four* sleeping pills. The secret service agent was standing just a few feet away from Benjamin holding the phone all the while starring at him waiting for him to take it. "Alright, alright, exclaimed Benjamin! Give me the damn phone."

When Benjamin took the phone his first words were, "what the hell is so important that you have to call me at two forty—five in the morning Mr. Nash?"

"Mr. Nash answered I will tell you what is so damn important Doctor Stone! *Your* virus, *your* precious virus has mutated we have reports of several cases in the Asian and from African communities."

Benjamin barked, "It is impossible! I am sure of that."

"Doctor Stone we have people dying in the same manner as before who are most definitely *not* of Arabic decent. I need you to get dressed Doctor English is on the way to Twin Falls. He has a sample of the new virus and Doctor Stone I know you are not a religious man but I pray you are right." Mr. Nash then hung the phone up on Benjamin. The effects of the four sleeping pills that Benjamin had taken were suddenly gone; no doubt the sudden rush of adrenaline Benjamin's body had just received countered their effects.

Benjamin's mind was racing, how could this have happened, how was it possible he was so sure of himself? It was not long before Doctor English arrived with the sample virus. The two of them went to work immediately. By midday Benjamin could no longer deny the new virus was a mutation of the original strain.

The days and weeks went by and the two of them tried everything! But *nothing* seemed to work, this was a "true super virus", Doctor English told Benjamin that it had long been his belief that viruses would sometimes mutate in order to survive. It is nature's way; it is simply a survival tactic. The virus ran out of people to infect, it was dying; so it mutated. Benjamin laughed at that theory, "That does not even make sense," commented Benjamin.

"It does not have to make sense Doctor Stone, for all your intelligence, for all of you knowledge of advanced science, you *never* expected to be outmaneuvered by a simple virus. Mother Nature is much more powerful than we are Doctor Stone, *not* realizing that was your mistake."

Doctor English was right and that realization *terrified* Benjamin! It was not long before the virus was showing itself in the United States, killing both Asian and African Americans alike. It could not be worse, Benjamin received word that the President and his family had been affected or at least that is what Benjamin thought (it couldn't get any worse.) But once again, Benjamin would be proven wrong.

The virus mutated again, only this time it would concentrate itself on the Caucasian race showing no mercy.

Humanity was on the edge of destruction, and then it happened; Benjamin himself felt ill to the effects of the virus.

In the end even the "Great Doctor Stone" would not be able to save himself, or so it seemed; then suddenly from nowhere Benjamin woke up.

He had probably been thrashing about in bed, no doubt because of the nightmare he had just endured. The bed sheets were wet with sweat, his heart was racing, he must have finally fallen out of bed which caused him to wake up. Benjamin pulled himself up to the edge of the bed. He was still in a state of grogginess because of the sleeping pills he was taking. At that very moment Benjamin was not sure what was real or what was a dream. Benjamin went to the bathroom and took a long shower.

Afterwards Benjamin was able to collect himself. He now knew that it had all been just a dream. Benjamin felt that because of what Carl had said about "killing them, killing them all," coupled with the four sleeping pills he had taken along with a possible mixture of last night's dinner.

Benjamin had just endured the *worst nightmare of his life!*

There was no virus; two point eight billion people had not died, and there was no mutated virus. He was safe at Twin Falls with Carl and his friend Adam who was visiting. He could see Bart out by the stables, saddling a horse. The nightmare was over, as in any dream there is always some truth to be found.

In this case the Bilderberg Group is real and they are a danger to mankind. Benjamin *did* lose his mother, father, sister, and brother—in—law in a market bombing in Israel.

He did lose his wife, twin daughters, and father—in—law on 911, and his heart has grown hard towards the Arabic nation. However, after that day Benjamin read no more about Islam, the Qur'an, nor did he continue to follow the news concerning such things. Instead he went back to work in his laboratory. He wanted to get back to his research on androids.

(CHAPTER EIGHTEEN)

As time went on and as the years passed, Benjamin's heart softened he no longer hated the people of the Arabic nation. He forgave those who took what meant so much to him.

Benjamin was content with spending the rest of his life undisturbed by the outside world at Twin Falls. One day while sitting on the back porch reading a book and listening to the sounds of the falls just as Benjamin had done so many times before he heard a buzzing noise in the background. It was getting louder; it can't be thought Benjamin. The sound became apparent. It was the sound of five helicopters, four military, and one for the President of the United States. Benjamin had a look of horror on his face; he thought *this cannot be happening. He is either in a dream from which there is no escape; or was the dream he had endured in the past a warning of things to come.*

For those who have read the story of Doctor Benjamin Stone, keep in mind this is only one plausible way in which mankind *may or may not* destroy himself.

CPSIA information can be obtained at www.ICGtesting.com
Printed in the USA
LVOW040951030312

271221LV00002B/44/P

9 781462 632350